NEVER MIX SIN *With* PLEASURE

ALSO BY RENEE ANN MILLER

Never Conspire with a Sinful Baron

Never Kiss a Notorious Marquess

Never Deceive a Viscount

Never Dare a Wicked Earl

Novella

The Taming of Lord Scrooge

NEVER MIX SIN *With* PLEASURE

The Infamous Lords series

RENEE ANN MILLER

ZEBRA BOOKS
KENSINGTON PUBLISHING CORP.
www.kensingtonbooks.com

ZEBRA BOOKS are published by

Kensington Publishing Corp.
119 West 40th Street
New York, NY 10018

First Printing: July 2021
ISBN-13: 978-1-4201-5005-6
ISBN-10: 1-4201-5005-7

ISBN-13: 978-1-4201-5006-3 (eBook)
ISBN-10: 1-4201-5006-5 (eBook)

10 9 8 7 6 5 4 3 2 1

Printed in the United States of America

Mom, I miss your smiles, I miss our talks, I miss you.
Not a day passes that I don't think of you.

Chapter One

London, England

With barely a noise, the thief the London newspapers had nicknamed the Phantom tiptoed across the old floorboards and raised the lower sash of the window in the attic. Though it was May, the night was cool. A brisk breeze carrying the scents of the city swept inward to brush against her cheeks. She reached up and tugged her dark knit hat lower over her ears. While making her way across the rooftops, she couldn't afford to have the wind dislodge her long red hair from its chignon and whip it into her eyes.

She swung one leg, then the other out the window. The dark trousers and black knitted guernsey sweater she wore made leaping from one rooftop to the next easier than if encumbered by a dress. She lowered herself to the band of stone that ran the perimeter of the town house. Like so many of these Georgian homes, her employer's residence possessed a ledge wide enough to walk on.

As a child, she'd balanced herself on tree limbs much narrower, while imagining herself an acrobat. She glanced at the pavement below. Falling from this height would cause more than a sprained ankle or a broken leg. A fall would most likely end in death. Shoving that thought from her mind, she leapt from the ledge to the flat rooftop of the adjacent town house.

Like a specter in the night, she made her way across the flat surface and jumped to the next roof, several feet lower, rolling on the balls of her feet as she landed. Leaping from one roof to the next made her feel carefree, almost aimless. But she was not aimless. Her goal was set in her mind. And if all went well, she would prevail.

The rattling of harnesses and the clopping of hooves echoed on the street below as a carriage rumbled down the cobbles. Drawing in a deep breath of cool air, she stepped into the shadows and pressed her back against a brick chimney until the sound of the vehicle faded into the dark night.

As she slipped out of hiding, she briefly tipped her face to the moon, letting it bathe her in its gray light. The moon was both friend and foe. It allowed her to see, but could also allow her to be seen. Hunched low, she padded across the surface before darting into the shadows again.

Up here on the rooftops, she felt free from all the rules that had dictated most of her actions throughout her life. No one watched her. No one judged her. But most of all, no one made her feel less because of the circumstances of her birth. She was like a nightjar bird, nocturnal, fluttering free above the city, conjuring myths and tales.

As she reached the last town house on the street, she held on to the drainpipe. Her leather gloves protected her hands from the rough surface as she slid down, pressing the soles of her shoes into the cast iron to slow her descent to the ground—or perhaps it was hell. There were days she didn't know where she would end up, especially if she got caught. But she had made a promise to Helen before her dear friend's death, and she would fulfill it.

A gust of wind carrying the scent of chimney smoke swirled close, pulling her from her thoughts.

She needed to hurry. Lord Hamby would be preoccupied with his guests, while she would be rifling through his bedchamber, searching for his coin box.

She would keep her promise.

She would make him pay.

All of them would.

Chapter Two

Lady Winton resembled a pumpkin. Olivia Michaels wouldn't voice such an unfavorable opinion aloud. A paid companion to an elderly lady of noble birth knew better if she wished to retain her position. And this position was imperative to Olivia's plan.

As her ladyship turned before the cheval glass in Madame Lefleur's London shop, Olivia snapped her gaping mouth closed. The orange, overly embellished concoction, with an exceedingly large bustle, looked garish on a woman of advanced years. A subtler shade with less flounce would be more flattering.

"I look enchanting, don't I?" Lady Winton asked in her haughty voice, which always sounded as if someone was pinching the woman's nose.

Olivia shifted her weight from one foot to the other while she fought the urge to violently shake her head. Vicar Finch at All Saints Orphanage for Girls had proclaimed lying was the first step toward hell, but there was no avoiding it, and since coming to London a few weeks ago, she'd already set herself toward perdition.

"Yes, my lady," she replied.

Lady Winton cocked a gray eyebrow at Madame Lefleur, who stood in the corner of the fitting room looking a bit green. Though the modiste had sewn the gown, her ladyship had instructed the proprietor on the bright color and flouncy design.

"*Oui, très belle*." Madame Lefleur's thin lips formed a clearly forced smile. The woman had her reputation as London's premiere modiste to consider, but she also knew the noblewoman was a vicious gossip with a sharp tongue who could turn the *ton* against any merchant.

"I shall tell everyone how I designed my gown." Lady Winton tipped her long, thin nose into the air.

A relieved expression flashed on the modiste's face before she masked it.

"Perhaps I should have a matching turban with orange feathers made. I shall revive the fashion. What do you think?"

Madame Lefleur looked utterly speechless.

"Well?" Lady Winton snapped impatiently, turning to glare at the modiste.

"It would hide your lovely hair," the French woman answered.

"True." Her ladyship patted the sizable gray bun perched on the top of her head like a massive bird's nest.

Olivia knew it was a wig, since sometimes when her employer dozed off it slipped precariously close to her right eye.

One of the modiste assistants stepped into the room, walking at a ground-eating pace. She handed a newspaper to Madame Lefleur. "He's done it again," she said in a hushed voice.

As Lady Winton watched the two other women's reflections in the mirror, her eyes grew sharp. She spun around in an orange swirl of fabric. “What are you two whispering about?”

“The Phantom has robbed another residence.” Madame Lefleur bit her lower lip and continued to read the article.

Lady Winton stormed toward the women and without asking grabbed the newspaper out of the shop owner’s hand.

“Who did he rob?” Olivia asked.

“Lord Hamby on Duke Street,” Lady Winton replied.

“Oh, my!” Olivia set her hand against her chest and tried to appear shocked.

“Don’t look so terrified, you silly girl.” Lady Winton glared at Olivia. “The thief has no interest in any of your measly belongings. What would he get but a few ragged dresses? He is targeting members of the nobility. People like me.” Her haughty voice inched higher with each word, while her normally florid cheeks paled.

Well, that wasn’t exactly true. The Phantom wasn’t intent on robbing all the nobility. The thief was in London to exact justice on a few men. Men who’d forced their attentions on members of their female staff, leaving them enceinte and jobless. Leaving those poor servants with little choice but to beg Mrs. Garson at the orphanage to take their infant children. By-blows like Helen—born on the wrong side of the blanket—fathered by lecherous, wealthy men who cast them away with nary a thought.

Clearly agitated, Lady Winton tossed the paper onto a chair and pointed a plump, beringed finger at the stack of boxes that contained several boned corsets and cotton unmentionables. “While I change, Olivia, bring those parcels to my carriage.”

"Of course, my lady." Olivia lifted the weighty packages. She stepped out of the dressing room and into the main area of the shop. Cream-flocked paper covered the walls, the perfect foil to the colorful bolts of silk and taffeta.

The bell over the entrance jangled.

Olivia craned her neck to glance around the parcels.

A woman with pitch-black hair and dark eyes entered the dressmaker's shop. Her yellow silk gown and matching hat set off her rich complexion. The woman was not as much beautiful as she was striking.

A young shopgirl rushed forward. "Signora Campari, please come in."

Campari? The opera singer? Olivia's feet faltered. Only last week, Lady Winton had returned from Drury Lane Theatre and extolled about the soprano's extraordinary talent.

Olivia wished she could have attended the theater and heard the prima donna's voice. But her employer hadn't included her in the outing with the coterie of elderly noblewomen she'd attended with.

Peering around the stacked packages, Olivia made her way out of the shop to Lady Winton's shiny black carriage parked in front. Thankfully the steps were lowered. With the boxes balanced in one arm, she reached for the latch and opened the door. Ducking her head, she stepped inside. Her foot collided with something or someone.

As she stumbled forward, the parcels in her hands flew upward.

Large hands wrapped about her waist, and she slammed against a firm, but warm surface as the boxes rained down.

She swallowed the sudden lump in her throat and lifted her tumbled chignon off her face.

Lord Anthony Trent lay on the carriage seat. Worse, she was sprawled atop him—nearly every inch of her body in contact with his masculine frame that held the faint, tantalizing scent of soap and bergamot.

Lady Winton had proclaimed his lordship *beyond* wicked once when they'd passed him on the street. And when her employer returned from Drury Lane Theatre, she'd mentioned how Signora Campari was the gentleman's current paramour.

He was the perfect complement to the opera singer. Like the diva, he possessed striking features that made an onlooker wish to linger so they might ponder the symmetry. Though, in all honesty, at this moment Lord Anthony looked less regal, for a pair of Lady Winton's rather ample white drawers had escaped the constraints of a box to land atop his lordship's head.

Mumbling an apology, Olivia reached up and pulled the garment off, revealing his wavy dark hair and a wayward lock that hung over his left eye. Her fingers twitched as she battled the desire to brush the silky strands aside.

His lordship peered at her through sleepy, heavy-lidded eyes. Eyes so dark one might think them black, but up close they were clearly the color of coffee with the slightest dash of cream. She could not recall ever being this close to a man to examine his features the way she did his lordship, or perhaps she'd never felt so infatuated to do so.

Those eyes that had looked sleepy widened and a smile formed in his square jaw, exposing perfect white teeth that looked as if they should be used in an advertisement for Higgins Pearly White Tooth Powder.

His carefree expression made her wonder if women falling onto his lap was an everyday occurrence. She could understand a woman's motivation in doing so.

One of his large hands slid from her waist to her back. The heat from it filtered through her thin cotton dress, sending a wave of warmth into her.

"Are you hurt?" he asked, his voice a rich, delicious baritone.

"Forgive me. I tripped." Something she would not have done if she'd realized the carriage had an occupant. Why was he lounging in Lady Winton's carriage?

A female screech, capable of shattering glass, cut off her thoughts.

Olivia glanced over her shoulder. Signora Campari stood on the pavement by the carriage's open door.

"*Un bastardo*!" the Italian woman screamed, lifting her hands dramatically into the air. "The *minuto* I turn my back you stray like a dog. You . . . you . . . shovel!"

A clouded expression settled over his lordship's handsome face before it cleared. "I believe you meant *rake*, Maria," he said calmly.

"*Si*, rake. *Rastrello*!" The opera singer stomped her foot.

Olivia suddenly realized the lush upholstery in this carriage was a deep blue, not the muddy brown of Lady Winton's equipage. Even more disconcerting was the fact Olivia remained pressed against the gentleman's warmth, from her tingling breasts to her hips. Her breath suddenly felt locked in her lungs. She scrambled off him and began gathering the scattered garments.

His lordship sat up. "The girl tripped, darling. Nothing more."

The woman made a noise that clearly conveyed her

disbelief as she lifted one of Lady Winton's drawers off the step from where it had landed and dangled it in the air as if proof of an indiscretion. "Bah!"

Olivia's face heated. Did the diva believe those unmentionables were Olivia's? She opened her mouth to explain, but the singer threw the garment into the carriage and began another string of Italian that didn't sound the least bit musical.

Lord Anthony expelled a heavy breath. His dark-eyed gaze returned to Olivia. "Are you quite sure you aren't injured?"

"I'm fine, sir. I beg your forgiveness. I thought this was Lady Winton's carriage."

The way his nose scrunched up clearly indicated he knew her ladyship.

"Oh, Olivia!" Lady Winton said, stepping next to the opera singer on the pavement. "What in heaven's name are you doing in there, alone, with . . . *him*?"

The opera singer turned to Lady Winton and began another round of animated Italian, interspersed with the sporadic English word that branded his lordship a rogue, along with the occasional garden implement.

With a commiserating expression, her ladyship nodded at Signora Campari. "Yes, dear, all men are scoundrels and cheats. You cannot trust them. Especially *this one*."

A nerve ticked in his lordship's jaw. He looked as if he wished to strangle the old woman.

With her nose tipped in the air, Lady Winton stormed away.

Mumbling another apology, Olivia snatched up the last of the scattered garments and boxes, then scrambled out of the carriage. She sucked in a deep breath as she surveyed the crowd standing on the pavement, gawking and whispering.

Lady Winton was charging toward her own carriage parked farther up the street in front of Lord Anthony's. The old woman's breasts were thrust forward like a carved figurehead on the bow of a ship.

When Olivia caught up to her ladyship, the woman grabbed the parcels from Olivia's hands and thrust them at her coachman. "Biddles, put these in the boot. Olivia, you are dismissed!"

The blood drained from Olivia's face, leaving it cold. "Lady Winton, I can explain."

"Humph. I don't wish to hear your explanation." The woman's curt tone sliced across Olivia's skin like a blade.

"But—"

"I cannot condone such immoral behavior. I should have known a girl from an *orphanage* would not be a suitable companion." Her ladyship climbed into the carriage and rapped her fist against the inside of the roof.

Biddles offered Olivia a sympathetic look as he climbed up on the perch and urged the horses to move on.

Olivia bit back a wicked word. The type of word Vicar Finch proclaimed would send her straight to hell. She turned to see Lord Anthony standing on the pavement next to Signora Campari. The diva's hands were still in perpetual motion. But this time not in the air. Instead, she was using them to strike his lordship in the chest.

With one fluid movement, he tossed the opera singer over his broad shoulder.

The prima donna screamed and pounded her fist against his lordship's back. "Antonio, put me down, this *minuto*!"

"That'll teach 'er, gov'ner," a man in the crowd yelled.

Laughter erupted.

With the soprano slung over his shoulder, Lord Anthony ducked his head and disappeared into his carriage. The sound of shrieking Italian could be heard as the equipage moved up the street, leaving Olivia the only player left in this fiasco.

"Damnation," she mumbled. When the ground beneath her didn't open and send her spiraling to purgatory like Vicar Finch claimed it would, she said the word again.

Now she'd have to grovel at Lady Winton's feet to get her position back. The thought of begging that sour-faced old bat made her want to retch, but she needed to stay in London. And the woman and her old gossiping friends were a plethora of information.

Information Olivia needed.

She squared her shoulders and started toward Lady Winton's town house. She would swallow her pride if it meant completing what she had come to London to do.

Chapter Three

Anthony stared at the various financial reports scattered across the mahogany desk and attempted to ignore the sharp pain that lanced across his temples like a harbinger of doom. He'd rather be in bed with Maria than contending with this. Well, perhaps not. After yesterday's debacle, she was more apt to castrate him than ease the anxious energy coursing through him.

He snatched up the invoice before him. How his brother, James, the Marquess of Huntington, contended with this amount of work, along with the House of Lords, was beyond him. He glanced at the calendar tucked into the edge of the blotter. Unnecessary to stare at it. He knew, damn well, that later today his brother James, his sister-in-law, Caroline, and their two sons, along with Anthony's youngest sibling, George, would take the rail to the Lake District for a monthlong vacation. During their holiday, James wished Anthony to deal with the family's latest acquisition, Victory Pens, and handle the ledger for his sister-in-law's newspaper, the *London Reformer*, along with the books for several of his other businesses.

What the bloody hell was James thinking asking him to handle such responsibilities? His brother deserved a holiday, but surely there was someone better qualified than himself to handle the task. And why did James have to be so involved in his various businesses anyway? He had solicitors, bankers, and Walters, his man of affairs, who worked out of the family's Bond Street offices. Why didn't he delegate what James normally oversaw to one of them? Surely, they were better suited to the task than him.

You can do this, a voice in his head whispered, battling the other inner voice that proclaimed, *you cannot*. He glanced at Walters, sitting in the chair that faced the desk.

The bespectacled man of affairs pushed his glasses up the bridge of his thin nose and offered a weak smile.

There was no avoiding it. With a resigned inward sigh, Anthony perused the bill in his hand. The amount on the invoice seemed an outrageous sum for a printing press, but what did he know? He handed the paper to Walters. "Send Phelps and Company a cheque for two thousand one hundred ninety-three pounds."

Anthony picked up the ledger for the *London Reformer* and opened it. As he scanned the business ledger to where he was supposed to enter the expenditure and his initials next to it, he twirled his pen between his fingers.

Walters cleared his throat.

Anthony glanced up.

The man's face flushed as he nervously wet his lips. "I believe it is one thousand two hundred and ninety-three pounds, my lord."

A bead of sweat trickled down Anthony's back. Without looking at the invoice, he knew the man of affairs was right.

Knew he'd twisted the numbers about as he always did. As if a casual slip of the tongue, he waved a nonchalant hand in the air. "Yes, of course."

The *thump, thump, thump* of a cane forewarned of Grandmother's approach. Strangely, he looked forward to the harridan's arrival. It would be a welcome reprieve from the numbers that danced around in his head like a puzzle. He casually pressed his back into the leather chair and tried to appear as though he knew what the bloody hell he was doing.

Without knocking, the dowager flung open the door and entered the office. The disapproving scowl on the old woman's face clearly indicated that Lady Winton had wagged her vicious tongue, relaying the incident with Maria yesterday.

"Walters, leave," Grandmother snapped.

The man of affairs stood so fast the papers balanced on his lap fluttered to the floor. Mumbling an apology, the fellow gathered them up and darted from the room.

The door clicked closed.

Anthony stood and motioned to the chair Walters had vacated. "Grandmother, why don't you sit? I hope you've had a favorable afternoon receiving callers."

She pounded her cane against the carpet. "Humph! I did not. How could I when the main topic on everyone's lips was the blatant disregard for propriety my grandson engaged in on Bond Street with an opera singer and another woman? Do you have no shame?"

He forced a carefree smile. "I assure you it was a misunderstanding."

"Am I to assume that tossing that diva over your shoulder

like a sack of coal for all of London to see was a misunderstanding as well?"

"No. That was deliberate." He did not wish to stand before a crowd as his hot-tempered mistress screeched and pummeled him.

"Yes, I'm sure it was. I'm positive that harpy Lady Winton has told everyone about the spectacle. It is bad enough your sister-in-law continues her political rants in favor of the suffragist movement in that radical newspaper she publishes, but now you've created a public spectacle. You are already a favorite subject in the gossip columns. Does this family have no sense of propriety?"

Anthony expelled a heavy breath while fighting the urge to rub at the steady pounding at his temples. "Caroline's opinions may not reflect yours, but I warn you, madam, I will not tolerate you maligning my sister-in-law in any way."

The dowager smirked. "Careful, boy, your unrequited love for your brother's wife is rearing itself."

He held the woman's steely regard for a long minute. He *did not* carry a torch for Caroline. If he defended his sister-in-law, it was because he admired her.

A vision of Caroline, James, and their children settled in Anthony's mind. In truth, he envied his brother's marriage, knowing he would never have such a relationship. A mistress he could hide his secret from. A wife would be a different matter entirely. Yet, with each passing year, his desire for something he both cherished and feared grew within him. A woman who looked at him the way Caroline looked at James. A woman who thought him beyond brilliant and would hold him in the utmost regard.

"Do you really think your string of mistresses will drive thoughts of Caroline from your head?" Grandmother asked, interrupting his thoughts. "At twenty-seven years of age, you should finally take a wife. Have your own children. A gaggle of brats, as mischievous as you, will distract you better than your meaningless lovers."

He liked children, but what if *his* inherited the affliction that plagued him?

"You are mistaken, madam. You know nothing about what I feel or think." Trying to hold his rising temper in check, Anthony moved to the door and jerked it open. He'd wanted a distraction, not a lecture. Worse, he'd promised James he'd live here with Grandmother for the next month because of the recent robberies in Mayfair. He must have been drunk when he'd agreed to that. Grandmother could take on any robber and come out the winner. And there was an army of servants at the Park Lane residence to jump at her beck and call.

"I have work to do, Grandmother. You might think me useless, but James does not, and I do not intend to disappoint him." He swallowed the thickness in his throat. Was that what he really wished to do? Prove to James and Grandmother—to everyone—he could run some of the family's business affairs?

The sound of the butler conversing with Caroline floated toward them, announcing his sister-in-law's arrival home.

Grandmother turned and arched a gray brow at him.

"James," Caroline called, stepping into the room. Upon seeing him and Grandmother, her feet faltered. "James is not home yet?"

He noticed the disappointment on her face. There was no denying how much she loved her husband, or how much James loved her. They had a happy marriage—one rarely seen in the *ton*. His sister Nina and her husband, Elliot, who were traveling in Europe, had the same type of relationship.

Shoving his thoughts aside, Anthony stepped forward and brushed a kiss to Caroline's cheek. "No. James had some political meeting to attend to. He thought he'd arrive home before you."

"I left my newspaper's editorial meeting early. I'm beyond famished. I even contemplated eating an old tin of biscuits I found inside one of my desk drawers. I realized I must return home when even the fuzzy green growth on them looked appealing." As she spoke, Caroline's hand settled tenderly on her rounded belly. She was with child, again. Caroline's gaze shifted to the dowager. "Grandmother, have all your callers left?"

"Yes, thank God," the old woman replied.

"A trying afternoon?" Caroline tipped her head to the side.

Grandmother grunted her affirmation.

"Well, after I visit the nursery to check on my dear boys, I intend to raid the pantry." She patted her tummy again. "This little one is demanding to be fed. Either of you care to join me for a light repast?"

Grandmother peered at him, waiting for his response.

He wanted to join Caroline, if only to escape the ledgers on the desk that taunted him. "I can't, Caroline. I've got too much work to do."

"Grandmother?" His sister-in-law's green eyes peered at the dowager.

"No. I've got a few unexpected letters to write. A hail-storm is upon us, and I must calm it."

A smile turned up Caroline's lips, and she tossed him a wink.

His body tensed. "Don't tell me even you've heard?"

Caroline waved a hand in the air. "The *ton* is forever making up prattle. Don't let it bother you, Anthony." And with that said, his sister-in-law swept out of the room.

Perhaps that was another reason he liked Caroline and enjoyed spending time with her. Because she thought the best of Anthony, when no one else did, no matter how damning the evidence.

As Olivia walked up Park Lane, she flexed her fingers against the handle of her battered leather valise. Yesterday, she'd gone to Lady Winton's residence to beg for her job back, only to be handed her suitcase. The woman had refused to see her—even refused to pay the wages due her or give her a letter of reference.

Her ladyship's actions reinforced Olivia's opinion that many members of the nobility were a cruel and nasty lot.

She stopped in front of a grand residence. It had taken her a full day to learn where Lord Anthony Trent lived. Biddles, Lady Winton's coachman, had said the gentleman lived at the Colbert Hotel, but a jovial man exiting the building had winked and given her this Park Lane address.

Stiffening her spine, she marched to the door and with firm determination rapped the knocker against the yellow lacquered surface. She needed to insist his lordship explain to Lady Winton that she and Signora Campari had misunderstood the situation.

A butler, with bony cheeks and a balding pate, answered. His gaze drifted over her suitcase and plain, navy cotton dress before settling on her face. His nose twitched as if inspecting a fishmonger's malodorous offerings.

Self-consciously, Olivia lifted a hand to her chignon, making sure none of her ginger locks dangled out of place from the tight bun she'd swept them into this morning.

"Yes?" he inquired in a stern voice.

She held her chin high. "I'm here to see Lord Anthony."

He thrust a silver tray in front of her. "Your calling card, *madam*."

The emphasis on the latter word implied he thought her nothing of the kind. And the fact she didn't possess a card would seal the butler's less-than-favorable opinion. She nibbled her lower lip. "I am without a card, sir, but I must see his lordship. It is a matter of urgency."

Without uttering a word, the man closed the door on her face.

She resisted the urge to mumble a blasphemy. She'd tempted damnation twice yesterday, perhaps a third time was not wise. Taking a deep breath, she pounded the knocker again.

The door swung open. The butler peered down his over-long nose. "Madam, if you do not remove yourself from here, I shall summon a constable."

Boom. The door shut again.

The squeaking of hinges drew her regard to the servants' area below street level. A brown-haired maid, wearing a white apron and gray dress, stuck her head out the basement's entrance. "Ole pinch-faced Menders won't let you in there. You're at the wrong entrance. Maids enter here."

"Maid?"

"Ain't you the new maid the agency sent?"

No, but if saying so would get her inside his lordship's residence, she'd pursue such a ruse. She wet her dry lips and nodded.

"Mrs. Parks wasn't expecting you until tomorrow."

"Mrs. Parks?" Olivia echoed, descending the steep stairs to the basement.

"That's the housekeeper. Didn't the agency tell you anything?"

This question she could answer truthfully. Olivia shook her head. "No, they didn't."

The rooms belowstairs were redolent with the scent of something savory. A thin woman with graying dark hair pulled into a taut bun stepped from the kitchen into the corridor. The keys jangling at her waist proclaimed her the housekeeper, and she looked as brittle and unbending as the butler.

"The agency sent the new maid, Mrs. Parks," the servant said.

The housekeeper narrowed her hard, brown eyes. "How old are you, girl?"

"Twenty-one, madam."

"You better be more competent than the last girl they sent. I won't tolerate bad behavior. No followers here. No giggling like a schoolgirl. And no fraternizing with the footmen. If you don't adhere to the rules, you'll find yourself out the door in a trice. Do I make myself clear?"

"Yes, Mrs. Parks. Perfectly," Olivia replied.

"Very well. What is your name?"

"Olivia, ma'am. Olivia Michaels."

The housekeeper nodded, then turned to the maid. "Katie, get Olivia a uniform."

"Thank you, Mrs. Parks." Olivia bobbed a quick curtsey.

"This way." With a sweep of her hand, Katie motioned to the narrow servants' stairway at the rear of the corridor.

As they made their way up, Katie turned to her. "Don't be nervous. Mrs. Parks is a bit brisk but better than most housekeepers. And his lordship is a kind employer."

"Is his lordship in?"

"Now don't go getting any high ideas about his lordship."

"High ideas?" Olivia blinked.

"You know. Trying to get a bit too cozy so he'll favor you and buy you some pretty baubles."

"Oh, no! I have no intention of throwing myself at the man." She only wished to speak with him. Surely not get *too cozy*. She didn't even know how to flirt. There had been few men at the orphanage except for Vicar Finch and a groundskeeper, and both men were ancient and old enough to be her grandfather. The latter thought made her feel a bit melancholy. She'd never had any family. Never known her parents or grandparents.

"That's best 'cause he's head over heels in love with his wife," Katie said, breaking into Olivia's thoughts.

Wife? She'd thought Lord Anthony a bachelor. No wonder Lady Winton called him a scoundrel. Well, men in love with their wives didn't dally with opera singers. How could the staff not know the man was a cad? Olivia harrumphed, then smacked a hand over her mouth and feigned a cough.

Katie glanced over her shoulder.

"A tickle in my throat." Olivia offered the excuse but didn't miss the questioning expression in the maid's eyes. Obviously, his lordship had them all bamboozled.

"And you won't find no mistress better than her lady-ship. Sweet as sugar, she is."

Poor, poor woman to have such a wicked husband.

"Now the dowager . . ." Katie tsked. "She's the one to avoid."

They stepped into the maids' quarters in the attic. A line of beds with mattresses thicker than the thin one she'd slept on at Lady Winton's were set under the dormers. Lace curtains covered the windows and a cheerful yellow paint brightened the walls.

Katie opened an oak wardrobe and removed a gray cotton dress and apron identical to hers. "This should fit you."

"Thank you." She took the garments.

"And that'll be where you sleep." The maid pointed to one of the beds.

If all went as planned, she'd be gone shortly. She just needed to talk to his lordship.

"Hurry back downstairs. Mrs. Parks doesn't tolerate dawdling." Katie headed out the door, pulling it closed behind her.

Olivia's fingers fumbled with the buttons that lined the front of her dress. This was madness, pretending to be the new maid. But what other options did she have? She stepped out of her garment and quickly hung it in the armoire. Her job as Lady Winton's companion was imperative. Old biddies like her ladyship enjoyed nothing more than gossiping. The more information Olivia could gather from those chinwaggers, the less risk she took. She needed to know about every gathering these highborns were planning. Who would be attending? When? Where? If she wasn't careful, she'd get caught and find herself behind bars in some dank prison cell.

She sat on the bed. Perhaps she should just ask Vicar Finch for her teaching position back—not finish what she'd come to London to do. A groan eased from her lips. By now Lady Winton, the old windbag, might have already written the stoic clergyman claiming Olivia a jezebel, closing the option of returning to the orphanage and her old life soundly in her face. And what of her deathbed promise to Helen?

Helen's gaunt face flashed in her mind.

"You'll make them pay for their sins, won't you?" Helen grabbed her hand—her grip weak.

"Yes, if you wish it."

As she nodded, Helen's cracked lips formed a smile. A minute later, the girl who had been like a sister to Olivia in the orphanage drew in her last rattling breath and closed her eyes as if the promise of retribution released her soul from her young, yet frail body.

Olivia blinked at the tears threatening to fall. She had two more men on her list. Helen's blackguard father was one of them. She would see this through. She stood before the square mirror that hung above one of the low oak dressers and slipped on the maid's dress and apron, then poked her head out of the door.

With quiet, measured steps, she descended the narrow servants' stairs. At each landing, she listened for his lordship's richly toned voice.

The sound of footfalls moving up the stairs set the hairs on her neck on end. Was it Mrs. Parks? Had the housekeeper realized Olivia was an imposter?

Chest tight, she stepped off a landing and dashed into the corridor. The footfalls grew louder. A quick glance revealed three doors. She crept to the closest one, inched it open, and slipped inside.

Chapter Four

With her palms on the door, Olivia pressed her ear to the wood and listened.

The footfalls moved past the room and faded.

She exhaled a heavy breath.

A feminine giggle broke the silence.

Heart thundering, Olivia swung around and flattened her back against the door. Her gaze landed on the massive four-poster bed with damask drapes that concealed the occupant.

Olivia froze. The only thing that moved were her lips, which silently prayed the woman would not hear the pounding in Olivia's chest.

"Oh my," the woman said in a voice that oozed anticipation. "I'm so anxious for a taste, I'm salivating."

Olivia's gaze shot to the sound. It wasn't coming from the bed, but an open doorway to her right, in the far wall. A sitting room or changing room perhaps. Slowly, she inched her fingers across the door until they clasped the cool metal handle.

"Ah, you greedy puss, let me put it in your mouth," a deep baritone responded.

The weight of Olivia's body settled back against the door. Her moist hand slipped off the handle. The voice sounded like Lord Anthony. She froze, fearing even the slightest shift in her weight would cause her knocking knees to buckle beneath her. She wished to speak to him, but not while he was otherwise engaged.

"Is it really as silky as everyone claims?" the woman asked.

His lordship chuckled. "Open your mouth and find out."

"Mmmm, it is."

She wasn't sure what they were talking about, but Olivia experienced a flush of warmth. She snapped herself out of her pillar-like state, curled her fingers about the door handle, and slowly turned it.

A woman dressed in an emerald green gown stepped out of the adjacent room. She was lovely, with rosy cheeks and startling green eyes. She held a small golden-colored cardboard box while licking the tips of her fingers.

The woman gasped. Her steps faltered as her free hand dipped to her rounded belly, yet she smiled. "Goodness, you scared me."

Was this her ladyship? Oh, his lordship was more of a villain than she first thought. His poor wife was obviously with child. The scoundrel! How could he be so free with his affections? While growing up in the orphanage, she'd always dreamed of a family and his lordship did not cherish his.

She pushed her near frozen body off the door and offered a quick, awkward curtsey. "I'm sorry. I seem to have taken a wrong turn, madam. I'm the new maid."

The woman glanced back at the doorway from whence she'd come. "Can you keep a secret?"

A secret? Perhaps she wasn't her ladyship. But if she wasn't, then who was she? A lover? Oh, could his lordship be such a scoundrel? To bring a paramour into his house was beyond the pale. Olivia forced herself not to gape at the woman's belly. "Yes," she said.

"You must think his lordship and I wicked."

Indeed, I do.

"I beg of you not to tell Cook you saw me with . . ." The woman paused and glanced down at the box. It was then, Olivia realized they were chocolates. "Cook is forever trying to make a batch as scrumptious as the confectioner, but I fear, she hasn't succeeded, and I'd prefer not to hurt her feelings. His lordship snuck a box in today."

"Who are you talking to, darling?" A man who resembled Lord Anthony, but older, stepped out of the adjoining room. He smiled, crinkling the skin near his eyes.

The green-eyed beauty turned to him. "James, we have been found out."

"Ah, only a matter of time, Caroline." He drew the pad of his thumb over the corner of her lip and held it up for inspection before licking the dab of chocolate off his finger. "Evidence," he said, grinning.

An odd sensation fluttered in Olivia's belly as she watched the interaction between these two. The way they gazed at each other . . . like they . . . Well, she didn't know what it was, but it seemed beyond anything she'd witnessed. As if tangible sparks shot between them.

The man turned to Olivia.

She curtseyed. Perhaps this was who Katie had spoken about. Yes, it made sense. This was his lordship and his wife. An older brother. The master of the house.

"Excuse me. I beg your forgiveness." She turned and grasped the door handle, hoping to make a quick escape.

"Wait," the woman said.

"Damnation," she mumbled under her breath, hoping this time the ground *would* swallow her up. She pivoted around.

The woman smiled and handed her the box. "If you can keep a secret, you may share these with the other maids. I shall be as big as a house if I keep indulging in my cravings."

Slowly, Olivia released the taut air in her lungs. Her ladyship was truly kindhearted. So much nicer than that nasty Lady Winton.

"Thank you, madam." Olivia backed out of the bedchamber. In the corridor, she slipped the box of chocolates into the largest pocket of her apron, wiped her damp palms on the garment, and tiptoed down the servants' stairs to the floor below.

She needed to find Lord Anthony fast. Perhaps he wasn't even home. She stopped before a set of open double doors and peeked inside a lovely drawing room with cream-colored walls, two blue upholstered sofas, and a massive fireplace. Her gaze narrowed on a gray-haired woman, dressed in black, who sat at a mahogany secretaire.

The woman glanced over her shoulder. "You, come here!"

Was this elderly woman the dowager Katie spoke of?

"Just don't stand there gawking." The woman stood and punctuated her words with two dull thumps of her cane on the blue and gold carpet.

Olivia stepped into the elegant room and curtseyed.

The woman's piercing gray eyes narrowed. Her gaze drifted over Olivia. "You're new?"

"Yes, madam."

"Your name?"

"Olivia, madam." Stomach fluttering, she curtseyed again.

"Stop bouncing up and down, child. You're making me seasick." The old lady pursed her lips and stepped closer. "You look familiar."

Olivia's throat constricted. Was this woman one of Lady Winton's cronies? Had she visited with her ladyship while Olivia was present? "This is my first day, madam."

As if bored with the conversation, the woman waved a hand in the air and handed Olivia a stack of letters with red wax seals. "Give these to Menders."

The haughty butler? She stifled a groan. Her fingers flexed against the missives. She'd hoped to get out of here before seeing him again.

"Tell Menders they must be put in the post today."

"Yes, madam. Right away." She exited the room.

A door farther up the corridor opened. A lanky, blond-haired gentleman with wire-rimmed glasses stepped out of a room. A member of the family? Doubtful, his clothes were simple, and he didn't resemble Lord Anthony or the other dark-haired nobleman she'd just met.

"Have a good evening, Walters," a man inside the room said.

The deep voice sent a shiver of recollection down her spine. *Lord Anthony.*

"Thank you, my lord." The thin man pulled the door closed behind him.

"Sir, is Lord Anthony in there?" Olivia offered the

fellow her most congenial smile and lifted the wax-sealed letters, implying they were to be delivered to his lordship.

The man nodded and continued past her to the narrow stairway the servants used. The sound of his footsteps faded as he descended the wooden treads.

She slipped the letters into the pocket of her pinafore and knocked on the door.

"Yes, enter."

Taking a deep breath, she stepped into the room. The walls were lined with floor-to-ceiling bookcases. A tall ladder hung on a brass bar. It appeared to slide in front of them, so one could remove books from the top shelves. A massive mahogany desk dominated the center of the office. The leather chair behind it was turned around, leaving the occupant hidden.

A thickly muscled arm, its sleeve rolled up to its elbow, came into view. The man held a crystal glass with honey-colored liquid that sparkled as the light from the lamp on the desk reflected off the cut tumbler.

"Did you forget something, Walters?"

Olivia opened her mouth, but nothing came out. She couldn't pull her gaze away from the muscles that shaped his lordship's arm, or the way his thumb slowly stroked the side of the glass he held. Once again, that odd, foreign heat, like the one she'd experienced while lying on top of his lordship in the carriage, sparked in her belly, flooding her body with warmth.

"Walters?" The casters on the chair made a noise as Lord Anthony swiveled around to face her.

His eyes widened. "You're not Walters."

She shook her head.

He set the glass down on the blotter. "Yes?"

She squared her shoulders. "I need you to explain what happened between us yesterday."

A clearly puzzled expression settled over his handsome features.

It appeared he didn't even recognize her. A heavy weight perched on her shoulders.

"Yesterday?" He narrowed his dark eyes. "Are you trying to blackmail me, love? I might be branded a cad, but I always remember whom I've been with." His gaze drifted a slow path over her body. "And I assure you, if we'd dallied, I'd remember you."

She was positive he would. She looked nothing like Signora Campari. The opera singer's dark hair looked as luxurious as sable and her complexion was clear, while Lady Winton had told Olivia that her red hair looked garish and her freckles distracting. Vicar Finch had said worse things about her hair, and once he'd instructed Mrs. Garson to cut it short. But he'd rued the day, since he'd insisted it only came back brighter.

"Yesterday, I entered the wrong carriage in front of Madame Lefleur's shop."

"Ah, you look different without your hair in your face. And since you landed on me, what precisely am I to explain?"

"That is was an accident. That we weren't . . ." Heat singed her cheeks. She took a deep breath. "Lady Winton thinks we were . . . um, acting inappropriately."

He laughed.

"It's not funny, sir. Her ladyship has dismissed me without a letter of reference."

The smile on his face vanished. Standing, he braced his

hands on his desk and leaned forward. "The old battle-ax sacked you?"

She'd never been this close to him when he stood. He was even taller than she thought. The room seemed to grow smaller. "Yes. Will you go and explain to her that we weren't . . . cavorting?"

He motioned to one of the upholstered chairs that faced the desk. "Please, sit."

She nodded. As she settled into the soft fabric, Olivia tucked the skirt of her dress beneath her.

Lord Anthony came around the desk and leaned against the surface. Without his coat on, she realized that the breadth of his shoulders was not due to padding or the skill of his tailor.

"Miss . . . ?"

"Michaels. Olivia Michaels, my lord."

"Miss Michaels, I fear whatever I say to that nasty old bird won't change the woman's opinion."

The hope in her chest deflated, leaving an ache. She needed that job or at least one comparable to carry out her plan.

"By the look of your uniform, it appears you've already found another position. Has Mrs. Parks hired you to work here?" he asked.

She shook her head and explained how she'd let them believe she was the new maid. "When the real maid arrives tomorrow, I'll be tossed out on my ear."

Lord Anthony rubbed a hand across his shaven jaw, already growing dark with stubble. "Don't worry. I'm sure I can find someone who needs a maid."

Being a maid wouldn't allow her to sit with women from the top tier of society and hear their gossip. "I wasn't a maid, sir. I was her ladyship's companion. Do you know anyone who would wish to employ me for my company?"

"Yes, but"—he shook his head—"you wouldn't wish to work for them."

"But I would. I'm desperate."

"I assure you, you aren't that desperate." A crease dissected the smooth skin between his brows. "Do you know what type of employer I mean?"

"A noblewoman as high strung as Lady Winton?"

"Worse." His gaze slid over her body.

His perusal sent a rush of warmth through her veins. She suddenly understood what he meant. Her cheeks grew hot.

"You're as innocent as a newborn puss, aren't you?"

I'm far from innocent, my lord. She knew things—had done things that would shock him. Not things of a sexual nature, but things that no one would suspect her of.

He strode back to his chair and folded his long frame into it, then opened the ledger in front of him. He released a heavy breath. "Give me a moment to add this dashed column of figures, then I shall try to think of who might be in need of a lady's companion."

His lordship wrote several numbers on a sheet of paper. He scratched one of the figures out, then wrote another. Raking his long fingers through his hair, he mumbled a blasphemy. The type of word Vicar Finch insisted would send one to hell. He might be handsome beyond compare, but he sure took an inordinate amount of time adding the figures up.

With his sensual lips pinched into a straight line, he wrote a number into the journal, then peered up at her.

"Now, who could use a companion?" he mumbled as if thinking aloud.

Breath held in her lungs, she waited.

He tapped the tip of the pencil against the blotter. "I cannot think of anyone."

"No one?" Olivia's hopes sank like a lead weight into water.

A thumping noise like someone walking with a pegged leg or a cane resonated through the ceiling from the floor above.

The rhythmic tapping of his lordship's pencil stilled, and he peered up. A slight smile curved up one side of his mouth. "Do you have a strong constitution, Miss Michaels?"

"Yes, I believe so."

"Well, there is one old woman, but she is rather *difficult*. Cantankerous is the best word to describe her, but you've had experience with belligerent individuals if you've tended to Lady Winton."

Hope made her scoot closer to the edge of the chair.

"How are you at ducking flying objects?" his lordship asked.

Flying objects? "Um, I presume as competent as the next person."

"Good, then I will hire you as a companion for my grandmother."

She thought of the sharp-toned woman she'd met earlier. She might be worse than Lady Winton, but with no other prospects and no references she could not be picky.

* * *

Anthony watched as the corners of Miss Michaels's lips turned up into a smile.

Obviously, the young woman knew very little if anything about his grumpy grandmother, or she would be running from the room. "She doesn't pay a great deal of calls, but when she does my sister-in-law, Lady Caroline Huntington, usually accompanies her, and she is leaving today for holiday. And the dowager receives a prodigious number of callers and occasionally goes to the theater."

A brief flash of excitement lit up Miss Michaels's eyes.

"Have you ever attended the theater?"

"No, my lord."

"Well, then I'll hire you to be her companion. But the task will not be an easy one."

"I understand, my lord. I will do my best."

He wasn't sure doing her best would be enough. Grandmother was hard to please, along with abrasive. But it was better than Miss Michaels ending up on the street, and with no references she might end up there. "I'll inform her after I finish adding one more column in this ledger."

"Thank you, my lord."

Anthony nodded, then removed a piece of parchment from the paper tray. Carefully he wrote the figures he needed to add and double- and triple-checked to make sure he'd written them correctly. A headache began to throb at his temple. He fought the urge to rub at it. "Two hundred fifty-seven plus five hundred and ninety-eight," he mumbled.

"Eight hundred and fifty-five," Miss Michaels said in a low voice.

Startled, he glanced up. "What did you say?"

She blinked. "I beg your forgiveness. I did not mean to overstep."

He waved his hand in the air. He wasn't concerned about her apology; he'd only found it difficult to comprehend how she'd added the figures together without even seeing them on paper. It seemed incomprehensible to him. "Forget about that, just repeat the figure you said."

"Eight hundred and fifty-five."

He wondered if she'd seen what he'd written down. "Really, then what is eight hundred and fifty-five plus one hundred and forty-two?"

She folded her hands in her lap. "Nine hundred and ninety-seven, my lord."

He wrote down her answer and carefully compared it to the answer he'd written down earlier. They were the same. Good Lord. He glanced up at her. "You're correct."

"I've always possessed a strange ability to calculate figures. Mrs. Garson, the matron at All Saints Orphanage, realized it and not only gave me a teaching position, but the job of handling the orphanage's ledgers."

Usually companions were down-on-their-luck women of genteel birth. "Did you grow up at All Saints?"

"Yes, my lord."

"And how is it you became Lady Winton's companion?"

"Her ladyship is a second cousin to the village squire. He gave me a letter of reference."

Anthony nodded. He slid the ledger across the desk, pointed to a column, and handed Miss Michaels the pencil. "Can you add this?"

She looked down at the three figures. "Two thousand eight hundred and eighty-nine."

He rubbed the back of his neck and blinked. Again, the same figure he'd taken a protracted time to calculate. "Miss Michaels, I'll only hire you to be my grandmother's companion if you agree to one other stipulation. Let us call it a proposition."

Chapter Five

Olivia Michaels stared at him like a rabbit caught in the gaze of a hungry fox. What type of position did she think he wanted her for?

Unbidden, a wicked image of her naked body lying in his bed flashed in his mind. He pushed it aside. "I assure you, the position I offer you is not nefarious. I'm in need of a clerk. Someone skilled with figures. So, I'll hire you as my grandmother's companion, if you agree to work for me in your spare time."

She nibbled her lower lip.

Obviously, that old battle-ax Lady Winton had filled Miss Michaels with scandalous tales about him being a womanizer. "I'll treat you the same way I treat my brother's man of affairs. And believe me, I've no interest in the chap besides his competency."

"If you employ such a fellow why would you need me?"

Because Walters really worked for James, and if they spent several weeks together, he was sure the man would find out about Anthony's problem—the way numbers imposed themselves out of order. He'd kept this secret his whole life, feigned laziness and disinterest. Gotten himself kicked out of several schools with his bad behavior as soon as he believed someone was catching onto the truth.

He couldn't risk Walters finding out and reporting this knowledge to James when he returned from holiday. Miss Michaels could be a buffer between him and Walters. She could handle the mathematics that seemed to get twisted about in his head.

"Walters spends most of his time at the Trent family's offices on Bond Street. We have a weekly meeting to go over several expenditures and ledgers, but there is a great deal of work to be handled here. You'll be paid for the additional time."

Her hazel eyes widened, and he realized they were a pretty mixture of amber with little specks of gold toward the outer edges of her irises. "What do you say?"

She glanced down at her hands, folded primly in her lap, then returned her regard to him.

"You need a job, Miss Michaels. I am offering you not one, but two. And both will pay exceedingly well."

"Thank you, my lord. I accept. What am I to tell Mrs. Parks?"

"I'll handle both her and the butler."

She reached into her pocket and removed a stack of letters.

"What are these?" he asked, taking them from her.

"I believe I have already met your grandmother. She asked me to give these to the butler."

She possessed a strong constitution if she'd met his cantankerous grandmother and still accepted the job. It proved how desperate she was, which was a godsend for him. He stood and pulled the bell rope. As he waited for Menders to enter the room, Anthony's gaze traveled over

Olivia Michaels, who was a good seven inches shorter than his six feet. She possessed an oval face with freckles on her cheeks and the bridge of her nose. Her hair, pulled into a tight bun at the back of her head, was a bright shade of red. His gaze dipped a little lower. Her breasts were small, but her derriere was rather shapely. The type of bottom a man could hold onto while she rode him to the point of ecstasy. He shoved that thought aside. He didn't dally with those in his family's employ.

Noticing his regard, she looked self-conscious and once again peered at her lap.

He pulled his gaze away.

A knock sounded on the door.

"Come in," Anthony said.

Menders stepped into the room. The butler's gaze shifted to Olivia. The man's eyes grew wide. Frowning, he opened his mouth.

"Menders," Anthony said, cutting the butler off before he could utter a word. "This is Miss Olivia Michaels. She is the elder Lady Huntington's new companion. Please show her to the bedchamber across from my grandmother's."

The butler blinked. "Yes, my lord."

Anthony folded his arms over his chest. "Menders, sadly Miss Michaels had to pretend to be a maid to gain admittance into this residence. She doesn't recall which footman closed the door on her face when she inquired whether I was in, and doesn't believe she'd recall his face if she saw him again, but I want the staff to know they will be severely reprimanded if they turn callers away before they inquire into that person's business."

"Of course, my lord." The butler gave Miss Michaels a sideways glance and an expression of relief flashed over the man's face. Hopefully, he'd feel indebted to her now. It would make her transition into being Grandmother's companion easier, for the old woman surely wouldn't make it so.

Anthony picked up the stack of letters and handed them to the butler. "These need to be put in the post, but beforehand show Miss Michaels to her room."

"Yes, my lord."

Miss Michaels stood. "Thank you, Lord Anthony."

"Miss Michaels, when you are settled, please return here." Anthony rounded the desk and sat, ending the conversation.

The door clicked closed behind them.

He peered at the ledger and frowned at the numbers in a long column, wondering if he was seeing them correctly. With any luck, Grandmother wouldn't scare the chit away. He needed her help.

James entered the office. "What were Menders and the new maid doing in here?"

"I've hired her to be Grandmother's companion."

"Grandmother's what?" Razor-thin sharpness edged James's voice.

"Companion," Anthony repeated. "Grandmother has become accustomed to Caroline accompanying her. With your wife away, I thought it a good idea."

"Anthony, what's this about?" James asked, a suspicious glint in his narrowed eyes.

His brother was too smart. Anthony drew in a breath. "The woman lost her position as Lady Winton's companion."

"And you had something to do with it? What did you do?"

Damnation, he was tired of everyone asking him that question. "I bloody well did nothing."

"You're not responsible?"

"I'm not. She climbed into the wrong carriage yesterday."

"Really?" His brother's voice dripped with disbelief.

"James, I was out with Maria."

"Yes, I heard."

Good Lord, news traveled about London at lightning speed. "After Lady Winton saw the girl with me in my carriage, she fired her. The old bird won't even give her a reference."

"So, you think you're doing her a favor by setting her up to deal with Grandmother?"

"Better that, than being on the street."

"I suppose you are right but do me a favor. Don't tell Grandmother until after Caroline and I leave. I do not wish to hear her reaction. And that poor chit, if she thought Lady Winton a wretched employer, she might have just made a deal with the devil."

"I'll handle it."

James nodded. "We are leaving. Caroline and your nephews wish to say goodbye."

They strode into the entry hall where a flurry of activity commenced. Caroline was holding her elder son Michael's hand. Thaddeus, age two, dressed in a sailor's suit, was crying in his nanny's arms and reaching for his mother.

"Someone is in need of a nap." James took Michael's hand, so Caroline could take the weeping child in her arms.

Caroline smiled and rubbed Thad's back. "I'm sure he'll fall asleep on the train."

His sister-in-law always possessed remarkable calmness in the face of chaos, especially when it involved her children. Most women he knew would have instructed the nanny to contend with the child, but not Caroline.

Anthony caught the look his grandmother was bestowing on him. It said it all. Move on. She didn't understand. He did not lust after his brother's wife. He lusted over what James and Caroline had. His sister-in-law's total devotion to his brother. She loved James and her children and would do anything for them. The same was true for James regarding his wife and sons.

Grandmother thumped her cane against the marble tiles in the entry. "Well, you best get going." The old woman looked as if forced to endure another moment with the children, her cold heart might turn to ice and shatter within her.

"Yes, time to shove off." James clapped a hand onto Anthony's shoulder. "We will see you in a month's time."

Both Caroline and James kissed Grandmother's papery cheek.

Anthony bent down in front of his nephew Michael. Unlike the Trents' dark midnight-colored hair, the boy possessed light brown locks with threads of gold, like Caroline's. He tousled the boy's hair. "You be a good lad now."

The child nodded and clutched at Anthony's sleeve. "Uncle Tony, won't you come with us?"

"I can't, little man. I need to stay here and hold the fort. And you need to be a good boy for Mama and Papa. I shall see you when you return. I expect to hear all about it." He stood and followed them outside to where two carriages waited.

Apprehensions over tending to the completion of

Victory Pens's new manufacturing building, along with the other businesses, including the accounts for Caroline's newspaper, drifted through the back of Anthony's mind. He should have told James the truth. Should have told him of his trouble with figures. The reason he'd given his tutors and teachers such a hard time. The reason he'd left university to travel the Continent.

Caroline turned to him. Her hand clutched his as she leaned close. "You shall do fine, Anthony," she said as if reading his thoughts. She kissed his cheek and Caroline and James climbed into their carriage.

You cannot do this, that naysaying voice in his head whispered. *Tell James.* He took a single step toward the carriage, then froze. He needed to try.

"Move on," the coachman of the first carriage called to the horses.

The two vehicles moved up Park Lane. He turned to see Grandmother standing in the doorway, her gray gaze locked on him. She still didn't understand the emotions churning within him.

"Don't say a word, madam," he said sharply as he strode past her. "Do I make myself clear?"

Grandmother arched a gray brow but kept her guidance to herself.

He stepped into James's office—his office for now—and closed the door and paced the length of the navy and gold Turkish carpet.

Someone knocked.

Damnation, he should have realized Grandmother would need to make her opinion known. He didn't have the patience to converse with her right now—too many thoughts were going through his head. Tomorrow he would visit his mistress and end their arrangement. Right now, he needed to contend with a high-strung mistress like Maria as much as he needed a bullet in the head.

He jerked the door open.

Olivia Michaels gasped and reared back. He could imagine his expression. He probably looked like the devil. He forced a smile and motioned to one of the chairs that faced the desk. “Come in, Miss Michaels.”

Sitting, she, once again, folded her hands primly in her lap. The plain navy dress she wore wasn’t much nicer than the gray maid’s uniform she’d worn earlier, perhaps worse, since the darker color washed out her pale face.

“Are you all settled?” he asked.

“Yes. The bedchamber Menders showed me to is lovely.” Her eyes sparkled with pleasure.

They were expressive with a kaleidoscope of colors. And when she smiled it transformed her simple face.

“I’ve never slept in such a room. It’s . . .” She blushed. “Forgive me, I’m prattling on.”

“I’m glad you’re pleased.” Hopefully, the room’s elegance would compensate for the woman having to contend with his irritable grandmother. He didn’t feel like dealing with the matriarch anymore today. “Tomorrow morning report here, and I will introduce you to the elder Lady Huntington.”

“Am I to help with the ledgers this evening?”

They had already given him a headache and he needed to go buy Maria a gift for when he ended their arrangement tomorrow. Afterward, he intended on going to his club. “No.”

* * *

The following day near noon, Anthony stepped into his office to see the little redheaded mouse he'd hired as his grandmother's companion sitting in one of the two chairs that faced his desk. He mumbled a curse under his breath as he remembered he'd told her to meet him here in the morning.

"Forgive me, Miss Michaels, I overslept."

She nodded but did not say anything.

"Have you been waiting long?"

She glanced at the clock on the mantel. "No, my lord, only four hours."

Since eight? Who the bloody hell got up that early? He supposed those who'd not gone out drinking with their chums and gotten pissing drunk. He pulled on the bell rope.

A few minutes later, the butler entered the room. "Yes, my lord?"

"Is the dowager in the blue drawing room, Menders?"

"She is."

"Has she had her tea yet?"

"No. I was just about to bring it."

"Very good. Ten minutes after you do so, I want you to show Miss Michaels to the drawing room. She'll wait for you here."

"Very well, my lord." Menders nodded and left.

"Miss Michaels, you must be resilient when dealing with the elder Lady Huntington. In simple words, she can be rather difficult at times." That wasn't completely true. Her mood didn't shift, she was usually always cantankerous, but it would be best if Olivia Michaels thought it only a momentary lapse, not a perpetual state.

"Yes, my lord."

"Very well, I will go and inform her of your employment." Anthony strode from the first-floor office, took the stairs two at a time, and entered the blue drawing room.

Grandmother sat in one of the two damask chairs that faced the sofa. She held a book in her gnarled fingers and peered over its edge at him.

"I need to talk with you."

"About?" She closed the novel and placed it beside her on the cushion.

Menders entered the room, carrying a silver tea service.

As the butler set the tray on the mahogany table beside the matriarch's chair, the dowager stared at Anthony.

"Do you wish me to pour, madam?" Menders asked.

With a flick of her hand, Grandmother shooed the butler away, and the man strode from the room.

"Let me get that." Anthony sat in the chair adjacent to hers and poured her tea into a delicate cup and saucer that felt too small in his large hands.

The old woman's sharp, gray eyes studied him.

"You like it with three lumps of sugar." It wasn't a question; he might have trouble with figures, but he was observant.

She nodded, but her astute gaze narrowed. She knew he was up to something. He enjoyed having tea with her as much as he enjoyed being thrown from a horse.

He lifted the tongs and added the cubes of sugar to her tea. His brother James always said that after ingesting so much sugar one would think it would have sweetened the old bird's disposition, but it hadn't. Smiling, he handed her the cup and saucer.

"What are you up to, Anthony?" Soundlessly, she took

a sip, yet her shrewd eyes continued to watch him over the rim of the cup.

"Up to?" He stood and moved to the massive marble fireplace. In mock indignation, he pressed his fingers to his chest. "You offend me, dear Grandmother. Whatever do you mean?"

"I'm old, not senile. You wish to share tea with me as much as the devil wishes to converse with a saint."

"What an interesting analogy. So, which one of us is the devil in this scenario?" He leaned an arm on the mantel. "I've hired you a companion."

"A what?" Grandmother slammed her teacup onto the tray, causing the teapot to rattle. The spoon slipped from the saucer and clanked against the polished tray.

"A companion," he repeated in an elevated voice, insinuating her hearing was deficient.

"I'm not deaf, Anthony. I heard you loud and clear. I don't need or wish for a companion. I demand you dismiss the woman."

"She'll be company for you. And with Caroline and James away, she can accompany you to the theater. You know I have little interest in sitting in the family box and watching a play."

"True. You would rather go to the actresses' dressing rooms and act the scoundrel."

"Yes, well, that's neither here nor there."

"I insist you sack the woman."

He straightened. "I won't. Now, I think it's time you met her."

"Have you gone mad? I said no." She thumped her cane against the rug.

"And I said it is already done."

"I don't wish for anyone's company. I prefer my own."

"Perhaps that is the problem."

The butler stepped into the room. Miss Michaels stood behind him in the corridor. This was going worse than he predicted. The woman would have to have a strong backbone if she was to deal with Grandmother on a daily basis.

"Come in, Miss Michaels."

"My lord. Lady Huntington." She bobbed a curtsey.

"You?" Grandmother scowled. "I thought you were a maid."

"No, my lady. There was some misunderstanding. I've been hired to be your companion."

Grandmother's gaze drifted over Olivia. "Who are your people?"

Anthony stiffened. He needed to deflect the old woman away from her prodding. He opened his mouth. "She—"

"I am an orphan, my lady," Miss Michaels said, her chin tipped up. "I was most recently employed as Lady Winton's companion."

Anthony cringed.

Grandmother stomped her cane again. "Good Lord, Anthony, is she the woman your mistress caught you dallying with in your carriage?" A red flush of anger blossomed on Grandmother's bony cheeks.

"I was not dallying with his lordship," Olivia Michaels replied, her voice infused with steel.

Both his Grandmother's and his gaze swung to Olivia. He'd give her credit, very few people addressed his grandmother without cowering. She'd caused several maids to quit and even more to cry.

"Madam, you may defame my lack of status, but my morals are pristine. I entered the wrong carriage. There was no improper behavior. And Lady Winton quickly rose to condemn both me and your grandson. Unjustly."

Grandmother seemed momentarily shocked. Speechless. Rarely did anyone defend themselves when the old bird made accusations, least of all those employed in this household.

Anthony contemplated rushing Olivia Michaels from the room before a cup or saucer or even a cane was hurled at her. He stepped toward her so he might shield her body from any objects Grandmother might be inclined to throw.

Grandmother's gaze shifted from Olivia to him, then volleyed back to her new companion. She was as angry as a hornet that's been swatted at repeatedly. "Out! Out! Out!"

Chapter Six

"Well, that could have gone better," Anthony said as he and Olivia stepped out of the drawing room. "Since your time is free, you can help me with the ledgers. Hopefully, tomorrow my grandmother will be more agreeable, and we will try again." Anthony turned and strode away without any further explanation. He glanced over his shoulder.

Olivia Michaels was staring longingly at the door as if she wanted to try to win Grandmother's regard today. Not a wise move. When the old woman was in a wretched mood it was best to leave her alone.

"Tomorrow, Miss Michaels." His voice was firm and unbending. He was known for his devil-may-care nature, but Anthony also realized the power of his family and the rank of his birth. That, along with a stern voice, could accomplish a great deal. He'd witnessed his brother's use of it often enough.

She nodded and followed him to his office.

He grabbed one of the wooden chairs, which was set against the wall, and placed it on the opposite side of the desk, facing him. "Have a seat and we will get started."

As she sat, he saw the disappointment in her expressive eyes. "Miss Michaels, I could overrule my grandmother and insist you stay in the room when her guests arrive, but it is better she accepts you."

She nodded.

He hated disappointing people, but he seemed to be gifted in that regard. He was half-tempted to dismiss the woman. But whether he wished to admit it or not, he needed her as much as she needed him. Anthony opened the ledger for Victory Pens. His brother might come across as stern, but James had bought an old building in the East End that would house his self-feeding pen factory and was making substantial improvements to the building. Improvements that would help working conditions for the employees.

Anthony lifted a stack of invoices and handed them, along with the ledger for the company, to Miss Michaels. He opened the book to the page with the expenditures. "Miss Michaels, please enter these invoices onto this page. In the first two columns write the company who provided the work and in the next the improvement. In the last column enter the amount. Then total the figures. Any questions?"

"No, my lord." She picked up the pen in the holder and looked oddly at it before her eyes scanned the desk. "Forgive me, sir, I do not have an inkpot."

"You do not need one. This is a self-fed pen. The ink is already in the writing instrument."

The sorrowful look on her face since walking away from Grandmother shifted to one of intrigue. She examined the pen like an anthropologist would the discovery of a fossil.

"I've never seen such an instrument." She peered at him—eyes larger than normal. "How do you replace the ink?"

"The top unscrews and using a dropper you can refill it. A bit messy, but the convenience of having a pen that you can use without dipping into an inkpot gains the user a great deal of convenience."

"Ingenious," she mumbled, still examining the writing instrument. "One could even use it while riding on a train."

"Indeed." He sat in his chair across the desk from where she sat. "You may keep that one."

She looked startled—as if no one had ever given her anything before. "Thank you, my lord."

As she wrote the first entry, Miss Michaels made a tiny sound of pleasure.

If she became that excited over a pen, Anthony wondered what little noises she would make while being tangled with a man in bed. He discarded that wicked thought. When Maria reached her pleasure, the soprano sang as if she were onstage. He'd always found it a bit unsettling. Well, he wouldn't have to worry about that any longer. This evening he would visit his mistress, give her the bracelet he'd bought, and end their tumultuous arrangement. He forced his attention to the correspondence Menders had placed neatly on the blotter.

A knock sounded on the door.

"Come in."

The butler entered the room. "My lord, um . . . your parrot seems in an agitated state."

By *agitated state*, he presumed Menders meant the winged beast was spewing profanities. A week ago, he'd won the parrot in a card game. Though now that he was in possession of the foul-mouthed bird, he wondered if his opponent had lost the hand on purpose.

"I fear he is chatting so robustly that your grandmother's guests might hear him when they arrive." The butler's concerned expression reflected his belief that such a thing would cause the old woman to throw a tantrum.

That was all Anthony needed. Grandmother was already fit to be tied. He didn't need her wretched mood getting worse. "I'll take care of it, Menders."

The butler nodded and left the room.

"You have a parrot, sir?" Miss Michaels asked, her voice full of excitement.

"Yes, by chance do you know of any recipes for parrot soup?" He stood.

The joy in her expression slipped away and her mouth gaped.

"Don't fret, Miss Michaels, I was only joking." He hoped.

Relief flashed across her face.

"I shall return shortly." Anthony strode out of the room.

As soon as the door closed, Olivia contemplated marching down to where the Dowager Marchioness of Huntington would be entertaining guests. She squashed the idea. Perhaps Lord Anthony was right, and she should try again tomorrow. She released a frustrated breath. She'd learn very little of the *ton's* events cloistered in this room. What would she do if the woman continued to refuse her company? It would be almost impossible to gain a position as a companion without a letter of recommendation. She could try talking to Lady Winton again.

She gave a humorless laugh. That would be a fool's venture.

Olivia forced the nervous tapping of her foot to remain still and glanced at the correspondence on Lord Anthony's desk. Her fingers itched to riffle through it and see if there were any invitations to social events there. She needed any information she could gather on the last two noblemen on her lists.

She drew her lower lip between her teeth and glanced at the doorway. How long would it take Lord Anthony to get his parrot? Her gaze volleyed back to the stack of correspondence on his blotter. Without further thought, she walked around to his side of the desk and sifted through the posts, looking for invitations that might help her to know the comings and goings of the *ton*.

She stopped at an invitation to a ball and noted the title of the nobleman giving the event. His name wasn't familiar, but the information might be helpful. She grabbed a sheet of parchment from the paper tray and jotted the name, date, and time down, then continued to peruse the rest of the correspondence, stopping whenever she came across an invitation to a ball or any other gathering.

Footsteps approached.

Heart beating fast, Olivia scurried back to her chair, and shoved the paper in her pocket.

Lord Anthony strode into the room with an enormous bell-shaped birdcage with a canvas cover draped over the upper portion of it.

Her breaths sawed in and out of her lungs a bit faster

than normal, leaving her thankful he only gave her a cursory glance.

The butler followed him into the room and set a bird's perch next to the desk.

"Thank you, Menders." Lord Anthony set the cage down on a round table in the corner of the room.

The manservant walked out of the office and closed the door behind him.

Squawk! "Let me out of here!"

Olivia blinked. She'd never heard a parrot talk. It sounded almost human.

"Just hold on, you rascal," Lord Anthony grumbled.

Olivia couldn't tear her eyes away as she waited for his lordship to lift the cloth off the cage.

He removed the cover, revealing a sizable bird with bright green plumage and black eyes circled with yellow.

The bird pivoted its head. Its beady eyes appeared to spot her, and it whistled.

Olivia blinked.

"He likes you." Lord Anthony opened the door to the wire cage.

The bird climbed onto his hand, and his lordship set him on the perch.

Squawk. "Yo ho ho, wench!"

Lord Anthony released an exasperated sigh. "I should warn you, Miss Michaels, Atticus has a colorful vocabulary."

"Did you teach him to talk, sir?"

"Good Lord, no. I won him in a card game only a week ago."

Squawk. "Hey, sweetie, give me a kiss."

Olivia's cheeks grew warm. A silly reaction. One should not blush over a parrot who flirted, since he was only repeating what he'd overheard or been taught. "Are you sure it isn't you who taught him to speak?"

"I should feel offended that you would ask me that. Not once, but twice." His voice held an edge as if affronted, but his lips lifted into a warm smile.

Offended? She doubted a man who tossed his mistress over his shoulder on a busy street was easily offended. Olivia wondered if he had smoothed out the misunderstanding with Signora Campari.

"Pinch me fanny," the bird said, drawing her from her thoughts.

The bird was outrageous. Vicar Finch would have keeled over if he'd heard the brightly feathered fellow. She pressed her lips together to stop herself from grinning.

Lord Anthony shot the bird a lethal look. "Miss Michaels does not care for your ribald talk. And I can see by the look in her lovely eyes, she blames me for your bawdiness, even though I am quite innocent."

Olivia kept her eyes on the bird, even though she wanted to look at Lord Anthony. No one had ever said she possessed lovely eyes. But like her reaction to the bird, she should not be flattered. She presumed Lord Anthony Trent was a natural flirt who easily passed out compliments to enchant the ladies. Well, she would not be so easily flustered by such a cad.

"Now stop it, Atticus," Lord Anthony chastised.

"Killjoy. Killjoy." The parrot squawked.

"I'm tempted to give you back to Lord Hamby," he said, returning to his chair.

Olivia's gaze jerked to him at the mention of Lord Hamby.

He must have noticed her startled expression, for he tipped his head slightly to the side. "Do you know him?"

No. But she knew of the vile man. He'd been one of the men she'd robbed. "I do not. Is he a friend?"

"Friend? No. The earl is a wretched person."

She knew that. "Yet, you play cards with him."

"Unavoidable."

She waited for him to expand. Hoped he would, but he picked up one of the invitations and read it. She presumed many of the nobility moved in the same circles, especially during the season.

"Hamby claims the bird spoke that way before he bought him from an American sailor. Though if I were to venture a guess, I'd say Atticus's skill in lusty phrases is from both men."

She could imagine being in Hamby's home the bird had seen a great deal. Like the way Hamby liked to push his maids into a dark corner and have his way with them. Whether they were willing or not.

"How are you doing with those invoices?" he asked.

"I'm over halfway through entering them."

He flashed a purely male smile.

Her heart skipped a beat. She wondered how many times he'd offered his knee-weakening smile and won a woman over. Too many times she presumed.

He picked through the correspondence, glancing at some, while taking his time to read others.

While he was preoccupied, she couldn't stop herself from looking at him. Though his lashes were long, it didn't make him look feminine in the least. Not with the hard, masculine angles of his square jaw. She should not be taken in by such a handsome face. He was a scoundrel. Not villainous like Lord Hamby, but still wicked. But there was a kindness to him. He had given her the pen and her job. But she couldn't let herself become swayed by his handsomeness or the impressive breadth of his shoulders. She could not become distracted from what she had come to London to do—fulfill her promise to Helen.

Lord Anthony glanced up.

Olivia, realizing she was still staring, peered down at the invoices in front of her and continued writing the figures.

The bird started bouncing up and down on its perch again.

"My lord, do you have any idea what it means when he does that?"

He frowned at the bird. "I have no idea whatsoever."

"I think it means he is happy."

"Do you now? Well, you might be right. All I know is that it is preferable to his chatter."

Smiling, Olivia continued working on the ledger.

Squawk! Squawk! Squawk!

Lord Anthony narrowed his eyes at the bird.

Olivia covered her mouth to hide her smile.

"I swear I'm going to ask Cook to find a parrot soup recipe if you do not stop."

"Blow the man down!" the bird said.

A laugh bubbled up Olivia's throat that she couldn't contain.

"You think it's funny, Miss Michaels?"

She evened out her expression. "No, sir."

As if he was fighting his own reaction, a slow smile settled on his face.

Goodness, he truly was a handsome devil. *Devil* being the most prominent word in that sentence.

Someone knocked on the door.

"Enter," he said.

The butler stepped into the room and handed Anthony a note.

"Thank you, Menders. Have all my grandmother's callers left?"

"Yes, she said she is suffering with a headache and told me to not accept any more callers today."

He nodded, and the butler exited the room.

Lord Anthony unfolded the piece of parchment and released a long breath. "Miss Michaels, my grandmother has summoned me to the drawing room. I shall return shortly."

Hope filled Olivia's chest. "Do you think she has changed her mind about me?"

"Doubtful. I was most likely the subject of conversation precipitating her megrim, and she wishes to chastise me."

"I apologize, my lord."

"For?" He cocked his head slightly to the side.

"I realize that if I hadn't stepped into the wrong carriage . . ."

He waved a hand in the air as if it was not of great import. Then a slight smile curved his sensual mouth. "I have an idea, Miss Michaels. Please accompany me to see my grandmother."

"Might I inquire what your idea is?"

"You will see." He stood and threw the note into the rubbish pail by the side of the desk.

She followed him as he strode to the door.

He glanced back at the bird. The animal was bouncing up and down on his perch again. "Behave," he said, then opened the door and motioned for her to precede him.

As they moved down the corridor, Olivia wondered what he had planned. She didn't think it anything nefarious, yet she'd seen a devilish gleam in his lordship's eyes, and she couldn't wait to find out what he was about.

Chapter Seven

Standing shoulder to shoulder beside Miss Michaels, Anthony strode through the open double doors of the blue drawing room.

His grandmother, who sat in a straight-backed chair, looking imperious, narrowed her eyes. "What is she still doing here?"

"Did you think just because you said to send Miss Michaels on her way, I would?"

"I should have known you would not. You are as stubborn and set as the rest of the Trent men. I shall have no peace from any of you until I am in my grave."

"I can see you are in one of your pleasant moods," Anthony said.

"Why should I be in a good mood? I summoned you here to inform you that all anyone wants to talk about is you, my rapscallion grandson."

"It is only a matter of time until the scandalmongers find something new to entertain them."

"Humph. The only good news I've had is that Lady Winton has sprained her ankle and is bedridden and won't be spreading more gossip about you. If you care anything about me, you will leave me in peace and take"—she pointed a gnarled finger at Miss Michaels—"her with you."

Menders walked into the room. The leery expression on the butler's face, along with the fact he held a newspaper in his hand didn't bode well. Anthony was sure the butler had skimmed the on-dits before walking in here.

The butler cleared his throat. "Excuse me. I have the copy of the *London Globe* you asked for, your ladyship."

Grandmother held out her hand for the newspaper, and the man hurried out of the room. Not a good sign.

Anthony turned to Miss Michaels. "There is about to be an explosion."

"An explosion?" she echoed.

Before he could explain, his grandmother flicked to the middle of the newspaper. A flush of red moved up past the collar of her black gown to color her normally pale cheeks. Her fingers curled into the edges of the paper in a white-knuckled grip that contrasted with the color on her face. "Damn plague!"

Standing next to him, Olivia Michaels's eyes widened.

"What's wrong?" Anthony asked, knowing quite well what had ruffled the old bird's feathers.

"What's wrong you ask! Once again, you have made the scandal sheets." Scowling, Grandmother released an exasperated huff and shook the newspaper in the air.

Anthony took the newspaper from her and scanned the gossip column.

> It's rumored that the infamous Lord A, brother to the once notorious Marquess of H, was seen tossing one of London's

favorite sopranos over his shoulder and depositing her into his carriage.

Releasing a sigh, Anthony held up his hand, halting the old woman from saying anything further. "I have a bargain to suggest that might help calm things down."

"A bargain?" Grandmother's thin lips formed a straight white line in her flushed face.

"Yes. Hear me out. I will end my relationship with Maria if you agree to take Miss Michaels on as your companion."

"That is blackmail." The old woman's eyes turned to narrow slits. She grabbed her cane from where it leaned next to her and thumped it against the rug.

"I've always thought the word 'blackmail' to be unsavory. I think it would be better we call it a compromise." Anthony tried not to grin, knowing he held all the power to give the matriarch what she wanted. His subservience. But since he intended to end his relationship with the fiery diva, he thought it an ingenious plan.

Her fingers clutched at the gold knob of the cane.

Anthony had a feeling she was considering swinging it at him. Better that than at Miss Michaels, who stood silently next to him.

"That will not do," she spat.

"Why?" Anthony almost growled the word. "I thought you would be overjoyed. It will soothe the gossip that is upsetting you as badly as if you suffered from a case of gout."

"Because ending your relationship with the opera singer will not be enough. I wish you to go about in society and repair the damage you have done to your own reputation, along with this family's. You need to be viewed as respectable. I surmise the best way to handle that would be for you to accompany me to several social events."

"Grandmother, you must think me a fool if you imagine that I believe that is the only reason you wish me to escort you."

"Why else?" she asked, feigning an innocent expression that seemed so out of character for Grandmother that it was almost comical.

"You want to force my attention on the new crop of debutantes whom I have no interest in."

"Well, you cannot go on thinking that your unrequited love for your—"

"Grandmother," he said in a low, warning voice, "be careful what you say."

The old woman's steely gray eyes shifted to Olivia Michaels, whose keen intelligence seemed to be absorbing every nuance and word spoken. Grandmother's expression revealed she realized she was precariously close to divulging her ridiculous belief that Anthony carried a torch for Caroline. If the servants got wind of such an untruth it might not be contained solely in this house. If she thought the gossip now unsettling, that tidbit would cause a firestorm that would not only touch him but Caroline, and ultimately James.

"If we are engaged in a compromise, those are my terms." Grandmother arched one thin brow.

He glanced at Miss Michaels. He needed her help. Damnation, he felt trapped between his grandmother's demand and the work his brother had foisted upon him.

He drew in a deep breath. "Very well. I will accompany you on *one* ride through Hyde Park."

"Not a carriage ride. I wish for something more formal."

The hairs on the back of his neck lifted. He didn't like the gleam in his grandmother's eyes. "Do tell."

"You will accompany me to a ball instead."

It would probably be a ball hosted by one of her cronies like Lord Pendleton—an event as dull as tarnished silver. But if it would get his grandmother to stop acting as if she might have a coronary he would comply. "Very well, Grandmother, if you agree to take Miss Michaels on as your companion, I will sever my relationship with Maria and accompany you to a ball." He held up his index finger. "But just that one event."

The old woman's regard narrowed on Miss Michaels. "But she cannot accompany us. If she is seen people will recognize her and believe she is your lover."

The color drained from Miss Michaels's face.

"Doubtful."

"Why is that doubtful?" Grandmother thumped her cane.

"Because Miss Michaels's hair was in her face, and I doubt anyone who saw her would recognize her."

"Lady Winton would," Grandmother shot back.

"Didn't you just say she is bedridden?"

"Yes, but eventually she will recover, and when she finds out she will wag her tongue."

"Then I suggest you preempt her vicious gossip by sending her a letter telling her how unjustly she treated Miss Michaels, and that you have decided to take her into you employ to show her that not all members of the *ton* are so quick to judge."

The dowager tugged on her earlobe. "That might work,

but if you think it will shame her into taking the girl back it will not."

He was exceedingly aware of that. And he didn't want Miss Michaels to leave. "So, we have a deal?"

Grandmother grinned. "Yes, we have a deal. However . . ."

The word *however* along with the shrewd glint in his grandmother's eyes forwarded that there was going to be a stipulation. An uncomfortable feeling, like the type one experienced when their carriage took a fast turn and momentarily balanced on two wheels settled in his gut.

Grandmother pinned Miss Michaels with a hard stare. "There must be rules. You will only speak to me when spoken to, and I can't stand giggling. Do you giggle, girl?"

"I will be sure to never do so in your presence."

"Are you being cheeky, Miss Michaels?" Grandmother's eyes shot daggers.

"Definitely not."

"And no pawing at me. I hate being fussed over."

"Yes, my lady."

"Then you may stay."

Anthony exhaled a silent breath of relief.

As a teacher, Olivia had dealt with unruly children at the orphanage. Like Belinda Fraser, who took pleasure in pulling other girls' hair, and Henrietta Smith, who'd hidden all the pieces of chalk. Surely, after dealing with those rapscallions she could deal with the Dowager Marchioness of Huntington. And of course, there had been Lady Winton, whom Olivia had cowed to, knowing it the only way to deal with the old battle-ax, but she sensed that the dowager needed a sparring partner, and if it meant

Olivia could stay in Mayfair, she was up for the job, even if it resulted in the occasional tongue-lashing.

The old woman pointed a gnarled finger at Olivia. "Come closer."

Olivia had once read a story about a cunning fox who'd feigned blindness on an unsuspecting rabbit, and when the animal moved within reach, the fox swallowed him whole. She squared her shoulders and strode forward.

"Anthony, leave us."

His lordship crossed his arms over his sizable chest. "I'm not sure I should."

"I won't bite the girl."

His lips twitched. "Promise?"

"Of course."

Lord Anthony turned to her. "Miss Michaels, I shall be in my office. If you should need me."

After he pulled the door closed behind him, the dowager tapped her index finger to her lips and studied Olivia like an entomologist would a bug in a glass jar. "You said you were raised in an orphanage?"

"I was."

"Where?"

"All Saints Orphanage for Girls in Kent, my lady."

"And how is it someone of such parentage became a companion to Lady Winton?"

"The town squire is a second cousin to her ladyship, and it was through his patronage."

The older woman nodded her head and shifted in her chair, knocking a book to the floor. "Pick my book up and hand it to me."

Olivia was nearly positive the dowager had purposely

let it fall. She forced a smile as she picked it up. "Do you wish me to read to you?"

The woman snatched the book out of her grasp. "I'm quite capable of reading to myself." She pointed to a wooden straight-backed chair. "You may sit there."

"I have a book in my room. May I get it?"

The woman motioned with a flick of her hand toward the door. "Go on."

"Thank you, my lady."

She exited the room and slammed right into a solid mass of male. She glanced up into Lord Anthony's dark eyes.

One of his large hands settled on the turn of her waist. Warm and steady.

"I'm so sorry, my lord."

One side of his mouth tipped up. Releasing her, he stepped back.

"It's not your fault. I was spying."

"Spying?"

"Eavesdropping, my dear girl. I wanted to make sure the old crow didn't attempt to scare you away."

Olivia's chest tightened. No man, well except for Vicar Finch, had ever worried about her. And the vicar had worried more about the damnation of her soul than her actual being. "I am more resilient than I look."

"I'm sure you are," he replied.

For a long moment, he held her gaze with those warm coffee-colored eyes of his.

Her stomach fluttered. "I should get going. The elder Lady Huntington said I might get a book to read."

"Of course."

She tried not to dash away too quickly but couldn't help

glancing over her shoulder to watch his lordship stroll down the corridor.

Abruptly, he spun around. "Miss Michaels?"

"Yes, my lord."

"You do not need to help me with the ledgers tonight since you've already done most of the work. Besides I will be going out again."

She nodded and watched as he turned to continue down the corridor, his broad shoulders looking even wider in the narrow space. She wondered if his lordship was going to see Signora Campari.

She scoffed at her thoughts. What did she care? It made no difference to her if he spent the evening with the opera singer. She had no interest in a handsome lord who possessed a body that could tempt an angel.

No interest whatsoever.

Chapter Eight

After dinner at his club with a few chums and several hands of cards, Anthony knocked on the door of Maria's suite of rooms at the Fontaine Hotel on Broad Street. Maria had all but said she could not trust him and would not listen to reason. It was time to sever the relationship.

Maria's petite maid, Alina, answered. The young servant's eyes widened. Obviously, she feared a fight comparable to a tsunami was about to commence.

"*Ciao, mio signore.*" The woman bobbed a curtsey and bit on her lower lip, so hard, Anthony feared she might draw blood.

"Alina, I wish to speak to your mistress."

The maid nervously glanced over her shoulder, then stepped aside. *"Entra, signore."*

Green damask fabric trimmed with gold velvet covered the upholstered furniture. The suite of rooms was upscale in comparison to what the other members of the opera company stayed in while performing in London. Anthony knew it to be a costly apartment, since he paid for it.

The door to the bedchamber opened, and wearing a

sheer white peignoir, Maria fluttered out of the room. The gossamer fabric draped over her body did little to hide the full globes of her breasts with their tawny-colored nipples and the triangle of dark hair between her legs.

There was a momentary hesitation in her step as she spotted him. She narrowed her dark eyes. Her angry glower swung to the maid. "Alina, I told you not to let his lordship in if he called."

The maid's shoulders drooped. "He is *muscoloso*. I did not see how I could stop him."

Maria scowled. "Bah! Get out of my sight, girl, before I send you back to live in that shack with your *madre* and seven siblings."

The servant scurried out of the room, her hands covering her head as if she feared her mistress would throw something at her. Anthony suspected with Maria's volatile temper, she had probably hurled something at the young maid before.

His gaze shifted from Alina to Maria just in time to see a vase being thrown at him. He ducked as it whipped by his head. With an explosive noise, it struck the wall sending shards of blue pottery into the air to scatter like a burst of color from a firework.

Bloody hell. He should have known not to take his eyes off the woman. "Now, Maria, let us talk like sensible adults."

"*Mascalzone*!" She reached for a porcelain figurine of two cherublike angels and cranked her arm back.

Hell and fire. Anthony might not be a mathematician, but he knew if Maria continued to throw things at him, he was going to owe the hotel a great deal of money. He rushed forward and snagged the piece from her hand.

"Good Lord, woman. Must I repeat myself? You misunderstood the situation. The woman stepped into the wrong carriage." He set the figurine down.

"Bah! I do not believe you. Lady Winton said you are a scoundrel and not to be trusted. She said you are a snifter of skirts."

He presumed Maria meant sniffer of skirts. "Lady Winton is a nasty piece of work who wishes everyone to be as miserable as she is."

As if he hadn't even spoken, Maria continued her tirade, interspacing English and Italian. Maria sniffled. Bloody hell, was she going to cry? He'd never seen the woman do so. He hated when women cried. It made him think of his poor mother. She'd been treated rather shabbily by his sire, and he didn't want to be anything like his discontent father, but it seemed he was destined to be.

He gently clasped Maria's shoulder, but before he could say anything, she cracked her open palm against his face. Anthony drew in a slow breath. As he had presumed there would be no working this out. It was clearly over, and relief washed over him.

"I should have known better," Maria said with a sniffle. "I turned down Lord Bramble for you. He will be a duke one day."

The young heir was not even twenty. Anthony doubted the boy even shaved. The woman would eat him alive and leave him a stuttering mess.

The door to Maria's bedroom opened.

"What's going on?" The young pup in question stepped out of Maria's bedchamber looking like he'd hastily dressed.

"It appears, Maria, you did not turn him down." Anthony cocked a brow.

She had the good graces to blush. He doubted she did it often.

"L-L-Lord Anthony . . ." A lump moved in the younger man's throat and his skin glistened with sweat as he finished tucking the ends of his white shirt in.

Anthony presumed he better say something before the man wet his very costly trousers. "Bramble, how are you?"

The young nobleman blinked as if he feared it was a trick question.

Maria narrowed her eyes.

Anthony presumed she had wanted him to fight for her or pummel the fellow. He reached into the inside breast pocket of his jacket to extract the jeweler's box with the bracelet he'd purchased as a parting gift.

As if fearing Anthony was withdrawing a pistol, Bramble took flight and flew behind a settee. The sound of whimpering could be heard from where the young fellow hid.

"Bramble, my good man, I am not in the least bit upset. I came here to end my arrangement with Maria. You are more than welcome to her. May God help you." Anthony tossed the jeweler's box on a marquetry table adjacent to the sofa and strode to the door.

He'd just about reached it when another vase came flying by his head and struck the wall several feet away from him.

Thankfully, Maria's aim was wretched, Anthony thought

as he slipped out of the room, or he would have been sporting one hell of a goose egg on his head.

Unlike the sparse bedchamber Lady Winton had provided Olivia, the room Lord Anthony had instructed the butler to give her was beyond lovely. Everything about it looked costly. The violet-colored counterpane with delicate flowers matched the swagged curtains. The walls were draped in silk coverings and the carpet was thick and plush under one's feet. On one of the low dressers sat a floral porcelain water basin and pitcher with hand-painted flowers under the shiny glaze. She could not imagine the queen's bedchamber being any more elegant. It was a room a prized guest would be honored to have.

As Olivia paced back and forth the generosity shown to her caused a stab of guilt over her subterfuge. Guilt she'd not experienced while staying at Lady Winton's residence. Her old employer was the embodiment of everything negative Olivia had come to feel about the nobility.

She strode to the armoire in the corner of the room. Crouching, she reached under it and withdrew the pocket-sized notebook she'd hidden there earlier. She sat on the edge of the large tester bed and removed the fancy self-feeding pen Lord Anthony had given her, along with the paper from her pocket with the times and locations she'd seen on the invitations on his lordship's desk. This information might come in useful. After she wrote it in the notebook, she stood and tucked it back under the armoire.

An image of Lord Anthony's face floated in her mind. The man acted like he possessed a devil-may-care attitude, but his dark eyes were alert. Smart. She would need to be careful around him, not only because of his intellect but also because when around him she experienced an odd fluttering in her stomach that was not solely due to nerves.

Tucking a loose tendril of her bright red hair behind her ear, she uttered a dull laugh. The man had no interest in her. She was nothing like Signora Campari. The woman was striking. Men would clamber over each other to be the diva's lover. No one would do so for Olivia, yet the way Lord Anthony glanced at her while he said he knew men who would wish to hire her for a position had made her feel desirable.

Olivia pressed her palm to her forehead, knowing she was letting her thoughts ramble. She needed to concentrate on her plan. She opened the drawer in the table beside the bed where she'd seen a box of matches and moved to the fireplace. She crumbled the parchment she'd written the information on and shoved it into the grate before striking a match and setting the paper on fire. Gray smoke spiraled upward as the edges darkened before the crumpled paper burst into a ball of orange flames, leaving nothing more than a pile of ash.

Olivia strode to the window and unclasped the lock. She raised the lower sash and was pleased it moved freely—without making a noise. Yesterday when she'd been shown to this elegant bedchamber, she'd peered out the two windows the room possessed to see if either was near a downspout. Luckily one of them was. More fortunate, both windows possessed a small wrought-iron balcony. Not the type one would place a chair on and sit, but a much narrower one that elevated the exterior of the house's aesthetics. But if she held on to the rail, she could place her feet on the ledge and carefully move to the downspout and make her way to the ground. She tapped her foot. Going down would be much easier than getting back up. She thought of the window in the office. If she unlatched the ground-floor window, it would be easy to climb through it.

Thinking of the two men she still needed to rob, she pulled the window closed. Restless, she paced before forcing herself to sit in the damask-covered chair in the corner of the room.

A memory floated through her mind. As if it were yesterday, she could clearly see Vicar Finch standing over Helen's simple wooden casket, intoning a psalm. She could almost feel the bitter January air and hear the whistle of the wind in the graveyard adjacent to the rectory. The recollection caused gooseflesh to prickle the skin under her sleeves. She rubbed her hands over her arms and pinched her eyes closed, attempting to stifle the memory, but it only grew more vivid.

". . . for they rest from their labors," Vicar Finch's words echoed in her head. She recalled how he'd closed the black leather book in his hand as Mrs. Garson motioned to the girls to line up in a single file, but Olivia had felt rooted to where she stood, reluctant to leave Helen there, alone.

The kindhearted matron had set a gloved hand on Olivia's back, given her a quick hug, and prompted her to join the others.

This had not been the first time the girls from All Saints Orphanage stood in the graveyard as one of them was laid to rest. *Laid to rest.* The words seemed odd in Olivia's mind, for the frozen, dew-covered ground had not appeared hospitable.

Nor had the tidy rows of headstones with green moss at their bases. Helen, like all the orphaned and friendless girls buried there, did not have a tombstone. But Olivia knew exactly where her friend was laid to rest, since the day after the funeral, she'd placed three large stones atop the grave.

She swallowed the lump in her throat and opened her eyes. The elegant room was now blurred by her unshed tears.

With the backs of her hands, Olivia swiped at her eyes and glanced at the bed. Doubtful sleep would come easily, and she'd finished her novel from the lending library. Her mind centered on the plethora of books that lined the shelves in Lord Anthony's office. It would be wrong to take one without asking. She almost laughed. Her conscience was squabbling over borrowing a book without permission when she'd done so much worse. But not to Lord Anthony. He might be a rascal, but he had shown her he had a good heart, unlike so many other members of the *ton*.

She walked to the door and inched it open. No sounds reached her ears from the dowager's suite of rooms, and Lord Anthony had left several hours ago. He probably wouldn't return for a while, and the servants had gone to bed. On the tips of her toes, she made her way down the stairs to his lordship's office.

From where he sat in the leather chair in the corner of James's office, now temporarily his office, Anthony stared at the small sliver of moonlight that cast a narrow streak of light into the dark room. After visiting Maria, he'd played a few hands of cards at his club, then returned home to be alone with his thoughts and a glass of his brother's exemplary brandy.

He rested the back of his head against the leather chair and closed his eyes. *Bugger it!* Was Grandmother right? Had he used a string of lovers to distract himself? Not from Caroline, but from what truly bothered him?

It would explain why finding Maria with another man had not infuriated him. He hated to admit that Grandmother was correct about anything. If true, it would also explain why he'd chosen someone as volatile as Maria. Things were never dull with her. The fiery diva had been a grand distraction.

He swigged another mouthful of brandy and enjoyed the warmth as it made its way down his throat to pool in his gut. As he lowered the tumbler, his gaze followed the single shaft of moonlight from the slit in the curtains. It cut across the desk to cast its subdued beam on the bloody ledgers on the corner of the wooden surface, then to the wall of shelves filled with books. He should have grabbed the decanter of brandy and hightailed it to his bedchamber, where he would not be mocked by the ledgers' presence—testaments to his failings and inability.

Though at one time, when only a tot, he'd enjoyed being in this office. Enjoyed the scent of smoke from his father's cheroots and the smell of the leather-bound ledgers, but that had been before he'd come to realize that the latter would torment him when he tried to read the columns of numbers written within their pages.

In the gloom, he peered at the portrait of his father that hung above the mantel. Father had possessed no sense when it came to finances. If it wasn't for James's business acumen, they'd have ended up destitute.

A memory flashed in his mind of him sitting on the hearth rug playing with his toy soldiers, while his father went over the ledgers with James. As the second son, he'd known his place was in the background unless something happened to James. The thought of that happening had always made his stomach curdle. Not because he feared he'd be thrust into the position of marquess, though that was rather terrifying, but because he cared deeply for James. One could not ask for a better brother.

He rubbed at the tight muscles in his neck. He could not let everything that his brother had worked diligently to attain be ruined because of his pride, or because Caroline had told him he would be fine. She didn't know what ailed him. He should write James and tell him the truth. That he was not competent enough to do this job. Yet, he wanted to do it. Wanted to succeed.

He stared at the amber liquid, then tipped the glass to his mouth and took another sizable swallow. Perhaps with Miss Michaels's help with the ledgers he could succeed. He would give himself one week to try. To attempt what felt like the impossible.

The hinges on the door gave a low-toned squeak as it swung inward. He narrowed his eyes. Who the bloody hell was up at this hour? Surely not Grandmother.

Olivia Michaels, still wearing her drab navy dress, slipped into the room.

What was she about? Thievery? Perhaps he'd been too trusting of the woman. Perhaps the incident in his carriage was not the reason that old battle-ax Lady Winton had sacked Miss Michaels.

Quietly, she moved across the room.

For a moment, he thought she was heading to the desk, but she stepped beyond it and up to the bookcases where the shaft of moonlight illuminated her back.

A part of him felt angry. He wanted to be alone with his thoughts. Olivia Michaels was infringing on that. Yet, he said nothing as she perused the books.

Olivia picked up a large tome with gold lettering, and he wondered what it was. Was she a lover of poetry, romance, or history? She placed it back on the shelf and moved to the rolling ladder. She set her hand on the rail and climbed up the first rung, then several more until she was a good seven feet above the floor.

Good Lord. Obviously, heights did not frighten her. Was she just exploring or had a specific book grabbed her attention?

As she reached for a book, she made a little noise of pleasure. The same, almost erotic noise she'd made while examining the self-feeding pen.

The sound made something spark within him. He wanted to know what title brought her such joy, yet he remained silent, knowing if he spoke now and startled her, she might topple off the ladder.

After examining the book in her hand, Miss Michaels placed it back on the shelf. Had she thought it a different title? She gave the ladder a strong push. It slid sideways on the brass bar and rollers it was attached to. Like an acrobat, she extended one of her legs backward, leaving her precariously balanced on one foot.

His stomach pitched. Was she mad? She could tumble and break her neck, yet she appeared fearless.

After the ladder reached the end of the shelves, she

started moving down the rungs, then as if frozen in time, she stopped.

Even in the dark, he could see her body tense as if she suddenly realized she was not alone. Had he made a noise? He didn't believe so.

For several long seconds, she just stood still as if her senses were heightened to any nuance of noise, then she twisted her body so fast, he feared she would truly topple down and snap her neck.

Chapter Nine

The small hairs on Olivia's neck stood on end. She wasn't alone. Heart beating a steady tattoo, she spun around to see Lord Anthony bolting across the room with ground-eating steps.

"Good Lord, woman, are you trying to break your neck?" he asked, his voice harsh as if he thought she should be committed to Bedlam.

Before she could answer, his large, warm hands gripped her waist. She peered down into his dark eyes, even darker in the dim room.

"Careful," he said. "I've got you." His voice sounded less sharp, more anxious.

She bit off the urge to tell him she wouldn't have fallen. Her tumble in the carriage was an anomaly, brought about from her tripping on his booted foot and her inability to see it because of the dashed packages she carried.

His fingers tightened against her waist as he lifted her down. For a second, she was suspended in midair before the front of her body brushed against the hard surface of his chest. Her hands instinctually moved to his shoulders as he slowly lowered her to the carpeted floor.

This close she could smell the soap on his skin and the scent of spirits on his breath. But he didn't appear drunk. His eyes looked too alert. His speech was not slurred. Nothing like the time she'd gone for a walk at the orphanage and found Mr. Leeman, the jack-of-all-trades, as drunk as Davy's sow, lying in the tall grass singing a ribald tune.

"Thank you," she mumbled, her hands still on his shoulders.

His were still on her waist.

She liked the pressure of his fingers and the warmth of his palms filtering through the thin material of her cotton dress. She shook away her wicked observations, while chastising herself, then stepped back.

He released her.

She should shift farther away, since she could still feel the heat of his skin radiating off him, encircling her like a blanket on a cool night.

"May I ask what you are doing in here, Miss Michaels?"

Though not drunk, his mood was darker tonight. His carefree nature discarded for one much more solemn.

Olivia forced herself to take another step backward. She wet her lips. "I couldn't fall asleep. I thought perhaps I could borrow a book. Forgive me, I should have asked permission, but I didn't realize anyone was awake."

"Take what you wish." He waved a hand toward the bookshelves.

"Thank you, my lord."

He strode to a table in the corner of the room and picked up a glass with amber liquid.

"Were you working on the ledgers, sir?"

Briefly, his gaze shifted over them and his lips curled slightly.

With his dark mood, she should grab the book closest to her and return to her room, but the solemn look on his face made her hesitate.

For a long moment, he continued to stare at the ledgers, then, as if suddenly realizing she still stood in the room and he'd not answered her question, his dark-eyed gaze shifted to her. "No. I couldn't sleep and thought a glass of brandy might help." He lifted his glass in the air. "Care for a libation? It might help you to sleep better than a book."

She imbibed the occasional glass of wine, but the color of the liquor almost matched the color of the whisky bottle Mr. Leeman had cradled in his hand. "I think a book shall do the trick."

He walked over to a sideboard topped with several decanters and refilled his glass. She noted the steadiness of his hands. No, he wasn't drunk. But something had caused his dark mood.

"Why are you sitting in the dark?" The question sprung from her mouth before she could halt it.

He strode to the desk and leaned back against it. "Inquisitive, aren't you?"

"Forgive me. I shouldn't have asked that. I'll return to my room."

"Whatever you wish, Miss Michaels."

Something in his voice made her think he was challenging her to stay. A foolish thought. He didn't want her company. He wanted to be alone. If he wanted company, he would have been with his mistress. Her stomach fluttered as she imagined what he and the diva did together.

Her mind wasn't as naive as her body. When teaching one day, she'd found three of her students huddled together giggling. She'd stepped up to the girls and found them peering at a book. Not a tale of adventure or love, but a book with pictures. Naughty pictures. If Vicar Finch had seen it, they would have been severely struck with a birch switch. But instead, Olivia had confiscated it from them intent on burning it. But that night, she'd flipped through the pages and been both titillated and shocked by what she'd seen.

"I like the dark. It's peaceful," he said, answering her earlier question and pulling her from her thoughts.

She stared at him. She liked it as well. The anonymity it provided. One could behave differently when others could not see them. There was a sense of freedom. An illusion because no one was truly ever free of their circumstances.

"I do as well, my lord."

"Then we have that in common."

It was most likely the only thing they had in common, she read books to escape her life. He didn't have to. He was privileged. She would always hold a position of servitude. He was a nobleman. She was most likely a bastard and unlike Helen not the by-blow of a nobleman.

"I should return to my room."

"You haven't chosen a book."

She wanted one now more than when she'd entered the room. If not distracted by a novel, she would be left to her own thoughts. And right now, they centered on Lord Anthony and the scent of his skin, and breath, and how his large hands had felt on her waist. She turned away from his dark, penetrating eyes and strode back to the shelves.

The gold letters on a novel bound in faded red leather caught her attention. *Miss Murphy's Adventures*. She'd never heard the title before. As she lifted her hand to remove it from the shelf, she felt the heat of Lord Anthony's body as he stepped behind her. A fresh wave of gooseflesh settled on her arms. She fought the urge to rub her palms over her skin to settle the sensation.

"I'll take this one." Normally she would have read the first few pages to see if the story interested her, but instead she clasped the book to her chest like a barrier against this man who unsettled her, then she pivoted to face him.

"Thank you, my lord. I will make sure to return it to the same spot when I've finished reading it."

He nodded, then leaning against the desk once more, he stretched his legs out before him, and crossed them at the ankles.

"Good night," she said.

He saluted her with his now nearly empty glass. "Good night, Miss Michaels."

She bobbed a quick curtsey and headed toward the door. As she stepped from the room, she fought against her desire to glance over her shoulder and take one last look at him before returning to the solitude of her elegant bedchamber.

Instead, as fast as her legs would take her, Olivia made her way to her bedchamber, ignoring the way her body always tingled after she'd been in proximity with his lordship.

She tiptoed past the elder Lady Huntington's bedchamber, swept into her room, and quietly closed the door behind her. She leaned against the hard surface as if trying to bar the hounds from hell. But it wasn't anything tangible she tried to escape. It was her own lustful thoughts and they were much harder to hold at bay.

"You must fight against your desires." Vicar Finch's words echoed in Olivia's head. *"Illegitimate children are infected with their parents' wickedness and lustful inclinations."*

Olivia bit her lower lip. She'd thought the man's warnings poppycock until she'd met Lord Anthony. Every time he touched her, her skin prickled with anticipation. Perhaps wickedness did course through her.

She removed her dress and used the pitcher and basin to wash, then slipped on her white nightgown. After propping the pillows up against the headboard, she settled against them with the book. She'd only read a few pages when she found her mind wondering. Lord Anthony was not the happy carefree man he pretended to be. Tonight he'd been mercurial. She could not help wondering what caused such a dark mood.

She stared down at the page she'd been reading and tried to redirect her mind to it. His lordship was not her concern. Nor were his problems. She had her own agenda. She had made a promise to Helen and she needed to see it through.

Chapter Ten

The following day, Olivia sat in a chintz upholstered chair only a few feet from where the elder Lady Huntington sat. The matriarch accepted callers at two in the afternoon. Olivia was anxious to hear every bit of gossip that might help her with her plan to rob the last two men on her list.

The butler rolled a serving cart with a silver tea service, along with several delicate floral-patterned cups and saucers, into the room and maneuvered it into the spot between Olivia's chair and the one the dowager sat in, then he exited the room.

Trying not to tap her foot impatiently, Olivia glanced at the tall longcase clock, while she smoothed a hand over the skirt of her navy dress. Over the last hour, she'd peered at the timepiece more than a dozen times. The chimes of the clock rang twice.

"Why are you fidgeting, girl?" her ladyship asked.

Olivia straightened her shoulders and held the woman's direct gaze. "I wasn't fidgeting."

"Yes, you were." The dowager's glower caused the wrinkles in her face to deepen.

Olivia tipped her chin up an inch. If she was to get this old woman to respect her, she had a feeling she would need to show a more forceful resolve.

A knock on the door ended the battle of wills. Menders stepped into the room. “Lady Fairchild and Lady Chambers wish to know if you are receiving callers, madam.”

“Show them in.”

What seemed like an eternity later, the butler stood at the threshold and announced the two noblewomen who wore black silk and mourning veils. Lady Fairchild was gray-haired, short, plump, and moved at a turtle’s pace. Lady Chambers, also elderly, but thin as a rake, only walked slightly faster with the use of her cane.

Impatiently the dowager sighed. She turned to Olivia. “I might be dead by the time they sit.”

“What did you say, Camille?” Lady Chambers asked, placing a hearing trumpet to her ear.

“I asked if the weather outside has warmed up?” the dowager replied in an elevated voice as both women finally sat on the settee.

“Still a bit on the cool side,” Lady Fairchild replied.

Lady Chambers adjusted her black skirts and stared at Olivia. “And who is this?”

“My new companion, Olivia.”

Lady Fairchild brought her pince-nez to her eyes and stared at Olivia as if she’d seen her before but could not place where.

Seeming to realize what Lady Fairchild pondered, the dowager slyly drew her attention away by clearing her throat. “Do either of you wish for tea?”

“No,” both women replied.

Olivia listened intently as they talked about how Lord Hamby had been robbed last week.

"He has offered a reward for the Phantom and sworn he will see that the thief rots in jail," Lady Chambers said.

"I heard the thief stole over three hundred pounds." Lady Fairchild's rheumy eyes widened.

"A travesty! This burglar must be stopped." Lady Chambers released a heavy breath that made her bosom rise. "In other news, did you hear that Signora Campari will be the entertainment at Lord and Lady Garwood's ball?"

The dowager visibly stiffened.

Olivia tensed as well, but it was not from the mention of the opera singer's name, but the mention of Lord Garwood. The gentleman wasn't on her list, but she listened intently hoping someone on it would be mentioned. The three elderly women talked about how crowded Grosvenor Square would be that night with the influx of carriages.

"Will you be attending, Camille?" Lady Fairchild asked, a sly expression on her face.

"No," the dowager said stiffly. Obviously, she realized the reason for the other woman's expression.

"I have a bit of juicy gossip." Lady Chambers smiled like a cat eyeing a canary who fluttered from its cage and was now free game. "Did you hear what happened with that rapscallion Lord Anthony on Bond Street in front of Madame Lefleur's shop? The modiste herself told me about it."

Lady Fairfield's eyes bulged as her gaze jerked to her companion sitting next to her. And though she had stepped into the room at the speed of a turtle, she appeared ready to flee at a much faster pace as her regard volleyed to the dowager's scowling expression.

As if counting to ten, the dowager drew in an exceedingly long breath.

Lady Fairchild elbowed Lady Chambers.

"Ouch, Georgiana, what was that for?"

"I believe she is trying to remind you who Lord Anthony is related to," the dowager said in a calm voice, but the look in her piercing gray eyes and the way her hand flexed on her cane revealed she was anything but calm.

"Related to?" Lady Chambers echoed. "Why, isn't he related to the Lady Compton?"

Next to the woman, Lady Fairfield was shaking her head like a mangy dog trying to dislodge an invasion of fleas. She stood and grabbed her companion's arm, prompting her friend to stand.

"Georgiana, what is wrong with you?" Lady Chambers asked.

"Nothing, I just remembered I locked my cat in my bedchamber, and he might shred my curtains if I do not return soon." She turned to the dowager. "Camille, forgive us for rushing off."

The dowager said nothing.

As the two women strode from the room, Lady Fairfield bowed her head to her companion and whispered something.

The other woman lifted her hearing trumpet again. "Dash it all, speak louder. I cannot hear a word you are saying."

"I said Lord Anthony is Camille's grandson," the other woman shouted.

Lady Chambers cocked her head to the side. "Are you sure?"

"Of course I'm sure. I thought Camille was going to strike you with her cane."

Olivia had feared that as well.

"It shouldn't be me she strikes. It should be that rapscallion grandson of hers."

"Hush, you are talking too loud."

"What?" Lady Chambers asked.

"Never mind. Can't you walk any faster?"

Lady Chambers lowered her hearing trumpet and glanced over her shoulder to where the dowager was shooting her a lethal stare.

The two women scurried out of the room much faster than they had entered.

"Senile old windbags," the dowager mumbled, and thumped her cane. "That's it! I refuse to see any more callers today. In fact, I will not see any for the next week until this gossip dissipates."

What? That wouldn't do. How was Olivia to get any information if the dowager didn't host callers?

The butler stepped into the room. Before he could even open his mouth and announce who was calling, the dowager said, "I don't care if it is the queen herself, I will not be receiving another caller today."

The butler nodded. "Very well, madam."

"And have a carriage readied for me. I am going out." She turned to Olivia. "Get your shawl, girl, you are coming with me."

Where were they going? Olivia hoped the dowager wasn't intent on having her carriage run over the two old women who'd just left. Though, she looked angry enough to do it.

"Yes, my lady, right away."

As Olivia sat next to the dowager in a grand carriage with blue velvet upholstery, she brushed her fingers against the nap of the material and wondered if this was the same vehicle she'd mistakenly stumbled into outside of Madame Lefleur's shop. She couldn't help her thoughts from veering back to herself sprawled across Lord Anthony's solid and muscular body.

"Are you unwell?" the dowager asked.

"No, madam. I feel fine."

"Your face is flushed."

"Is it?" Olivia asked.

"If I say it is, then it is." The old woman released an exaggerated huff.

The carriage pulled up to the address the dowager had given the coachman.

Olivia peered out the window. The sign over the shop read MADAME RENAULT MODISTE.

As the coachman jumped down from his perch, the carriage shifted slightly. The man opened the door, and the dowager exited the vehicle without a word to Olivia.

Was she to follow like an obedient lapdog or stay in the vehicle?

As if reading her thoughts, the coachman lifted one shoulder, then rushed forward to open the door to the shop for her ladyship.

Not quite sure what she was supposed to do, Olivia hesitantly stepped onto the pavement.

With her cane thumping loudly, the Trent family matriarch marched through the door.

Olivia followed her inside.

A shopgirl who'd been peering at them from the large bow window rushed to the dowager's side. "Might I help you, madam?"

"I am going to help you!"

A puzzled look settled on the girl's face.

"Tell Madame Renault that the Dowager Marchioness of Huntington is here."

The shopgirl's eyes widened, then she did an about-face and bolted from the room.

Olivia glanced around. Though the gowns displayed were lovely, the interior of the shop did not have the elegance of Madame Lefleur's shop. There were no crystal chandeliers or silk paper on the walls. Her gaze stopped at a gown near the window. The rich blue color along with the sheen of the fabric and the intricate beaded detailing almost made her breath catch. It was lovelier than any gown she had ever seen.

A tall, slender woman, wearing a dark purple dress, stepped out of the back of the shop. The shopgirl, still flush in the face, trailed her. "Lady Huntington, you honor me with your presence in my shop."

The dowager pointed to Olivia. "I want to order Miss Michaels five gowns. An evening gown, a walking dress, and three day dresses."

The modiste's eyes widened. "*Très bien.*"

Olivia blinked and set the palm of her hand to her chest. Had she misheard? "For me?"

"Yes, I cannot go around with you if you are to look like a schoolmarm."

"But I do not have the funds for such clothing." Olivia's heart pounded. Was the dowager like Lady Winton? If a servant broke anything in her last employer's household it was deducted from their salary. Would she be indebted to the elder Lady Huntington for the rest of her life?

The woman waved a hand in the air. "I am purchasing them."

A broad grin settled on the modiste's lips.

Olivia blinked. "But . . ."

The dowager turned her steely gray eyes on her, halting her words.

Something seemed off. The old woman didn't strike Olivia as generous. She struck Olivia as a woman whose actions were clearly thought out. A woman who did nothing without an ulterior motive.

The glimmer in the modiste's eyes revealed her pleasure as she motioned to the colorful bolts of fabric. "Do you have a preference in colors, my lady?"

The dowager turned an assessing eye on Olivia, then she pointed to the lovely blue gown on the mannequin near the window. "I wish the gown to be something similar to this one, but in yellow."

Olivia's jaw went slack.

"Bronze for the walking outfit," the dowager continued. Her gaze drifted over the navy dress Olivia wore, and she flashed a look of disgust. "Miss Michaels may pick out the fabric for the day dresses, but no muddy browns, navy, or gray."

The modiste looked as if she'd just won some grand prize.

Two hours later, having picked out the fabrics and been measured, Olivia and the elder Lady Huntington left the modiste and settled in the carriage.

Besides the costly dresses, the dowager had also purchased her a pair of new stockings made of silk and several unmentionable garments. Olivia remained baffled. She realized that this shopping excursion was not solely for her benefit, but she could not figure out what the dowager was up to, but surely something was afoot.

Olivia's gaze jerked from the window to the dowager sitting across from her as they pulled in front of Madame Lefleur's elegant shop.

"Come," she said to Olivia. The woman didn't wait for the coachman to open the door. She set her feet to the pavement and, without a backward glance, marched into the shop.

The bells over the door jangled as they entered.

Two shopgirls dashed over to them. They curtsied and smiled at the old woman as if overjoyed she had decided to grace them with her presence.

Smiling broadly, Madame Lefleur, who stood near the counter, rushed over as well and shooed the shopgirls away.

"Lady Huntington, you know I would have come to your residence," the French woman said in her lilting accent. "What is it I might help you with?"

The dowager's eyes glinted. She walked over to a bolt of shimmering green silk and rubbed the material between her fingers. "Hmmm, I just ordered five gowns from Madame Renault, I thought perhaps . . ." She gave a cursory glance around. "No, there is nothing here I want. I've already spent a king's ransom."

The modiste's mouth fell open. "At Madame Renault's shop?"

"Yes, I hear she is less apt to gossip. You may close out my account and that of the Marchioness of Huntington's as well, along with my granddaughter's, Lady Nina Ralston. We will not be purchasing any gowns from your establishment in the future. I cannot abide tattlers."

"But, my lady . . ."

The old woman held up a hand. "No amount of groveling will change my mind. I will make it my life's ambition to see Madame Renault is the new premiere modiste in London."

Tears shimmered in Madame Lefleur's eyes. "But she isn't even French. She is a fraud."

"I don't care if she grew up on Whitechapel High Road in a bordello. Discretion is a virtue I hold rather dear when it comes to my family and you do not possess it." And with that said the dowager spun on her heel and headed toward the exit.

As Olivia followed the old woman, she glanced over her shoulder at the modiste's face, which had turned ashen.

Madame Lefleur knew the power some of these elderly matriarchs possessed, and the Dowager Marchioness of Huntington appeared to be the queen bee.

At dinnertime, once again, Olivia was served her dinner in her room. She was tempted to take her tray of food and head down to the servants' dining hall, but she had learned at Lady Winton's that as a companion she lay somewhere in an abyss as far as her place in the household. The staff at Lady Winton's had worried she would repeat what she heard to their mistress, while Lady Winton treated Olivia as if she was not good enough to dine with her. It seemed she was in the same position here.

She forked a spear of asparagus in a cream sauce and slipped it into her mouth. One thing she could not deny was that the meals here far surpassed the meals at Lady Winton's.

Olivia glanced at the gilded mantel clock with ornate scrolls and a tiny brass bird perched on it. After the dowager retired, she was to meet Lord Anthony in his office.

She finished her dinner and wiped her mouth. Standing, she set the linen napkin on the tray and strode to the cheval glass. Studying her reflection, she filled her cheeks with air and slowly released the breath. After being in Madame Renault's shop with the shimmering bolts of costly fabrics, she realized how dowdy her clothes were. She ran her hand down the cotton skirt of her navy dress.

Olivia gave herself a mental scolding. Her attire had never bothered her before. She wasn't a vain person, yet suddenly she desperately wished she had one of the dresses the dowager was having sewn for her to wear before she met with Lord Anthony.

Her low laugh was more bitter than full of mirth. Stupid to even think about his lordship. He had no interest in her, and she should not be fancying thoughts about him. She needed to remember that and *not* the way her body warmed when it had slid against his.

Yet, she peered at the clock again, feeling agitated that the hands on the timepiece's face moved so slow.

Chapter Eleven

Anthony glanced up as Miss Michaels stepped into the office. Last night as he lay in his bed, he'd thought about the woman. There was something about her. Perhaps it was nothing more than he was lonely in his bed. But as he studied her now, he wondered if it was the scattering of freckles on her face that intrigued him or the way the lamplight made her hair look like flames. Or perhaps it was nothing more than the innocence in her expression. Surely, there had been nothing remotely innocent about Maria.

"Good evening, my lord," she said, her voice low and husky.

Perhaps it was that. The tone of her voice. The throaty quality of it when she spoke low. It seemed incongruent with everything else about her. It reminded him of a woman in the throes of passion right before she reached her climax.

He shoved his lurid thoughts from his mind and cleared his throat. "Miss Michaels."

She slipped into the chair across from him and glanced around. "Where is Atticus?"

"Thankfully, the little feathered beast is sleeping in my bedchamber."

She smiled back at him. "I have a feeling you actually like him."

The bird did have his charms, but he responded with a disgruntled *humph*. "I hear my grandmother and you went on a shopping expedition this afternoon."

She dipped her head and he saw red flush her cheeks. "Yes, she bought me several dresses."

Really? He tried to comprehend what the old woman was up to. His grandmother wasn't known for her generous nature in either actions or words. When she did things out of character it raised his suspicion, but he could not clearly see what ulterior motive would have prompted the old woman. Though there had to be one.

As if she saw the puzzlement in his expression, Miss Michaels gave a weak smile. "Your grandmother said she could not go about with me dressed as I am. But I would surmise that the real reason was that she wanted to let Madame Lefleur know she was displeased with her."

"How would buying gowns from the modiste do that?"

"That's it. She didn't buy them from Madame Lefleur. She purchased them from a Madame Renault."

"Ah, now I'm gaining a bit of clarity." He grinned. "Leave it to the old bird to stick her talons into someone who has displeased her. I presume after she went to Renault's she lorded it over Madame Lefleur."

"Yes. She closed her account, along with your sister's and sister-in-law's."

"Stuck a virtual knife in the woman's ribs and twisted it." Now that sounded more like his grandmother.

"She said I do not need to pay for the gowns, does that upset you?" Miss Michaels nibbled on her lower lip drawing his eye to the plump surface.

Maybe that was what he liked about her. That full, pouty lower lip that seemed extremely kissable. He could imagine her mouth on his body. He laughed to himself. He needed to stop thinking about Olivia this way. "If the dowager chose to purchase you gowns, then take them without hesitation."

"You're not upset that she spent an extravagant amount?"

"Not in the least. She has her own funds. Did she buy you a ball gown?"

"Yes. One made of silk. The yellow fabric shimmered and caught the light streaming through the shop's bow window." She blushed. "Forgive me. I'm rambling again."

The excitement on her face made some emotion within Anthony spark. He could have given Maria ten gowns like that and she would never have batted an eye. Caroline, on the other hand, would have grinned broadly and kissed James, but Caroline, like Grandmother, had her own funds and did not rely on someone else to give such things to her. If she wanted a gown, she had carte blanche and could buy one. Miss Michaels had obviously never received such a gift and could not afford to purchase costly clothing for herself.

"There is no need to apologize, Miss Michaels. I am delighted you are pleased. And I'm sure you will look stunning when you accompany Grandmother and me to whichever ball she drags me to." The thought of attending a ball with his grandmother felt as intrusive as he presumed a foot up the arse.

"You don't care for balls, my lord?"

Anthony enjoyed gatherings, but the type of ball Grandmother would wish him to attend would be full of matchmaking mamas and stuffy prigs. There would be no dancing where a man and woman could waltz close without censure, and no running off to the garden for an assignation with sultry kisses. That thought made his gaze center on Olivia's mouth again. There would be talk of weather and fashion and worse, his grandmother would toss young debutantes in front of him like breadcrumbs to a pigeon. Debutantes looking for marriage.

"Spending any time with my dear grandmother can be a trial and tribulation."

A slight smile curved her lips, and Anthony decided it was not only the raspy texture of her voice when she spoke low that brought out the lust in him, it was indeed the plump surface of her lower lip. He pitched his renegade thoughts from his head and handed Miss Michaels the ledger for Victory Pens, along with more bills. Ones from woodworkers, painters, plasterers, so on and so forth.

In a few days he would visit the factory in the East End and make sure that the improvements were going according to the architect's and James's specifications. He reached for the blueprints. Though they had dimensions neatly written on them, Anthony could grasp them better since they contained scaled drawings.

He unrolled the blueprints and weighted the corners down with two paperweights, the desk lamp, and the ledger for the *London Reformer*. His eyes scanned the architectural drawings of the factory's layout. Last night in bed, he'd pondered the placement of the various manufacturing stations. The production flow was well thought out, but if they moved the packaging station closer to the west side entrance that would save time getting the crates loaded onto drays. Then they would just need to add a loading dock at that entrance.

He took a piece of parchment from the paper tray and using a ruler as a straightedge, he drew up the changes. He compared his design to that of the blueprints. Both utilized the same amount of space, so the changes could be made.

Smiling, he glanced up at the clock on the desk and realized two hours had passed. "Miss Michaels, did I hand you a bill for carpentry work for areas five, six, and seven?"

"I don't recall coming across one yet." She ran her finger over one of the columns. "No, but let me check the last few receipts." She thumbed through the remaining stack of invoices. "No. It is not in these either."

"Good." Anthony grinned. Tomorrow he would visit the factory in Wapping and see if his changes could be implemented.

Feeling somewhat jubilant, Anthony glanced at Miss Michaels again. She'd been judiciously adding the bills and jotting figures into the ledger. She was a godsend. "Miss Michaels, if you are tired you may finish the rest tomorrow."

She peered at him. "I am adding the last few entries now, then I will total the columns and be done."

Well, that fact deserved a celebration. He stood and strode to the mahogany sideboard and poured two snifters of brandy. "It's been a productive evening. We need to celebrate."

She looked at the glass he handed her and stared at it as if he had handed her a bug. "What is it, my lord?"

"French brandy. Cognac."

"Is this what you were drinking last night?"

"Yes."

"I've never tasted it," she said.

He leaned on the edge of his desk and watched as she brought the glass to her lush lips. She tentatively took a sip. Her upper lip glistened with the liquor, and she drew her tongue over it.

The sight made him want to kiss her and tangle his tongue with hers to see how her mouth tasted. Instead he asked, "What do you think?"

She took another sip. "I taste vanilla and . . ."

"Yes?"

She took another sip. "Citrus."

He grinned. That was exactly how he would describe it.

She set the glass down and handed him the ledger as she stood.

Suddenly he didn't want her to leave. He wanted to celebrate. Accomplishments were few in his life, but after working on the blueprints, he felt as if he was slowly climbing a mountain and believed he might reach the peak before tumbling backward. Everything was falling into place, and he owed a great deal of thanks to Miss Michaels.

"Let me thank you for helping me. Let me take you somewhere to celebrate what we've accomplished."

This time she looked at him like he offered her the apple from the Garden of Eden.

He grinned. "Don't worry, love. Nothing nefarious. I thought I might take you to someplace like Finley's Music Hall."

She'd never been to Finley's or any music hall. Lady Winton had mentioned the place once. Though her ladyship had never been there, she'd heard that the couples who danced there stood too close and some even danced on the tables. "You have been there before, my lord."

"Yes. I think you would enjoy it."

She bit the inside of her mouth. She was curious, but . . .

"Come on, Miss Michaels, live a little."

"I don't have anything to wear."

His gaze swept over her. "What you are wearing is perfect. I will change into a simple sack suit."

A piece of her desperately wanted to go. "I shouldn't. It would not be proper of me to attend with you."

"Being proper is rather dull. And if you do not accompany me, I fear I will get into all sorts of trouble. You see, Miss Michaels, I am the black sheep of the family and not always on my best behavior. If I am not accompanied by someone of your moral standing, I will most likely fall in with a bad crowd and end up doing something outlandish. I'll end up with my name in the scandal sheets and give my grandmother an apoplexy. You do not want her death on your hands, do you?"

She tried not to grin, but instead look pious. "I do not think she will be any more pleased if she hears I accompanied you."

"My grandmother is safely tucked in bed. If I'm on my best behavior she will never know. Plus, you owe me."

She presumed she did. Her stepping in the wrong carriage had started this last fiasco. "But I didn't force you to pick up Signora Campari and toss her over your shoulder."

"Aww, you saw that?"

"I did."

"Would you have rather I stood there and let that she-cat strike me? She might have broken my nose. I hear it is my best feature."

Everything about him was a best feature. God had been generous to him.

"Well, if you do not wish to go, I'll head there myself."

"I will accompany you," she replied before she could halt her words.

The rascal's smile broadened. "Thank you for saving my wicked soul, Miss Michaels. I will consider your debt to me paid in full."

If he was looking for someone to save his soul, she was not the one to do it. But he didn't know that.

Chapter Twelve

The horse's hooves clopped on the cobbles as the hackney moved through the streets in the East End of London. With each bump in the road, the springs of the vehicle squeaked and jostled them about. Olivia glanced sideways at Lord Anthony. She expected to see a put-upon expression on his face, since he usually rode in a grand equipage, but instead he turned to her and smiled.

"We're nearly there," he said.

She forced a smile, even though her stomach fluttered with apprehension. Attending an event with Lord Anthony was wrong, yet beneath her misgiving she experienced euphoria. Vicar Finch would say it was due to the wickedness that lay within her. She could almost hear his voice resonating from where he stood at the pulpit in the church as he cast his dark glance at the girls from the orphanage and spoke of sin and vice. Perhaps he was right when it came to her, since she desperately wanted to attend the music hall.

Olivia ignored that thought. Tonight, she would *try* not to think of sin—hers or anyone else's.

The vehicle pulled in front of a brick building. Two

large gas lanterns illuminated the red double doors and the name FINLEY'S painted in white boxy letters on the brick façade.

Lord Anthony jumped down and offered her his gloved hand. As they stepped toward the doors, he leaned close. The puff of his breath touched her ear as he whispered, "Miss Michaels, while in this establishment it is imperative you call me Tony, and I call you Olivia. The crowd inside doesn't take kindly to aristocrats, and though I enjoy a good round of fisticuffs, one man against three hundred would not be favorable odds."

The gas lights next to the doors lessened the night's shadows on his face, and she saw the flash of his white teeth as he grinned.

How could he smile after such a statement? Was a nobleman in danger here? If so, why would his lordship wish to visit such a place? Her own internal thoughts seemed almost ironic considering the risks she took. Did danger cause a rush of exhilaration to course through him? Sometimes she wondered about her own choices. Did she solely rob these wicked men to avenge others, or was she seduced by the thrill of it all?

"Miss Michaels?" he said, waiting for her response.

Some inner part of her wished to call him by the nickname. There was an intimacy to such an act. "Yes, I understand."

His smile broadened. He removed his costly leather gloves and shoved them into the pockets of his simple wool jacket, which was nothing like the clothes he usually wore. And though the garment didn't look tailor-made the breadth of his shoulders and lean hips were not any less obvious.

He opened the door and they stepped inside. A large mahogany bar ran one side of the dim room and a row of booths with simple wooden tables and built-in benches lined the opposite wall.

Several men at the bar turned and peered at them. A few mumbled a greeting, then returned their attention to their tankards of ale.

The bartender nodded. "Tony, haven't seen you here in a while."

Olivia looked at his lordship. He must frequent the establishment if the bartender knew him by his first name. Or the nickname he'd given them. She wondered who they thought he was.

As if reading what was going through her mind, one side of his mouth turned up, and he winked.

Feeling her cheeks heat, she avoided his gaze and peered around. Though the pub wasn't exactly small, it was not as big as she had assumed it would be. There was no stage and not the number of people he had led her to believe. The place looked rather somber, and she experienced a flash of disappointment.

"This is it?" she asked.

"The music hall is in the back."

He'd no sooner spoken when the floor beneath Olivia's feet vibrated. The sound of singing and foot-stomping made its way into the small pub area.

With a jerk of his chin, his lordship motioned to another set of red double doors.

Olivia's gaze shot to where he had gestured.

A man stumbled out of the doors, swaying as though he'd imbibed too much for his own good. His gaze settled on her. "Hey, love, I was about to leave, but I think I'll stay and have a dance with you." His words came out slurred.

Lord Anthony drew in a deep breath and shot the man a lethal glare. "Put your hands on her, my friend, and you'll find them broken. Understand?"

The man's supercilious smile slipped from his face, and he lifted his hands out, palms facing outward as if to ward off an attack. "Just trying to be friendly, nothing more."

His lordship shot him one more scathing look, then whispered, "Some of the men in here get a bit rowdy, but next to me no one will bother you unless they are as drunk as that fellow. But do not worry, if need be, I'll take care of them."

"Who do they think you are?" she asked, unable to halt her curiosity any longer.

"Just a patron," he replied, his expression unreadable.

Olivia was sure there was more to it than that.

He offered her his arm and led her through the doors into a massive hall with a stage in the front with red velvet curtains draped back. Three long tables filled with men and women seated at them were centered in the middle of the hall. Smaller round tables crowded the perimeter. Patrons stood on a balcony that ran on the three walls facing the stage. Most held tankards of ale and sang along with the piano player and the fellow who stood onstage, belting out a song about the health benefits of drinking a pint every day. Whenever the word *pint* was mentioned in the song, everyone clanked their glasses to the person standing next to them and stomped their feet.

"Let's find a table," his lordship said, speaking over the boisterous crowd.

They weaved through the tables. A man passed them

and clapped Lord Anthony on the shoulder. "Haven't seen you here in a while. We had a fight here last week. We could have used you then."

"Hopefully, there won't be any tonight. I'm with a lady, and I don't wish to get my knuckles bloodied."

The fellow glanced at her, grinned, and walked away.

"Were you involved in a fight here?" Olivia peered at him as he pulled out a chair for her at one of the few round tables that didn't have patrons sitting at it.

"A small scuffle." His expression remained bland, giving little of his thoughts away.

She tipped her head to the side. "I doubt one gets bloodied knuckles from a small scuffle."

"Two drunks went at it. Somehow I ended up in the middle."

Now she understood why he considered himself the black sheep of the family. Not every nobleman visited places like this and brawled.

A buxom barmaid, who looked to be in her mid-thirties, strode up to their table. "How you doing, handsome? What can I get you?"

Lord Anthony shifted sideways in his chair and peered at Olivia. "Do you want an ale?"

She'd never had one and wondered if it tasted like the brandy he'd given her earlier. "Yes, thank you."

"Two pints." His lordship raised his hand showing two fingers.

The man on stage finished his song and started singing another rowdy tune. Two tables away a woman climbed on the scarred surface of a table and lifted the skirt of her dress to her knees and danced. The woman's legs were encased in dark woolen stockings with a hole near the knee that exposed the white creamy color of her pale skin. Men and women gathered around and clapped.

If the proper Vicar Finch saw such ribald revelry, he would have fainted or perhaps suffered a coronary. But Olivia couldn't help the feeling of delight that the rowdy group caused to settle within her. These people, no matter their lot in life, enjoyed escaping the confines of their day-to-day drudgery. People whose birth and circumstances set them squarely in one spot on the social sphere. A spot they momentarily left behind—only to be reminded of it when they awoke in the morning. In truth, they were no different from her. Tomorrow she would still be a companion whose class varied greatly from his lordship's, but tonight she was determined to absorb this experience.

As if Lord Anthony sensed the excitement within her, he grinned, and she could not stop herself from returning his smile. Somehow, he'd known this place would excite something within her. Was she so transparent to him? That should frighten her.

Her thoughts were interrupted by the return of the barmaid with their ale. As the woman placed his lordship's drink in front of him, she bent low, exposing the creamy flesh of her ample breasts. "Anything else I can get you, duckie, you just give me a whistle."

Lord Anthony's gaze dipped to the barmaid's bosom, but he didn't return the woman's cheeky smile as he slid several coins across the table. "No. That will be all."

Did some women just blatantly proposition him? He was beyond handsome and his physique rivaled some of the pictures she'd seen of Greek gods, but still . . . She glanced around and noticed even in his plain sack suit he drew the regard of both women and men. Perhaps it was that he was taller than most and stood out. Well, that didn't make a great deal of sense since he was sitting. Perhaps it was the aura about him, or that the fight he'd engaged in at an earlier date had been something to behold, causing him to be regarded with both caution and admiration.

"Why is everyone glancing at you?"

He stared at her for a long minute. "Perhaps it is not me that draws their regard, but you."

Her? Was he mad? She was not beautiful or striking. Surely not like his mistress. Olivia's hair was too brash. Her face was freckled. Yet, when he looked at her, she could almost believe he meant what he said. Almost.

He took a long draw on the ale in his tankard, and she watched the movement of his throat as he tipped his head back slightly. Even that seemed sensual.

Pulling her gaze away, she raised her own tankard to her lips. The taste was bitter, nothing like the brandy.

Her face must have shown she was not sure she enjoyed it because his lordship gave a short laugh. "You've never had ale, Olivia?"

The sound of her name on his lips shouldn't have sent a wave of warmth through her, but it did. "No. Never. It's more bitter than I expected. Nothing like the brandy."

"Would you prefer a brandy instead?"

She shook her head and took another sip, worried the brandy might go to her head faster than the ale.

The boisterous song ended, and the room exploded with applause. Two men helped the woman down from the table she'd been dancing on.

A man who sat at a table near the stage stood and announced the next act.

"Who is he?" Olivia asked, motioning to the fellow.

"They call him the chairman."

A man dressed in a white shirt with billowing sleeves and a small red cap on his head stepped onto the stage with an accordion and played an upbeat tune. The sound of chairs being pushed back as people stood resonated in the air. Men holding the hands of their dance partners moved to the rear of the hall. Those not dancing clapped and stomped their feet in time to the music.

Olivia couldn't help her own foot from tapping to the beat.

"Will you honor me with a dance, Olivia?" Lord Anthony asked.

Her breath caught in her throat. Dance? She had only danced the waltz with the other girls at the orphanage. They had hummed the music low, since Vicar Finch had not approved of the partnered dance, even though it had been accepted in society decades ago. She'd never heard music like this before or seen this fast-paced dance.

He bent close to her. Once again, his breath touched her ear. "Release those shackles, Olivia. Dance with me."

Shackles? She'd released them far more than he knew. She wanted to dance. "I don't know this dance, and I might step on your toes."

"It's a polka. Very simple. I'll guide you." He held out his hand for hers.

She placed her palm against his.

His fingers wrapped about hers—warm and reassuring. The touch caused her belly to flutter. Unlike her, he seemed unaffected. She couldn't stop herself from wondering how many women his hands had touched. How many women had he caressed?

She pushed her thoughts away and bit her lower lip as they made their way to the rear of the hall to where couples swirled around to the fast-paced music.

Her heart beat a rapid tattoo as she listened to Lord Anthony explain the steps.

"Place your left hand on my shoulder," he said as he set his right hand to her back and pulled her close. He grasped her other hand and extended it outward. "Just follow my lead."

He led her around the room. Before she knew it, she was grinning broadly as they moved across the floor in a hop and step fashion with the others. The room almost vibrated with the excitement of the dancers and those singing to the tune.

The song came to an end and the accordion player started another rousing tune.

Without missing a beat, the dancers continued.

Lord Anthony raised a brow, silently asking her if she wished to dance to this song as well.

She gave a quick nod, and once again they moved with the flow of those on the dance floor.

Olivia's cheeks hurt from smiling so much.

"You are doing rather splendidly. You've not stepped on my toes once."

"Be careful what you say. The dance is not over."

He laughed—a deep, jovial sound that made her feel as light as the atmosphere.

When the song finished. Lord Anthony set both his hands on her waist and swung her in the air, laughing. As he lowered her the front of her breasts brushed against the hard surface of his chest, the same way it had in the office.

Every nerve within her tingled.

Anthony took her hand in his, and they weaved through the crowded tables.

"You dance wonderfully," he said as they neared the table.

She turned around. "I think I almost tripped you, Lor—"

Before she could finish her words, his large hand slipped around the back of her neck bringing her mouth to his.

The press of his lips absorbed the rest of his name.

Chapter Thirteen

For a minute, Olivia's head spun with confusion as his lordship's mouth met hers, in a firm and demanding kiss. But then she realized she had started to address him as *Lord Anthony* where any of the other patrons might have overheard.

Was that why he was kissing her?

Of course it was, yet her mind discarded that knowledge to center itself on the physical pleasure—the warmth of his lips as they moved against hers in a way that made her want to react. She felt lost, almost overwhelmed by the sensations drifting through her.

The kiss did not solely affect her mouth, but her whole body tingled with awareness.

Without further contemplation, she pressed herself closer and slid her hands over the hard planes of his chest. Not to push him away but to experience the feel of his strong muscles beneath her palms.

Slowly his mouth left hers, but not before he tugged her lower lip between his own lips as if savoring their kiss.

His intense gaze settled on her face, and she wondered

if the potency of the kiss had startled him as much as it had her.

He retreated a fraction, and she realized that though his one hand drifted away from her nape, the other still pressed at the small of her back. A warm touch that was both intimate and comforting.

His gaze dipped to her mouth, and he leaned close.

For a brief second in time, she thought he was going to kiss her again. Anticipation swirled through her, and the beat of her heart, which was finally returning to a semblance of normalcy, quickened again. But instead his mouth moved to her ear.

"Forgive me, Olivia," he whispered, "but I couldn't have you addressing me as you were about to. As I said, one against three hundred isn't fair odds."

Suddenly, she realized that the hum of conversation had grown louder around where they stood.

A man whistled.

"You're a lucky lad, Tony," a man called out, his Irish accent unmistakable.

Heat warmed Olivia's face.

With his hand still on her back, Anthony prompted her to their table. His hand curled over the top of her chair, and he pulled it back with a quick jerk, causing the legs to make a scraping noise against the wooden floor.

Was he suddenly angry? Unsure what to say, she peered at the chairman, who was announcing a comedian. Feeling she needed to say something, she turned to him. "I'm sorry. I'll be more careful."

He gave a low laugh. "Olivia, do not fret over it. I'm not as sorry as I ought to be for kissing you."

She thought he would grin. That his last words were

nothing more than a way to lighten the mood, but he looked as serious as a mourner in a procession.

Did he honestly mean what he'd said? Had he enjoyed it as much as she had? She should look away, but she felt all flummoxed inside. Her stomach clenched as if danger grew near, or as if she had leapt from one ledge to another and nearly lost her balance. Yet, she realized it was not a sense of danger that made her feel that way but a mixture of pleasure and lust. She'd enjoyed the kiss. Tremendously.

With his gaze directed on the stage, she studied Anthony's handsome face—his square jaw, the slightly curved arch of his brows, and his sensual mouth that had touched hers. Without thought, she pressed her fingers to her lips. They still tingled. She doubted he knew that was her first kiss.

During the next hour, several different performers took to the stage, including an acrobat. At present, another comedian was on the stage. The fellow told several jokes at the expense of the nobility. Olivia was surprised to see Anthony grinning. He chuckled—a low sound that caused a shiver to travel up her spine.

When another accordion player took to the stage and began a rousing tune as fast-paced as the one they'd danced to, Anthony asked if she would honor him.

Honor him? A man of his station using such a word toward her seemed foreign. Without hesitation, she placed her hand in his and they joined the other dancers.

They did the same hop and step moves. Once again, she smiled until her cheeks hurt. Had she ever smiled so much? She could not recall. Though she had enjoyed teaching the girls at the orphanage, it was a repressed pleasure—it was such a somber atmosphere at the orphanage that when she laughed too hard, there was always Vicar Finch to make her aware of it. Being this carefree was a novelty. After several songs, the chairman stood to announce another comedian.

She and Anthony had just reached the table when the double doors that led from the pub to the music hall burst wide open. Several policemen rushed into the room.

A cacophony of sounds resonated in the air. Screams, the scraping of chairs against the wooden floors as people quickly stood, the sound of some toppling backward, the policemen's whistles.

"Bugger it. We need to get out of here," Anthony said over the chaotic noises. He took her hand in his and they made their way to the stage. Like a gazelle, his lordship leapt onto it, then turned around and reaching under her arms, he lifted her onto the platform. She glanced over her shoulder to see some of the patrons fighting with the policemen and others being struck by the bobbies' billy clubs as they resisted being dragged out of the music hall.

"Come, Olivia," Lord Anthony said, talking over the commotion. "It won't serve either of us well to be carted down to the police station."

With her hand still tightly gripped in his, they made their way through the area behind the stage where a warren of passages seemed to spread outward like a spider's legs. They moved left, then right. Ahead she saw a door. It burst wide open and two policemen rushed through it.

Lord Anthony pushed her through an open doorway before the bobbies spotted them. Quietly, he closed the door and slid the metal latch into place.

The room was almost pitch dark, except for the shafts

of moonlight seeping through a grime-covered window that was set high in the wall. As her eyes adjusted to the dimness, Olivia saw crates of bottled liquor stacked around the perimeter.

His lordship released her hand, climbed up on the crate below the window, and unlocked it. He pushed the lower sash upward, causing more moonlight to illuminate the tiny room.

"Olivia, we must move fast!" He held out his hand for hers.

In the corridor, she could hear policemen banging on doors. She took his hand and stood next to him. The window looked over a side alley.

"No one is out there, but for how long who knows. I'll boost you up." He leaned down and locked his hands together, forming a stirrup.

She placed her foot into his cradled hands, grabbed the sill, and hoisted her body upward.

The noise from the policemen banging on the doors in the corridor grew louder. Closer.

Any minute they would reach this room.

"Forgive me," he whispered, placing his hands on her bum and giving her a firm shove so half her body protruded out of the window.

Setting her knee to the sill, she twisted around and lowered herself to the ground.

Anthony hoisted himself up and followed her outside.

"Damnation," he mumbled, noticing, as she had, that the alley ran straight into another brick building, leaving them with having to move toward the street in front of the music hall.

Used to scaling buildings, Olivia peered at the wall, looking for a drainpipe and footholds, but the surface was completely smooth with not even a single window or ledge.

Hand in hand, they quietly moved up the alley to the main thoroughfare. They could hear the crowd on the street and the sound of a policeman's whistle screeching in the air. Loud footsteps on the pavement alerted them to someone's approach. A long, dark shadow cut across the opening of the alley, forewarning of the person's proximity.

With quick movements, Anthony swung her around and pressed her back to the cold brick of the adjacent building. He dipped his head and his mouth covered hers again. His lips were warm in the cool night. The kiss started out almost tender, as if he was reluctant to press his lips to hers, but then the pressure increased.

She heard her own moan as she tangled her hands about his neck and returned his kiss.

His mouth coaxed her lips apart.

Briefly, their breaths puffed against each other before his tongue slipped into her mouth to explore the recesses within. She had never experienced anything so decadent.

Tentatively, Olivia moved her tongue against his.

He made an unmistakable noise of approval and leaned farther into her. Her tingling breasts were flattened against his chest.

"Break it up! Break it up! Go home if you want to be rutting with each other."

Anthony pulled back.

The policeman stood only a few feet from them, holding

his billy club. Obviously, he didn't realize they'd been in the music hall.

"Sorry, sir," Anthony said, his normally authoritative voice contrite. "Just was taking me girl out for a stroll."

"Strolling, eh, is that what you call it?" the policeman asked. "Be on your way."

Without responding, Anthony placed her hand around the bend of his elbow, and they moved out of the alley. "Keep your head down," he mumbled as they stepped onto the pavement where several other patrons were being carted into a police wagon.

They had walked a good distance away when she noticed a grin on his face.

"That was a close one." His smile broadened as if he'd reveled in the excitement of it all.

They truly were more alike than he understood. "Why do you think the police raided the place?"

"There's an illegal gambling casino in the back room. It appears someone tipped them off to its presence."

An hour later, they arrived back at the Trent family's Mayfair residence. Thankfully, every window in the house remained dark.

As Anthony slipped his key into the front door, he turned to her. "I'm sorry the evening turned out the way it did. I hope you weren't frightened too much."

Is that why he'd been so quiet after they had found a hackney to take them home? She thought perhaps it was the fact that she'd not only kissed him back in the alley, but that she'd taken the opportunity to tightly wrap her hands around his neck and cling to him like a lost lover.

The knowledge that his reticence was not caused by her behavior sent a wave of relief through her. She was half tempted to tell him that the abrupt ending to their night out would never, could never, erase everything that had come before that. The laughing, the dancing, and both kisses would be etched into her brain until she took her last breath.

She stared down at her feet and tried to think of how to respond without sounding desperate or infatuated. She was neither. Well, perhaps a little of the latter. Or a great deal of it.

"I should not have taken you there. Forgive me," his lordship said, drawing her from her thoughts.

"There is no need to apologize. I enjoyed myself immensely."

"Did you now? Even though we had to climb out of a window to avoid being arrested? Even though I kissed you not once but twice without asking you first? Even though I felt you trembling in that alley?"

She hadn't trembled from fear. She'd placed herself in dangerous situations that far outweighed what had transpired tonight. She faced it every time she climbed out of a window. Every time she balanced herself on a narrow ledge. And every time she entered a residence to settle a long overdue score.

It was not fear from the bobby that had caused her to shake, it was what she experienced when Anthony's lips moved against hers that frightened her. It was longing. Throughout her life, Olivia had yearned for many things.

A family. A home. A sense of belonging. During her life, she might attain those things but longing for any attachment to Lord Anthony was a fool's dream since they were separated by a social chasm too great to bridge.

"It was a bit frightening when the police arrived, but I did enjoy myself tonight. I had never visited a music hall, and I liked the tempo of the music, along with all the other acts. Of course, the ending of the outing will be something I never forget."

He smiled. "Yes, it is not every day one is involved in a policemen's raid."

She'd not meant the raid, she'd meant the kiss, but Lord Anthony didn't need to know that. Like all her other secrets, she would take that to her grave.

For another long moment, they just stared at each other.

"You are full of surprises, Olivia."

If he only knew how many, he would most likely despise her.

He turned the key in the lock, and the front door swung inward on silent hinges. Together they moved up the stairs. Their bedchambers were on the same floor. His near the steps, hers at the end of the corridor across from the dowager's room.

"Good night, Olivia," he whispered.

"Good night, my lord."

As she turned to walk away his fingers wrapped about her hand. "After everything we have been through, I think you can call me Anthony when alone."

She opened her mouth and before she could utter a word, his finger pressed against her lips.

"I insist."

She nodded.

“Good night, Olivia,” he said again.

“Good night, Anthony.” She turned and walked down the long corridor. At the doorway, she could not stop herself from peering back to where they had stood. He was still there, watching her.

Heart beating fast, she stepped into her bedchamber and slumped against the door.

Chapter Fourteen

The following week, Anthony glanced across his desk to where Olivia sat, diligently transferring figures into a ledger, while he once again worked on the blueprints of the different manufacturing stations at Victory Pens.

Over the past several days, they had fallen into a companionable silence as they worked in the office late into the evening. Occasionally, the quietness was shattered by Atticus saying something ribald. When the bird did so, instead of appearing scandalized, a slight smile edged up the corners of Olivia's lips. More than once, he wondered if she understood some of the lurid words the parrot spouted as if the bird had studied Francis Grose's book *A Classical Dictionary of the Vulgar Tongue*.

Luckily, Atticus had drifted asleep several minutes ago.

Since his and Olivia's escapade at the music hall, Anthony had confined his conversations with her to the business accounts she helped him with, while his restless mind dwelled on other things, such as the kiss they had shared in the alley outside the music hall.

The memory of her lips hesitantly moving against his, then the fiery passion she'd eventually responded with, along with the feel of her small hands gliding up his chest were burned into his mind—clear as the view of the ocean if one stood at Whitesand Bay in Cornwall.

Something had sparked between them, leaving them kissing each other as if it was the last thing they would ever do. Contrary to her saying she'd enjoyed herself, perhaps she'd thought it would be. Perhaps she'd thought they would be carted off to prison.

She cleared her throat, and he realized she'd asked him something while he'd been lost in his thoughts.

"Sorry, Olivia, what did you say?"

She held out an invoice. "Is the final figure on this three hundred and ten pounds or three hundred and twelve? The printing is smudged."

He took the paper from her and concentrated on the last digit. If he looked at the whole figure, he might muddle the numbers around. "I believe it's a two."

"That's what I thought. Thank you." She lowered her head and entered the amount in the ledger, then ran her finger over the column of figures.

Anthony could practically see her mind working as she calculated the total. She was remarkably intelligent. What would it be like to be able to add such data in one's head?

I will never know.

He peered back at the blueprint spread across his desk and picked up a piece of the translucent paper he'd bought at a printing shop on Fleet Street close to where Temple Bar used to be. The thin paper allowed him to transfer the dimensions and add the changes he wished to implement. With his pencil and a protractor, he made more adjustments to the placement of the loading dock. Though he didn't like adding figures, he'd come to find out that he enjoyed working on the flow of manufacturing areas and finding ways to improve them. He hoped his brother would agree with the changes he'd made when he returned from holiday.

An hour later, the shuffling of papers caused Anthony to set his pencil down and look at Olivia.

The light from the gas lamp made the red in her hair look like glowing embers. Earlier, he'd spent an inordinate amount of time wondering how it would look tumbling over her naked shoulders, contrasting with her pale skin. He'd also wondered if the freckles scattered on her face were on other parts of her body.

Olivia glanced up, and he realized she'd caught him staring at her. The pink on her cheeks deepened.

"Sorry for staring. Your hair . . . The light brings out the vibrancy of the red."

As if self-conscious about the color, she touched the ginger ringlet near her ear, then as though realizing the action quickly lowered her hand.

"The color is lovely." His words seemed impulsive, yet he could not help himself from offering the compliment.

She looked at him with a startled expression—an expression of shock like he'd said her breasts were rather perky and he wanted to see them naked. Which he had thought about but would not voice out loud.

She uttered a sound, something between a laugh and a noise of disagreement. "My hair is a hideous color."

"What? It is anything but. What would make you think that?"

She looked off into the distance of the room, her gaze on the bookshelves, but he could tell from the blankness in her eyes that she really wasn't even seeing them but thinking of an event from her past. One he presumed was not completely pleasant. Suddenly, more than anything, he wanted to know who had made her feel so self-conscious.

He waited, hoping she would tell him without prompting, but she remained quiet. "Tell me who told you such a thing, Olivia."

Her gaze jerked back to him. For a long minute, he thought she would not answer him.

"Vicar Finch at the orphanage said my hair was a curse."

"A curse? I don't understand."

"The sign of the devil. Like being left-handed. He said it was why I was not always agreeable. Why I needed to be punished."

Devil? Punished? The two words slammed into Anthony's gut like a blow, almost knocking the air from his lungs. His hands balled into tight fists. He forced them to relax. "Did he punish you?"

"I deserved it. I did things I shouldn't have."

"Like?" he asked, unable to control the anger within him that was reflected in the tone of his voice.

"I picked apples from Mr. Jamison's orchard, which abutted the orphanage, and gave them to the other girls and myself. I knew it was wrong. Stealing, but they were a treat and from spring onward whenever a breeze drifted through the orchard, we could smell the sweet scent of the blossoms in the air. When autumn came the fruit glowed under the sun like red beacons. We'd talk about how juicy they must be, and . . ." Her cheeks flushed with color. "Sorry, I'm rambling again."

"You're not rambling in the least. You are answering my question. And you were punished for this?"

"Yes." She nodded.

"How?"

"With a birching."

The anger within him traveled through his body, making him tense. He could envision a young, perhaps even hungry, Olivia bent over while a birch rod struck her backside.

"How old were you?"

"The first time?"

"You mean you were struck more than once?"

She gave a laugh and the thought that she could do so over such a memory startled him.

"Well, the apple blossoms smelled sweet every year. And I wasn't always caught. Only twice."

"You mean after being hit, you did it again?"

"My lord, you live in a grand house. You do not understand what it is like to hear the growl of stomachs. To see girls you have come to love, just like sisters, be hungry for something they long to have, but cannot because of their circumstances."

Olivia was right. He'd lived a privileged life. Not wanting for anything material. But he knew what it was like to want things that did not come easy, like adding figures with competency, but nothing as simple as desiring an apple. In her position, he would have done the same thing. Punishment or not.

"I don't condemn you, Olivia. I think that was rather brave of you. And this Vicar Finch thought you were predisposed to this behavior not because you possessed a thoughtful nature, but because you possessed red hair?"

"Yes, just like he struck my friend Helen when she used her left hand to write. I presume it was why the two of us became the dearest of friends. It was also the reason the matron of the orphanage, Mrs. Garson, showed the two of us extra kindness. She did not agree with Vicar Finch."

"So, there was someone to side with you there?"

"Yes. She was instrumental in me becoming a teacher at the orphanage."

"May I ask why you left your position to become a chaperone to someone of Lady Winton's ilk?"

"I had my reasons, my lord. But I don't wish to speak of them." Olivia set the pen down. "I've finished entering the last invoice from today. May I retire?"

"Of course, thank you for your help."

She nodded.

Anthony followed her movements as she strode to the door and exited the room. He suspected that Olivia wasn't telling him something. Perhaps it was nothing more than the orphanage held unpleasant memories that were not easy to forget if she remained there.

The following morning, the sun cast its bright glow through the two windows in Olivia's bedchamber as she finished washing. She slipped on her navy dress and wondered if today the dowager would once again accept callers. The woman appeared determined to wait out the gossip about her grandson before allowing anyone to call on her.

In over a week, Olivia had gathered no new information on the goings-on of the *ton*. She had helped Lord Anthony several nights with his ledgers, but he'd never left the room, affording her the opportunity to peruse the pile of invitations on his desk, and though the dowager opened her mail in Olivia's presence, she never saw what any of the correspondence said.

A soft knock sounded on her door.

She glanced at the mantel clock. *Seven thirty.* Olivia fastened the top button at her collar and opened the door.

The same dark-haired maid who'd brought the silver breakfast tray every morning stood in the corridor with a bland expression on her face.

She took the tray from the maid's hands. "You're Galen, right?"

"Yes, miss."

"Galen, I think I'll take my meals in the servants' hall starting today."

The maid's expression shifted to one of uncertainty.

Understandable. Like at Lady Winton's residence, the staff here likely feared she would report every bit of chin-wagging back to the Dowager Marchioness of Huntington. They probably thought she was a gentlewoman down on her luck who'd taken this position. She would have to get them to trust her. If the dowager refused to see callers, perhaps eating meals with the servants would be the next best way to find out the goings-on in London. Servants passed gossip from one household to the next. Plus, she was tired of eating by herself.

She strode past the maid, down the corridor, and moved down the back staircase. Once belowstairs, the sound of chatter and utensils striking against plates resonated from the servants' hall. As she stepped into the room, the buzz of conversation lowered to a hum before ceasing completely.

Unlike at Lady Winton's residence, where the butler and housekeeper took their meals in their respective offices, here the two upper servants dined at the table with the maids and footmen.

Since several members of the household staff had gone with Lord and Lady Huntington to the Lake District, there were several unoccupied chairs. Feeling the gaze of those in the room on her like a hot branding iron, Olivia set the serving tray on an old oak sideboard and sat with her plate at the empty seat closest to the entrance.

"I hope you don't mind if I join you." She smiled.

The old butler returned the expression, but the housekeeper and several others looked less trusting.

"Not at all," Menders said when no one else replied.

Lord Anthony was right, not revealing that the butler was the one who'd slammed the door on her face had made him an ally. His lordship might not like doing calculations, but he was smart. Several other words sprung to mind. Handsome. Kind. Extremely skilled at kissing. She hurled that latter thought away.

Katie, the young maid who had shown her to the maids' quarters when Olivia had first arrived, gave a tentative smile.

Olivia smiled back, then lifted the lid off her dish. She was relieved to see she'd been served the same food as the other staff: eggs, sausage, and a slice of toast with jam on the side. Ignoring the eyes on her like she was a bug in their food, Olivia forked a piece of egg and slipped it into her mouth.

The cook strode into the room and placed a pitcher of milk on the table.

"I must say, the meals here far surpass anything I've had before," Olivia said to the woman.

A proud expression settled on the cook's face as she strode back out of the room.

"The servants' hall can get rather boisterous," the housekeeper said. "Are you sure you wouldn't rather eat in your room?"

"Oh, no, Mrs. Parks. I was raised in an orphanage and am not used to eating alone. The sounds of a crowded dining hall make me feel more at home."

"You lived in an orphanage?" Katie asked, her eyes large.

"Yes, in Kent."

One of the footmen pinned her with a curious look. "I grew up in Kent. Where?" he asked as if quizzing her on the authenticity of her story.

"All Saints Orphanage for Girls."

"Well, I'll be. I grew up not that far from there." He smiled and took a sizable bite of his toast.

"Me mom grew up in an orphanage," the scullery maid said, stepping into the room and removing the tray Olivia had set aside.

They asked her a few more questions and soon the conversation returned to a normal rhythm. Olivia breathed a sigh of relief.

These were her people. Not men like Lord Anthony. She needed to remember that. Needed to remember her place in the world. She knew what powerful men could do. Abuse the power they had, and though Lord Anthony was not like the men on her list, they still were of a different station in life. Fawning over the man was as foolish as leaping over the rooftops during broad daylight.

"My cousin," Katie said, "who's a maid for Lord and Lady Belington mentioned that they've been working like dogs to get ready for the ball they are having tonight."

The mention of the Earl of Belington's name pulled Olivia from her thoughts. She glanced up briefly, then as if uninterested lowered her gaze to her plate of food. Belington was one of the last two men on her list. Trying not to appear too interested, she listened to them chat about the gathering on Upper Brook Street.

"It shall be a grand affair," Katie continued. "A truck-load of flowers was delivered yesterday. My cousin says the guest list includes everyone of import. Some say even Prince Edward might attend."

"I heard one of the maids there dropped a vase and his lordship sacked her, right there on the spot," Galen said.

"Lady Huntington wouldn't do that to one of us," a little dark-haired maid said.

"No, she wouldn't," Katie replied, "but the dowager would."

The housekeeper's gaze settled on Olivia, then the woman cleared her throat rather loudly and all conversation about the elder Lady Huntington ceased.

"Is Lord Anthony going?" a pretty blond maid asked, looking at the first footman, Cline, who sometimes served as valet to his lordship.

"He's going out, but I doubt there. He's not interested in those debutantes."

"Why would he be when he has Signora Campari," another footman stated.

"I think he broke it off with her," Cline responded.

Had he broken it off with his mistress? What did she care? She wasn't interested in the job. Not that he'd ask her. But she was interested in the Earl of Belington. In retribution. Tonight, the man would have one additional, uninvited guest at his ball.

Chapter Fifteen

The Dowager Marchioness of Huntington roughly cleared her throat.

From where Olivia sat in the blue drawing room, she peered at the woman sitting across from her.

Over the edge of her book, the dowager shot Olivia a deadly glare with her steely gray eyes. "The tapping of your shoe is monotonous."

Olivia stilled her foot. She was restless. Once again, the dowager had not received any callers. The only information Olivia had been able to gather about Lord Belington's ball tonight had come from what the staff had mentioned during breakfast.

"If you are bored, I suggest you go help that scallywag grandson of mine."

What? How did the old woman know she was helping Lord Anthony?

"Help Lord Anthony?" She forced an innocent expression.

"Don't play the naiveté with me, child."

Olivia opened her mouth to respond, but the dowager raised her hand. "I have no issue with you helping that rascal. I'm sure he requires all the assistance he can get. Why my eldest grandson put him in charge of any of his business holdings I will never understand. By the time Huntington returns from the Lake District, I fear those businesses might teeter on the precipice of ruin. Though in all honesty, I'd say goodbye to bad rubbish if that radical newspaper Caroline runs toppled into financial ruin."

The woman's words about Anthony agitated Olivia. He'd been working diligently on the upgrades for Victory Pens. The changes he'd implemented were conducive to the flow of operations. Well, in her limited knowledge, they appeared to be.

Olivia squared her shoulders. "Lord Anthony is doing a wonderful job. You should see the improvements he has made to the layout of the pen factory."

The dowager arched one of her gray brows.

Olivia braced herself for a setdown. She didn't care. The dowager was too critical of his lordship.

An unexpected grin formed on the woman's thin lips.

Unsure what to make of it, Olivia wondered if that was the way the woman looked before tossing a vase at one's head.

As if the effort to smile was exhausting, the dowager's lips slipped back into a straight line. She waved her frail hand in the air like Olivia was a pesky fly at the dining table. "Go on. Off with you."

Olivia hesitated. If she dashed off and went to his lordship's office, it would confirm she was indeed helping Anthony. She hesitated, unsure what was best. But unable to stifle her desire, she stood and strode to the door.

A minute later, Olivia stepped into the office and paused.

Lord Anthony stood by his desk. She studied the way

his long fingers moved as he rolled up the blueprints for Victory Pens. Her gaze settled on his top hat on the blotter and the fact that he wore a jacket, instead of just his shirtsleeves.

Was he about to go out? The thought sent a dichotomy of emotions through her. If he went out and left her in the office, she would be able to rifle through the invitations, but then he would not be here. Why should she care about his absence?

She would only be lying to herself if she didn't admit she enjoyed his company. He was unlike most of the other members of the *ton* she had spent any time with. He was less stuffy. Less pretentious. More relaxed. She liked that. She liked him—far more than she should.

He glanced up and smiled. "How did you get out of my grandmother's clutches?"

She wet her lips. "The dowager knows that I help you. I'm not sure who told her."

The expression on his face remained the same.

"You don't look surprised." She stepped up to the desk.

"I already knew."

"Oh?"

"This morning she sent a note to my bedchamber, summoning me to her suite of rooms. The only thing I'm surprised about is that it took her this long to find out. She has spies." He grinned.

By spies, he probably meant servants who feared the dowager's wrath. Feared they'd find themselves out the door with no references if the questions she put to them weren't answered truthfully.

"She was worried I was botching things up and you

were my partner in the destruction of the family's coffers," he continued, his gaze on the blueprints as he tied a navy ribbon around them so they wouldn't unravel. "I told her she had nothing to fear. That you are extraordinary, since you possess the ability to calculate sums better than anyone could even imagine."

That he thought her extraordinary, even if he meant only her mind, sent a warm feeling through her body. Plus, he had given her a tremendous amount of credit. She had figured if anyone caught on to the fact that she assisted him, he would say she did nothing more than take dictation—that he would take all the credit for maintaining the ledgers. The fact that he didn't, shouldn't have surprised her.

He picked up his top hat and set it on his head.

"Are you going out?" she asked.

"Yes, I'm going to Victory Pens to see how many of the changes I've asked to be made to the layout have been brought to fruition." He strode toward the door, then pivoted back. "Would you care to accompany me?"

Startled by the invitation, she blinked. "Yes. I would like that very much."

"Then we should be on our way. The construction foreman is expecting me."

"I shall get my shawl and be back in a moment." Once out of his sight, she flew up the steps as if assisted by wings. Sparks of excitement flashed within her. She wanted to see the pen factory. Wanted to see what Anthony had been so diligently working on.

In her bedchamber, she grabbed her shawl and wrapped it about her shoulders as she rushed down the stairs to the entry hall. The little sparks in her stomach intensified at the sight of Anthony at the doorway, waiting for her. She attempted to ignore the sensation, along with the warm smile he offered her.

Outside, Anthony held out his gloved hand to assist her into the waiting carriage. He folded his tall frame into the seat across from her and stretched out his long legs, causing his feet to bump into hers.

"Sorry," he said. "Do you mind?" He motioned to the spot next to her.

She shook her head. "Of course not."

Anthony stood just as the coachman called to the horses to *move on*. The vehicle jerked forward. Caught off balance, he braced his hands on both sides of her shoulders to stop himself from tumbling onto her.

Their faces were close. Close enough she could smell the scent of mint on his breath.

His regard was intense. It seemed to examine every feature of her face.

For a moment, she wished her skin was absent the freckles that dotted the bridge of her nose and cheeks.

His gaze lowered to her mouth.

Her heartbeat spiked.

"Forgive me, Olivia."

The low, raspy tone of his voice sent a shiver down her spine. She swallowed her foolish desire to shift forward so their mouths touched, so she could experience his warm and demanding mouth on hers again.

Anthony held her gaze for several seconds, then mumbling something under his breath, he straightened and sat next to her. He stretched out his long legs, crossing them at the ankles. She studied the shine of his black shoes to distract herself from the heat emanating from his body and the way his shoulder touched hers every time they hit a rut in the road.

"Is something amiss?"

She wet her dry lips and turned to him. Once again, their faces were close. She quickly peered out the window. "No, nothing."

The grand town houses in Mayfair faded as they moved closer to the East End of London where the air was thicker from the smoke from the nearby factories. Several drays loaded with wooden crates of goods rumbled by them.

The carriage slowed as it turned onto a street and pulled up to a two-story brick building with arched windows on the ground floor and smaller windows on the second story. The factory was symmetrical with a center green door and two massive barnlike doors on the far ends. The one on the left was open and a delivery of lumber was being carried inside by men in their shirtsleeves.

Looking like an anxious young lad at Christmas, Anthony grabbed the blueprints, opened the carriage door, and leapt to the pavement. He turned and offered her his hand. On the way here, he'd taken his gloves off and tossed them onto the seat across from them, while she had rushed from the house and not put hers on.

His fingers curled about hers.

The warmth from his touch traveled from his skin to hers.

Why did her body and mind obsess over this man? Perhaps it was nothing more than the fact that he had looked at her like no other man ever had. Angered over her feeble contemplations, she removed her hand from his. He didn't appear to notice the hastiness of her actions, while she felt bereft.

He opened the door and they stepped into a center hall with offices on both sides. A cacophony of noises filled the air. The *tap, tap, tap* of hammers striking nails, the *whizzing* of handsaws working their way through pieces of lumber, and the chatter of workmen bustling about. The building had the strong scent of freshly cut wood, paint, and sweat. In front of them was another door. Anthony opened it and they stepped into a massive space with worktables on one side and machinery on another.

She examined Anthony's face as he glanced around. "Are you pleased?"

As if suddenly recalling she stood next to him, he glanced at her. His eyes were bright. He smiled. "Very much so."

She had a feeling he had spent a great deal of his life acting frivolous and now had something he could say he had accomplished. The happiness she saw on his face gave her immeasurable pleasure. She knew what it was like to test yourself. To step out of how you were perceived by others and challenge yourself to do something that no one would think you capable of doing.

Impulsively, she reached for his hand and squeezed his fingers. As if her actions did not shock him in the least, he squeezed her hand back.

A man in a dark sack suit strode toward them, and she hastily released Anthony's fingers.

"Mr. Gibbons," Anthony said, reaching out to shake the other man's hand.

"My lord." The fellow enthusiastically pumped Anthony's hand.

Anthony turned to her. "Miss Michaels, this is Mr. Gibbons, the construction foreman. Miss Michaels, is my assistant."

For a brief second the man's expression showed his surprise. She was sure hers most likely did as well. She had not thought she would be introduced by such an esteemed title.

"Mr. Gibbons," she said, holding out her hand to shake his.

He briefly hesitated then grasped her fingers in a loose grip.

He turned back to Anthony, then motioned with a sweep of his hand. "What do you think, my lord?"

Like Anthony, the man's expression radiated a sense of accomplishment.

The boyish pleasure from Anthony's face evaporated, and he suddenly looked all business. He moved to one of the long worktables, unraveled the blueprints, and used four boxes of nails to pin the corners of the curled paper down.

Olivia listened to Anthony asking about which changes had been implemented. As he and the foreman chatted, she kept her gaze on Anthony's face. She wished his grandmother was here, listening to him talk about workflow and the changes he had applied.

After a half hour, Anthony rolled up the blueprints and they walked through the building.

At one manufacturing station, Anthony stopped and ran a hand over his shaven jaw.

She could see his mind working.

He turned to Mr. Gibbons. "Upon seeing this, I realize the aisle is too narrow. We have enough room to shift this station two feet to the left."

The man listened intently, then nodded. "Yes, that would make more sense."

"I'll adjust the blueprints," Anthony said.

They strode to the loading dock. Anthony examined a newly built ramp, then lifted a crate and set it on the structure. Without a great deal of effort, he maneuvered the box downward. "Yes, this will work much better. The downward slope is not too great that the boxes of pens will topple over. It will make conveying the crates much easier on the men's backs."

Mr. Gibbons's eyes widened slightly as if startled by Anthony's concern for those men tasked with loading the boxes. The sudden smile on the man's face revealed Anthony had been elevated in the man's regard.

An hour later, as they drove back to Mayfair, Olivia could see the sense of satisfaction on Anthony's face. He was proud of what he'd accomplished.

As if realizing she watched him, he turned to her.

"You're feeling rather proud of yourself, aren't you?" she asked, smiling at him.

He grinned. "I am. I'm pleased with the changes I've implemented."

"You should be."

As if her words added to his pride, his grin broadened. He nudged her foot with his. "I think we owe it to ourselves to celebrate again. We are both doing a rather splendid job."

His use of the word *we* made her heart feel light.

"Why don't we go out again?" he asked.

Excitement sparked within her. She envisioned them on the dance floor moving in time to the beat of another fast-paced polka. Her euphoria faded as she remembered that tonight was Lord Belington's ball, and she would be attending. Not through the front door. Not dressed in a costly gown. Not drinking champagne with the other guests. But she'd be there just the same. There was only Belington and Helen's father's name on her list, and hopefully, after tonight, just that single blackguard's name would remain.

She bit her lower lip. "I cannot go tonight."

"No?" His jubilant expression faltered. "Finley's is still closed down, so we won't be going there if that is what concerns you. We'll go someplace else."

"No, that's not it at all. I liked Finley's."

"You did, didn't you?"

"Yes. Very much so."

"So, tell me why you cannot enjoy a night out?"

She searched her mind for an excuse. Nothing came to her. Lying to him had come much easier when she'd first met him; now it made her chest ache. But there was no avoiding it. She peered down at her lap, not wishing to lie to him while looking directly at his face. "I fear I feel a megrim coming on."

With his index finger under her chin, he tipped her face up, so their gazes met. "Then when we arrive back, you must go and rest. Do not worry about the ledgers tonight. They can wait until tomorrow."

His concern made the lie she'd told him even more painful. He was too trusting, and Vicar Finch was right. She was wicked and would most likely end up in hell.

Chapter Sixteen

In her bedchamber, Olivia paced from one end of the opulent room to the other. A couple of hours ago, Anthony had gone out to celebrate how well his redesign of Victory Pens was turning out. Every minute, up until the moment she'd heard him close the front door, she'd battled against her desire to go with him. When she'd heard him exiting his room, down the corridor, she'd almost run after him to say she'd had a change of heart. That her fictitious megrim was gone.

But she'd forced herself to not move an inch of her body until after she was positive he had left, then she'd cried. Not a heart-wrenching cry that makes one's shoulders shake and turns one's eyes puffy, but a slow cry like a drip-drip from a leaky pipe.

Olivia wasn't completely sure why she'd cried.

Hogwash. She knew exactly why. Dancing with Anthony had been one of the most wonderful experiences of her life. She'd enjoyed the way he'd twirled her around the room, the heat from his body drifting over her, and the way he held her gaze. During those splendid moments, no chasm of class separated them. It was as if she'd stepped into another world, and it was freeing. It was like the freedom she experienced as she jumped from one rooftop to the next. Yet, if she continued to think of him in such a fanciful way—as if they were equals in society—she'd not tumble to her death, as she could from a rooftop, but instead might end up with a broken heart.

One could not step out of the role life had given them for too long. Reality would settle back on them with even more weight if they believed they could escape their lot in life. And she needed to remember that when she finished what she'd come to London to do, she would abandon this city. Lately, she'd pondered the idea of taking a ship to America and leaving England and the life and sins she'd committed behind.

She didn't want the memory of Anthony to follow her and make her nights restless. She needed to forget him. Though even now, she wondered who he twirled around the dance floor. Who he smiled at, and if the woman was experiencing the same, almost tangible current Olivia had felt in his arms.

She stopped pacing and sat on the edge of the bed. An explosive gust of breath left her mouth as she flopped backward onto the soft mattress and stared at the ceiling above. The room was completely quiet except the *tick, tick, tick* of the mantel clock. Across the hall the Dowager Marchioness of Huntington had retired, leaving only the soft padded footsteps of the household staff who would soon take to their beds.

But even then, it would be too early to leave for Lord Belington's residence. She needed to wait until the party was in full swing. When those in attendance would be enjoying supper, closer to midnight.

She rolled onto her belly and slipped the book she'd borrowed from the office off the bedside table. She would read until it was time to get dressed. Hopefully, that would distract her.

Somewhere between stepping out of the family's Park Lane residence and climbing into his carriage, Anthony had changed his mind about going to a music hall and ended up at his club at St. James's.

Trying to keep his expression unreadable, he studied his cards, separating them slightly so he could count the two black clovers and two hearts on the pair he held in his hand to make sure he'd not read the numbers incorrectly. He had learned to compensate for his issues with adding by counting the symbols on the cards in a consecutive order and knew that court cards were worth ten points. Adding single digits had always come easier to him since there were no numbers next to them to invert.

He picked up a crown from the stack in front of him and pitched it onto the pile of coins in the center of the table.

His opponent, Sir Harry, narrowed his eyes to slits and studied him. "I think you're bluffing, Trent."

Anthony remained quiet. He was, but if he denied it the man would know it was true. Best to keep mum. There was a science to playing cards. One did not need to be only proficient at the game. One needed to be proficient at reading the other players at the table. That was where Anthony excelled. Sir Harry loved to gamble, but he possessed a terrible habit of rubbing the spot behind his ear when he was contemplating folding. He'd done it twice during this hand, so even though Sir Harry's cards were most likely better than Anthony's, the man feared he would lose. Tossing an extra crown on the table would ratchet up Harry's doubt and would most likely cause him to fold.

Anthony flipped a crown into the air. It made a *clinking* noise when it landed in the center of the pile already on the table.

As suspected, Sir Harry grumbled and tossed his cards on the table.

Anthony forced his expression to remain bland as he placed his cards facedown into the discarded ones before sweeping up his winnings.

Harry eyed Anthony's cards as if he desperately wished to know if he'd been duped but turning them over was against the rules. Releasing a gusty breath, the man shoved his chair back and stood. "Damnation, not my night. And I despise this bloody game. What the Americans see in playing poker I don't understand."

Next to Anthony, one of his closest chums Lord Talbot grinned. "I hear the queen has learned the rules."

"Perhaps I could beat her at a hand," Harry grumbled.

"I doubt she'd allow a rascal like you into the palace," Talbot said.

"Ha! She wouldn't allow you or Trent in either." The normally jovial smile on Harry's face returned. "I'm off, gents. I need to find a pretty bird to uplift my bruised ego."

Talbot's gaze followed Harry. When the man was out of earshot, Talbot turned to Anthony. "I bet he had you beat."

"Most likely." Anthony winked.

"Well, you scared everyone away. All of them lighter in the pockets. Now, what are we to do?"

Just then Lord Bramble, Maria's new lover, stepped into the room. The young buck turned a rather putrid shade of green upon seeing Anthony, then pivoted so fast he bumped into a waiter carrying a silver tray with two glasses of port.

The tray in the man's hands wobbled before crashing to the ground. The glasses shattered and port splattered all over.

Everyone in the room turned to gawk at Bramble, who was fleeing the room as if the devil himself followed him with a three-pronged pitchfork.

"What's gotten into Bramble? The young lad looked ready to piss himself." A line creased the skin between Talbot's brows.

"He's Maria's new lover."

Talbot wrinkled his nose. "You're joking?"

"No."

His friend's frown deepened. "The way he looked . . . Did you threaten the lad? I thought you were relieved to be without her."

Anthony gave a humorless laugh. "I am beyond pleased our arrangement is over. Maria will wring that pup dry of every penny he possesses, then toss him away when she gets a better offer."

"If that isn't putting you into a sour mood, what is? You've looked angry all evening."

"I don't look angry."

"Well, you've had a rather put-upon expression on your face since we arrived."

Had he? It surely had nothing to do with Maria. No. He'd been thinking of Olivia and why the idea of going to a music hall without her had lost its appeal.

He forced a smile. "Is that better?"

"No. I've known you too long not to realize when you're upset. You look as wretched as that time the headmaster sent for your brother James to come pick you up after being expelled."

Surely, I don't look that morose. James had been livid seeing as the reason Anthony had been sent away had to do with the headmaster's wife. And he'd wanted to be tossed out of school, though he'd not wanted to disappoint his brother again. "I'm living at Park Lane with my cantankerous grandmother. Isn't that enough to sour one's mood?"

Talbot let loose a hearty laugh, causing several other members in the club to glance their way. "It is, indeed."

An image of Olivia popped into his head. Anthony wished it was only his irritable grandmother that ailed him, but it was not.

"Trent, what do you say we go to that new gin palace that opened on Newgate Street?"

Gin palaces could be boisterous. Maybe that was what he needed to distract himself from thoughts of the lovely Olivia Michaels and her freckles. He wanted to kiss each and every one of them, especially if they were scattered like stars across other parts of her body besides her face.

Good Lord, where had that thought come from?

Talbot snapped his fingers in front of Anthony's face.

He realized his friend was waiting for an answer. "Very well. We'll venture to the gin palace."

"A second ago, you looked miles away. Could it be that you are distracted by that female clerk you hired?"

"Miss Michaels? Of course not." But he knew he was. He just didn't completely understand why she distracted him so much.

* * *

Olivia awoke and jerked upright in her bed. She'd fallen asleep. What time was it? She rubbed at her heavy-lidded eyes and peered at the mantel clock.

Goodness. It was nearly eleven thirty.

Hurry, a voice in her head demanded. Or you will arrive at Lord Belington's after the supper hour. She jumped from the bed. As she dashed to the armoire, she removed the small key from the pocket of her dress. She tugged her valise out from the bottom of the large mahogany armoire and slipped the key into the lock. Since it was old, she needed to wiggle it a few times before she heard the *click* of the latch releasing.

She reached inside and removed the secret false bottom, revealing the black guernsey sweater, woolen trousers, knit cap, leather work gloves, and her soft-soled shoes, purchased secondhand at Petticoat Lane Market.

Within a few minutes, she'd removed her gown and slipped on the men's clothing. She peered at her reflection in the cheval mirror as she slipped the knit cap over her head and tucked any loose strands of her flame-colored hair under it.

Her heart raced fast with a mixture of fear and anticipation as she opened the window and glanced at the thin ledge to the left of the wrought-iron balcony. Unlike Lady Winton's thick ledge, this one was thinner. She would need to balance herself on it for close to seven feet before she'd reach the drainpipe. If she wasn't careful, she'd end up splattered like a bug on the ground.

Don't think of that.

Carefully, she slipped one leg over the windowsill and

holding the bottom of the sill, she pushed up and pulled the other leg through the opening.

Putting one foot before the other, she took small steps, while leaning her weight toward the building. The already rapid beats of her heart picked up speed. A bead of sweat moved down her spine as she clamped her gloved hand around the drainpipe and swung her body onto the downspout. Slowly, she shimmied down and released the air locked in her lungs when her feet touched the ground.

As she moved to the back gate, she glanced over her shoulder at the town house, relieved to see all the windows remained dark. She bit her lip as she glanced at Anthony's window. Foolish to think of him right now and what he was up to. She needed to concentrate. One mistake and she would be thinking of him from behind bars or dead.

Olivia lifted the metal latch in the iron gate and breathed a sigh of relief when it swung open on well-oiled hinges. On almost silent steps, she darted into the dark night.

Chapter Seventeen

Using the back alleys and mews, Olivia kept to the shadows as she made her way to Lord Belington's town house. As she reached his street, carriages lined both the mews and the front of the residence.

Crumbs. Getting close enough to his town house without being seen would not be an easy task. Tugging her lower lip between her teeth, Olivia glanced around for a way to get to the rooftops. The home at the end of the street had an attached carriage house with a lean-to that was no more than nine feet above the ground. If she placed her foot on the stone lintel below the window of the structure, she could hoist herself onto it.

She scanned the back of the town house, searching for a way up to the roof. A drainpipe ran down the right corner. It was in line with the large protruding cornerstones that she could set her feet atop of to help hoist herself upward. From there she could move across the roofs of the attached town houses, which were of a similar height. It would be easy to leap from one to the other, but she'd have to keep low so none of the coachmen standing by their employers' carriages spotted her.

With a plan sketched out in her mind, Olivia set her foot on the lintel, then pulled herself onto the lean-to. Not wishing anyone to spot her, she crawled across the surface. At the corner of the house, she stood and reached for the drainpipe.

She glanced up. She needed to climb two more stories to reach the roof. Her stomach contracted, then fluttered with anxiousness. Inside her leather gloves, sweat coated her palms. She reminded herself how easily she'd climbed the trees at the orchard that was adjacent to the orphanage. She could do this.

Taking a deep breath, she wrapped her gloved fingers onto the cast-iron pipe and set her foot on top of a cornerstone. The muscles in her shoulders and thighs burned as she slowly inched up the cast iron. By the time she reached the roofline and hoisted herself up onto it, her breaths were coming in fast puffs from the exertion.

With her body crouched low, she stayed in the shadows and moved from one rooftop to the next until she reached Lord Belington's residence. Three dormer windows faced the street. Most likely the room where the maids slept. None would be in their beds tonight. They would all be helping with the party.

She peered to the street below. A couple stepped out of the residence in their finery and climbed into their carriage. Was the supper hour already over? Or were they just leaving early? She hoped the latter. Keeping her body low and in the shadow of a chimney, she reached the window. Olivia sent up a silent prayer that one of the windows would be open to release the oppressive heat that was usually found in these attic rooms.

A smile spread across her face as she noticed all three windows had the lower sash raised. Holding on to the windowsill with an iron grip, she poked her head inside the opening. As she'd predicted, it was the maids' quarters. Narrow beds lined the far wall, crammed close together with barely a foot between them. With both hands, she lifted herself through the opening.

A beam of moonlight revealed an open door across the room and to the left.

She crept through it, then to the servants' steps. As she made her way down the winding stairs, music and laughter drifted up from the ballroom. When she reached the second narrow landing, she opened the door and peered out. Gas sconces lit the empty corridor, highlighting the plush carpet and gold-flocked paper. All of it a testament to the wealth of Lord Belington, a man who had the morals of the devil himself.

On the tips of her toes, Olivia made her way to the first door and slipped inside. A massive bed with gold curtains swagged back at the four corners dominated one wall. The scent of masculine cologne and tobacco smoke, along with the dark colors of the bedding, absent flowers and frills, proclaimed it most likely his lordship's bedchamber.

Olivia moved to the highboy dresser and opened a drawer to quickly rummage through it. Finding nothing of value, she searched the next one. A grin tipped her lips upward when her fingers touched a wooden box tucked under a woolen pair of trousers.

With the box in her hand, Olivia moved to the window that overlooked the back terrace. The coin slots in the top proclaimed it his lordship's money box. Quietly, she set it down on the wide sill and angled it so the moonlight illuminated the lock on the hinged lid.

She slipped a hairpin out from her pocket and moved it around in the lock until she heard a *click*. Inside were three compartments marked *coins, silver, gold*. Instead of coins, the first section held a wad of banknotes, more than she could have dreamed of finding. She filled her trouser pockets with the money.

Olivia put the coin box back, wishing she were a fly on the wall and could see his lordship's face when he realized the Phantom had paid him a long overdue visit. She was about to exit the bedchamber when a woman's giggle drifted down the corridor, along with a man's deeper laugh.

Olivia glanced around, searching for a place to hide. She hastily scooted under the bed only seconds before the door opened.

"Good Lord, Estelle, is this your husband's bed-chamber? Perhaps we should find another room."

"No, here is perfect," she purred.

"Oh, you are so wicked," the man replied with a chuckle.

The mattress dipped as the two flopped onto it.

"Lift up your skirts, Estelle. We need to be quick."

Olivia heard the rustling of layers of material. With her hand clasped over her mouth, attempting to mask the nervous breaths sawing in and out of her lungs, she prayed to God they *would* be quick. She peered to the side and noticed one of the banknotes had fallen out of her pocket and lay next to the edge of the bed. The sight of it made her heart pound against her ribs. If the couple saw it . . .

The mattress bounced up and down above her.

The man grunted.

Slowly, Olivia rolled onto her side and carefully stretched

her hand out and curled her fingers around the banknote, then slipped it into her pocket.

"Did you hear something?" the woman asked.

"No. Now hush. I'm trying to concentrate." The man grunted once, twice, before he uttered a low, almost unearthly, sound. He jumped off the bed, and Olivia realized he still wore his trousers and shoes. "Now, we best get going," he said.

"What?" the woman screeched. "That's it? We are done?"

"Yes, we need to hurry back before your husband realizes we have both left."

"Yes, but—"

"Come now." His feet moved to the door.

"Damn you, Reginald. That was a bloody poor performance."

"Sorry, sweet." The man didn't sound sorry in the least. He poked his head out the door. "All clear."

Grumbling her discontent, the woman slipped off the bed and straightened the skirt of her costly looking blue gown.

Olivia released a heavy breath as they closed the door behind them.

That had been close.

Too close.

Heart still beating fast, she retraced her steps, made her way back to the attic, and climbed back onto the rooftops.

The following morning, when Olivia stepped into the servants' dining hall, several members of the staff glanced up, but most continued to eat without hesitation. Thankfully, they had come to accept her presence as one of them.

She strode to the sideboard, placed an egg and a raisin scone on her plate, and took an empty seat.

The cook dashed into the room, drying her wet hands in the folds of the white apron tied around her waist. "The Phantom robbed Lord Belington last night!"

Forks stilled.

Chatter stopped.

"How do you know?" Mrs. Parks asked.

"The greengrocer just dropped off my order and Mr. Hobbs said when he delivered to Lord Cranford's house across the street from Belington's there were a bunch of bobbies milling about outside. When he asked what was going on, they told him. Said there were even some fellows from Scotland Yard there, including the commissioner himself."

"No one saw anything?" Menders asked.

The cook shook her head. "Mr. Hobbs talked with Lord Belington's housekeeper. She said no."

Olivia, unlike the others who had stopped eating, slipped a piece of egg into her mouth.

The footman named Cline leaned forward and glanced at the door before speaking. "My uncle is a clerk at Scotland Yard. He says several of the detectives think it might be a nobleman. A guest whose attended all of the gatherings."

"A nobleman?" Katie echoed.

"Wouldn't that be a fine kettle of fish?" the cook said.

"Does this Lord Belington live in Mayfair?" Olivia asked, even though she knew exactly where the ghastly man lived.

"Yes, only a few streets away." The maid sitting next to

Olivia shifted in her seat. "My uncle, God rest his soul, used to work for him. Called him a dreadful man."

Several of the other servants mumbled their agreement.

"Some of them nobs are getting what they deserve," another footman mumbled.

"Yes, I hear he's a right old bastard," the coachman added. "I think someone should give this Phantom fellow a medal. Even if he is one of them."

"Do you really think it could be one of them?" Katie asked.

The coachman nodded. "The way some of them gamble . . . I wouldn't doubt it. I heard only last week Lord Hampshire lost two thousand pounds while playing whist at his club. Hard to even imagine such a sum."

"It is," Olivia agreed, thinking of how much the orphanage could have used such funds. Well, in a few days All Saints Orphanage for Girls would receive a rather substantial, anonymous donation. Not two thousand pounds, but enough to repair the leaking roof.

Shortly after breakfast, Olivia stepped into the drawing room to find the dowager sitting at the secretaire writing a letter.

The elderly woman glanced up, then returned her attention to her correspondence. "If James doesn't return soon, I fear the recently purchased pen factory will be a botched mess and teeter close to ruination."

Ruination? What poppycock. "You're still not willing to give Lord Anthony any credit, are you?" Olivia asked before able to halt herself from speaking her mind.

The woman's pen stilled. Her shoulders stiffened.

She narrowed her eyes to slits as she looked at Olivia like she was a bug she was about to smash flat. "What did you just say to me?"

She should beg the dowager's forgiveness, sit quietly in a chair, and keep her mouth closed. But she could not sit idly by while the woman belittled her grandson. "I believe, once again, you are reticent to give Lord Anthony the credit he should be given, and there is credit due."

The woman's mouth opened, then closed as if taken aback by Olivia's impertinence. But instead of screaming and tossing anything at her, she pinned Olivia with a challenging expression. "Anthony has fallen back into his old ways. He went out last night and didn't return until early this morning. He'll probably sleep the day away."

Even on the day they had gone to the music hall, Anthony had been up early the next day attending to the businesses his brother had left him in charge of. He was probably already in his office. He might not enjoy overseeing the ledgers, but he was a hard worker.

"Are you positive he's not in his office already, or are you just making an assumption?"

Bracing one hand on the arm of the chair and the other on the top of the gold knob of her cane, the dowager stood. "Has that smooth-talking rascal turned your head, Miss Michaels? Is that why you defend him?"

Heat singed Olivia's cheeks. Perhaps he had, but her defense of him had nothing to do with that. "No, madam. I defend him because I have seen what he has accomplished."

"If you are so sure he is there then let us see. Come."

Olivia stayed a step behind the dowager as they made their way to the office. She released a slow breath and sent up a silent prayer that Anthony was indeed attending to the responsibilities placed on him and not asleep in his bedchamber.

Upon reaching the office's door, the dowager stopped and without knocking flung it open.

Olivia held her breath.

The old woman glanced at her. The expression on her face was not an I-told-you-so-look, but one of bewilderment, which must mean . . . Olivia stepped next to her.

Anthony glanced up from where he sat at the desk, talking with Lord Huntington's man of affairs, Mr. Walters, who was there for his weekly meeting.

In truth, Anthony looked a bit worse for wear, but he was there and attending to business.

Olivia released the breath that had lodged itself in her chest.

Atticus, who stood on his perch, started flapping his wings as he gazed at the dowager. "Abandon ship. Old wench on starboard. Old wench on starboard!"

Olivia tried not to laugh at the expression on the dowager's face.

"Why haven't you made soup out of that bird yet?" she grumbled. "You've threatened to do it enough. If you don't have the stomach for it, I'll do it."

"I think I'm growing fond of him." Anthony grinned. "Is there something you need, Grandmother?"

"No, I . . . um . . . will talk to you later."

Olivia would bet money that the Dowager Marchioness of Huntington had never stuttered in her life. It was refreshing to see she was human.

One side of Anthony's mouth lifted into a lopsided grin.

She had a feeling he knew exactly why his grandmother was there.

The old woman turned away and started down the corridor again.

Anthony winked at Olivia, and her stomach did a slight flip. She turned to follow the dowager.

"Olivia," Anthony called after her.

She pivoted back. "Yes?"

"I hope you are feeling better today."

Better? She'd almost forgotten that she'd told him she had a megrim. Another flash of guilt swept through her. "I am, my lord. Thank you for inquiring."

He nodded and returned his attention to the man of affairs.

When they arrived back in the blue drawing room, the dowager didn't return to her desk; instead, she lowered herself into the stiff chair she usually sat in. Her brows were pinched as if in deep thought.

Olivia wanted to say something, but what more could she say? The scene they had just witnessed proved that Lord Anthony was taking his responsibilities seriously.

The dowager lifted her novel off the chair-side table and opened it to where she'd placed a green ribbon.

Olivia glanced at the clock. Were they to sit here all day in silence? If so, she wished the woman would allow her to help Anthony. Almost unable to help herself, Olivia cleared her throat.

The dowager glanced up.

"Do you intend to receive callers today?"

"No," the dowager said, returning her gaze to her book.

The fact that the dowager wasn't receiving callers didn't seem as detrimental to Olivia's plans as it had when she'd first taken the position, since during meals, the servants had proven to be a plethora of information. It seemed nearly every member of the staff had a relation at another Mayfair household. But sitting in silence with the dowager seemed a waste of time, especially when she could be helping Anthony.

Was that truly the only reason she wished to go back to his office? She feared not. She had come to enjoy her time with him. Almost cherish it.

Several minutes later, Olivia tried not to tap her foot, but when the dowager flung her an agitated look, she realized she was strumming her fingers on the armrest of her chair.

"Madame Renault will be bringing your gowns over shortly to be fitted." Without glancing up, the dowager flipped another page in her book.

As Olivia recalled the lovely gowns she would soon call her own, her stomach fluttered as if there were bubbles popping in it. She had never owned such finery. She tried to keep her lips in a straight line, but they tugged upward into a pleased smile.

"Thank you." The words slipped out of Olivia's mouth a bit raspy, as if her voice was dry or rusty from disuse.

The dowager glanced up; her thin gray brows pinched together as if she didn't understand the emotions sweeping through Olivia.

Olivia swallowed the lump in her throat and blinked away the burning in her eyes. Of course, the dowager didn't understand. She had most likely been born into wealth. Always bought her clothes from a modiste and not second-hand shops or from the carts of used clothes at Petticoat

Lane Market. She'd never added an additional piece of fabric to a hem or cuff to hide the frayed edge.

The elderly woman stroked her finger down the leather binding of her book as if contemplating Olivia's words. "After the modiste leaves, you might as well go and help my grandson."

Olivia didn't know which she was more excited about: that she would have new gowns or once again be able to spend the afternoon with his lordship.

Chapter Eighteen

At the exact moment the mantel timepiece in the drawing room chimed ten o'clock, the butler stepped into the room. "Madame Renault and her assistants are here, Lady Huntington."

The dowager nodded her regal head. "Show them in, Menders."

"Yes, my lady."

The gowns are here. Olivia didn't want to care about such things, but excitement exploded in her stomach.

No more than five minutes later, the modiste and two other women, whom Olivia remembered from the shop, stepped into the room with dresses draped over their arms, along with several garment boxes.

Olivia's gaze settled on the yellow ball gown one of the assistants carried. For a minute, she believed her breath stopped. Even from where she sat, she could see the sheen of the costly fabric and the canary-colored beads sewn into the hem. The cut glass reflected the sun streaming through the tall windows, causing prisms of light to sparkle like stars. It was the type of gown a member of the nobility would wear, not someone of her station. She subdued the urge to bounce out of her chair and run over so she might get a better look.

Stay seated, you silly fool, or they will think you gauche.

She glanced at the dowager. There was no expression of awe on the elderly woman's face. She was used to such finery.

"Well, stand up," the dowager said, but the normally sharp tone of her voice was subdued a fraction.

"Yes, we must see if the gowns need alterations." Madame Renault fluttered toward Olivia, smiling broadly. "Louisa," she said to one of her assistants, "we will try on the sapphire taffeta day dress first."

"Oui, madame." The assistant opened one of the sizable white boxes and withdrew the dress.

Olivia's breath caught. It had cloth buttons in a lighter shade of blue and ruffles on the cuffs and hem in the same subdued hue. There were several swags and appliquéd roses. Surely this was not a day dress.

But the modiste smiled as the other woman brought it over, betraying that the gown was indeed meant for her. "Now, we must remove your dress if we are to try this one on. We are all women. Do not be shy."

She wasn't shy, per se. She had spent most of her life undressing in front of other girls. It was more that she didn't wish to show her undergarments that were more worn than her dress.

Why should you care? a voice in her head asked. But she did care. She tipped her face downward, averting her eyes from the onlookers, and unfastened the buttons lining the front of her simple cotton dress.

When she slipped it off, she noticed the modiste examining her yellowed corset and chemise. But the woman said nothing.

Olivia didn't dare look at the dowager, for she could just imagine her expression of disgust.

"Louisa." The modiste turned to her assistant. "Bring me the new satin corset."

The woman nodded, then darted to where she'd set several boxes on a chair, and opened the top one. She withdrew a cream-colored corset with satin ribbons on it.

So she wouldn't gasp at the beauty of the garment, Olivia pinched her lips together.

The modiste begun unfastening Olivia's corset. "We must take off this one. It does nothing for the line of your breasts, while this one will lift them." Madame Renault took the new one from Louisa.

Up close Olivia could see there were small roses embroidered into the fabric. As the modiste secured the clasps, Olivia ran her hand over it. "It looks too pretty to cover up."

The modiste grinned. "But we must, mustn't we?"

"Of course," the dowager snapped, thumping her cane as if she wished everyone to know she remained to oversee what was going on.

Even the woman's vexed expression could not dampen Olivia's mood.

Louisa pulled a pair of silk, opalescent stockings from the same box and handed them to Madame Renault.

The modiste asked Olivia to sit and instructed her on the proper way to roll them onto one's legs so the delicate material wouldn't snag.

She'd just put them on and stood when the door opened.

Olivia's gaze shot to the door, as did everyone else's.

Lord Anthony stood on the threshold. His regard traveled over her body then down her silk-clad legs so slowly, one would think they were a mile long. His gaze settled on her face—his warm-colored eyes intense.

Heat blossomed on her cheeks. The warmth on her face nearly as scorching as the sensations shooting through her body.

"Forgive me," he said, and closed the door.

"Is that your husband, madam?" Louisa asked. "He is *si beau*."

"*Oui*." The other assistant nodded and blushed.

She swallowed. "No. That is Lord Anthony. We are not related." She didn't dare look at the dowager to see her expression. She could only imagine the appalled look on her face over such a notion.

After the modiste left, Olivia made her way to Anthony's office. She tried not to fidget with the cuff of her sleeve on the old cotton dress she'd slipped back on, but after being fitted for those lovely gowns, she felt like a pauper in her navy day dress.

"Just a few alterations, and I will deliver them back to you," the modiste had assured.

Perhaps her anxiousness was not solely due to that. While being fitted for the gowns, she couldn't stop thinking of Anthony's heated gaze as he'd perused her body. The intensity in his regard had left her stomach fluttering. No man had ever looked at her like that—as if she were as stunning as his last mistress, Signora Campari.

While he'd taken her in, standing there in that lovely corset and silk stockings, she'd not even felt the desire to cover herself up. No. His hot regard had felt like a warm blanket on a cool autumn night. Comforting.

Ha! *Comforting* was a benign word for what she'd experienced. Lust. Desire. Want. All were better suited.

She smoothed her chignon with her restless hand and stepped into the office.

Anthony glanced up and stood, while motioning to her chair across from his. "Forgive me, Olivia, for intruding earlier. I was unaware that the modiste had arrived."

"Understandable, my lord."

She glanced at Atticus. The bird was sleeping.

Anthony folded his tall frame into the chair. "I need to dictate a letter to you."

As she sat, she searched his countenance for the hungry look she'd witnessed in his eyes earlier. Maybe she'd imagined it. She removed a piece of paper, picked up one of the self-feeding pens, and waited for him to begin.

Silence.

She glanced up, and there it was. An unguarded look. One that seemed to say something. Convey some emotion. A frisson moved through her, causing the delicate hairs on her nape to stand up. A sense of jubilance shifted through her, like the elation she experienced after returning from one of her midnight rendezvous over the roofs of Mayfair.

No. It was more fulfilling.

As if realizing he was staring, he blinked, like one pulled from deep thought by the intrusion of a cough. "Are you pleased with your new gowns?"

Pleased? The word was too tame to describe her feelings. "They are beyond lovely. Madame Renault has to make some alterations but will have them delivered in a few days."

His gaze remained on her for a long moment. Was he thinking of how her body had looked in those garments? Did he know how much she'd thought of him after he'd left the room?

She glanced at the fraying cuff of her sleeve. Why did she continue to torture herself with wild thoughts of this man whose station far exceeded hers?

Plus, she wasn't what he thought. He believed her sweet. He believed her innocent. What would he say if he knew the truth? That he harbored the thief known as the Phantom? The thief who stole from members of his class. When he'd talked about Lord Hamby and how he'd won the parrot from the man, Anthony's expression had clearly revealed his disgust for his lordship, but that would not mean he would approve of her actions—that she'd robbed the man.

"I'm glad you are pleased," he said, pulling her from her thoughts. He picked up a letter from the pile on his desk. "I need to send a letter to Mr. Warren regarding the work Mr. Armstrong is doing."

She knew both men's names. Mr. Warren was the land steward at the family's Essex estate. And she'd seen several invoices with Mr. Armstrong's name. Not for Victory Pens, but for repairs to the tenant farms at their country home.

As Anthony dictated, he stood and roamed around the room. His long fingers picked up a paperweight from his desk, and he tossed it from one hand to the other.

He appeared so serious. Different than the scapegrace she'd met in front of Madame Lefleur's dress shop. Like most days when he worked in the office, he'd discarded his coat and rolled up his sleeves to a point just below his elbows. As he shifted the heavy weight back and forth, the muscles in his forearms flexed.

She swallowed and forced her gaze back to her dictation.

"Add the same valediction as the last business correspondence." He turned around, facing her once again.

She nodded and walked around the desk to set the letter on his blotter so he could approve it at his leisure. His muffled footfalls on the thick carpet revealed he'd stepped behind her. The masculine scent of his shaving soap wafted to her nose and the heat of his body radiated over her back.

"Excellent," he said. His breath ghosting across the back of her ear, exposed by the way she'd styled her chignon.

If she turned around their faces would be close.

Don't do it, the sensible voice in her head warned.

Go on, you want to, the less circumspect part of her urged. She turned, bringing their mouths into proximity.

Only a few inches separated them. His minty breath touched her lips. He shifted fractionally closer.

Her heartbeat ratcheted up.

She recognized the look in his eyes. It was the same heated look she'd witnessed earlier in the drawing room. If it wasn't one of desire, then she was a misguided fool. She held up the pen in her hand. "It's ready for your signature."

"I see." His voice sounded deeper, raspier.

Not moving back, not taking his gaze from her face, he took the pen from her. Their fingers brushed.

The contact, so simple, so benign, should not have caused the tingles that moved from the point of contact to shift through her whole body, even reaching her toes.

"Are you trying to tempt me, Olivia?"

"No," she replied, her voice barely a whisper. But she knew it for the lie it was. The look in his eyes said he knew it as well.

"Are you sure?" he asked.

"No. Not in the least."

She thought his mouth might quirk up into that smile he usually flashed at her, but his expression remained steady. Intense.

His body shifted closer as if pulled by gravity. As if she were the moon and he the ocean. The scant air between them evaporated, leaving the warmth of his chest pressing into her shoulder, yet he still did not lift his hands to touch her.

Was he waiting for her to make the first move? Without thought, she turned more completely toward him and skimmed her hands over his chest, slowly, allowing her mind to memorize the contours of his body beneath it.

His eyes drifted closed, then opened again. "This isn't a very wise move on either of our parts."

The ability to stop the desire rushing through her seemed a monumental task, but Anthony was right. She started to shift backward, but his hand skimmed up her arm, halting her movement.

And she knew without a doubt what he was about to do.

Chapter Nineteen

"I want to kiss you, Olivia," Anthony said.

Anticipation caused a delicious warmth to travel through Olivia's body. She wanted that as well. Desperately. But forming the words proved difficult. Instead she tipped her face up to his and shifted her right hand until it rested directly above his heart. The rhythm not only excited her but brought a sense of comfort.

Why? She didn't know. Perhaps because her life at the orphanage had been fraught with uncertainty and her recent actions only added to the sense that she was dangling from a loosely tethered rope. She wasn't sure where she belonged. A feeling of limbo followed her no matter where she was. She felt present but distant. But being close to Anthony seemed to chase away her fears and demons, leaving her experiencing a sense of *home*. A sense of belonging.

Foolish, woman, she scolded herself. It was beyond reckless to think such thoughts. Cruel to disillusion oneself with thoughts of them attaining anything more than an exploration of the desire that sparked between them. They lived in different worlds.

Nothing can come of this, the rational voice in her head whispered, but her body was already falling too deep into a state of want to heed the niggling.

His intense gaze dipped to her lips. Slowly, as if unsure if she would bolt like a scared rabbit, he lowered his mouth to hers.

Anticipation swirled through her. She let her eyes drift closed and centered every bit of her mind on the feel of his warm lips brushing against hers. Light. Delicious. Teasing.

He made a noise—a growl of sorts—and the contact shifted. Became stronger.

She kissed him back. Answering with the same hunger he gave. Answering the inner desire that clawed at her like a caged animal who wished to be released from the confines that held it.

Anthony's hand shifted to her waist, skimmed upward, leaving an indelible warmth and pressure in its path. His lips parted, causing hers to do the same. Their breaths mingled, then his tongue touched hers.

She stroked her tongue against his. The sensation was pure carnal delight.

He pulled her body tighter to his.

Olivia moaned—a noise of pleasure. Contentment.

His hands slid to her bum, lifting her slightly. Enough for her to feel the hard length under his trousers. She should think it wicked. She should pull back, but her own physical response to the contact was like a potent elixir, possessing the ability to leave her head a bit foggy. Like the feeling when you first wake up—when your body and mind lay somewhere between sleep and consciousness. Unburdened. When the weight of the day ahead is distant, and your limbs are almost weightless. That was what kissing Anthony was like. Yet, all her senses seemed fine-tuned to the feel of his lips, along with the pressure of his large hands. It was as if they were waking her body with every movement. She could even feel the tips of his fingers as they glided up and over her ribs.

If his one hand didn't stop it would soon find her breast. Was that where he wished to touch her?

That thought made them tingle and grow heavy with anticipation. Odd that her body understood this better than she did—that it nurtured a primal reaction.

When his warm palm did indeed cup her breast, she arched into it, wanting more.

As if he understood the need spiraling upward within her, his touch grew firmer, adding to all the sensations.

A knock on the door caused them to both freeze and pull back slightly. Their breaths sawed in and out of their lungs.

"My lord, I have Atticus's food," the butler said.

"Damnation," Anthony mumbled.

The parrot woke up and ruffed his feathers. *Squawk.*

Realizing the butler intended to enter the room, Olivia rounded the desk, brushing her hands over her dress as if to remove the visible prints Anthony's touch had caused. As she took her seat, he gave her a cursory glance as if assessing she didn't look like she felt—thoroughly kissed.

He sat as well and snatched the pen off his desk and appeared to examine the letter he'd dictated to her. "Enter."

Menders stepped into the room.

Olivia picked up an invoice and perused it.

Standing on his perch, Atticus squawked. "'Bout time, you scallywag!"

The butler sniffed as if being reprimanded by a bird was beneath him and placed the bowl of nuts on the table where the cage was.

"Thank you, Menders."

Menders stepped out of the room and pulled the door closed behind him.

Olivia felt the heat of Anthony's gaze on her. She forced herself not to look up. Too many thoughts were going through her head. Thoughts of what she and Anthony had done before the butler knocked. She fought the urge to touch her tingling lips.

The bird squawked and anxiously fluttered his wings, waiting to be transported like royalty on a palanquin.

"Be patient, you rascal." Anthony pushed his chair back with more force than necessary and strode to the bird.

With his back to her, Olivia took the opportunity to watch him as he set his arm in front of the bird and the parrot climbed onto it. Her gaze settled on his large hands as she recalled how they'd touched her. The memory caused a burst of heat to rush through her. She forced her gaze to the brightly colored bird who bounced up and down, then to the invoice in her hand.

"Don't push me today," Anthony said to the parrot. "Otherwise, I might open a window, then close it after you've flown out."

The parrot made a chuckling sound as if he knew it an idle threat. Anthony set the bird onto the table next to the dish of nuts, while his mind tried to figure out what he should say to Olivia.

Still unsure, he strode back to his desk. He could tell just by Olivia's tense posture that she didn't wish to discuss what had just transpired between them. But they could not bloody well ignore it.

He sat and peered across the desk. She looked thoroughly distracted by the invoice she held, but he doubted she was.

Good Lord, that kiss between them had seemed incendiary. He'd kissed women with passion before, but he couldn't recall any making him feel so . . . What? Lustful? No. He'd felt that before in abundance. He liked women. Liked everything about them from their sweet scent to the soft curves of their bodies.

So why had this seemed different? Frustrated by his own confusion, Anthony raked his fingers through his hair and tried to gather his scrambled thoughts. He peered at Olivia. There was something fresh about her. She was beautiful in her own way. And the hair he'd thought too bright upon meeting her now seemed lovely. He wanted to wrap his hands in it. How many times had he wondered how long it was and whether the silky mass covered her breasts when let down? His wicked thoughts had no place in their relationship; he could not afford to lose her.

He cleared his throat.

Olivia glanced up, and he saw how his rather unheeded kiss had caused her already sensual lips to look puffy. He needed to apologize. "Olivia—"

A rap on the door halted his words.

Anthony fought the urge to tell them to go away. "Yes, come in," he said, more sharply than he wished.

Menders stepped into the room; his brows lifted in puzzlement. "Forgive the interruption, my lord." He held up the mail. "The post has arrived."

"Thank you, Menders." Anthony outstretched his hand and waited for the man to once again leave. He'd just crossed the threshold when Grandmother appeared.

Good Lord, what was this, Victoria Station?

As she marched into the room, Atticus let loose another squawk. "Yo ho, danger ahead."

"Hush, you foolish bird!" Grandmother snapped. "Or I'll send you to a taxidermist and give you as a gift to Queen Victoria. I'm sure she'd be pleased to add you to her collection of birds."

As if the parrot understood the threat, he made a sound like a gulp and tucked his head under his wing.

Good Lord. Anthony blinked. The old woman had quieted the little beast with one threat. Or perhaps it was the steely look in her eyes that revealed she might not be making an idle remark.

Anthony's regard settled on the invitation with a broken seal in his grandmother's hand. So, the moment of truth had arrived. He was to pay his debt to her by attending some ball.

A time-to-pay-the-piper grin lifted her papery cheeks. "Lord Dayton is having a ball next week and we will attend."

Dayton? The man was a stick in the mud. He'd joined Prime Minister Gladstone several times on his walks in the East End in an attempt to reform prostitutes. Anthony could not imagine what a ball at his house would be like. Untrue. Sadly, he could. Instead of champagne they'd be served lemonade and tea. And during waltzes his lordship would peer down his overly long hooked nose to give haughty disapproving glares if anyone stood too close to their partner. Not to mention that the matchmaking mamas would be out in full force. He didn't trust his grandmother. She had probably planned for him to get caught with some prim girl who she thought would make him a good wife.

He glanced at Olivia. Lately, his mind seemed to center on someone else. Someone much closer in proximity.

"Very well." He outstretched his hand for the invitation. "I will make sure I attend. A deal is a deal. Even if done with the devil."

Grandmother's grin widened, then she pivoted and strode out of the room, her cane tapping an almost merry tune.

As soon as she pulled the door closed, he looked at Olivia. It was time he made pretty and apologized. "Olivia."

She peered at him. Her eyes were bright. Her lips were still puffy and red. Her freckled cheeks flushed. At this moment, she was the most stunning woman he had ever seen, and he wondered how he had not thought so before. The sultry look on her face made him wish he could paint, so he could save this moment in time on a miniature. One that he could carry in his pocket and glance at whenever he wished to brighten his day.

Another knock on the door had Anthony storming toward it. He was going to throttle whoever was on the other side and take an inordinate amount of pleasure doing it. He flung the door wide.

With an audible squeak, Menders jumped back.

Anthony experienced a stab of guilt. He didn't wish to give the butler a fright, but he was dashed tired of being interrupted. "What is it, Menders?"

The man's Adam's apple moved in his throat, and he held up an envelope. "A messenger just delivered a note from Huntington House. It's marked urgent."

"Well, hand it over, then."

Menders outstretched his hand holding the missive, looking as if Anthony was as rabid as a dog and might bite it.

"Thank you." Anthony took the message and read it.

Good Lord. The land steward, Mr. Warren, had been severely injured while helping some men work on the water wheel at Huntington House. The man had lost two fingers and was damn lucky he'd not lost his arm.

The butler still stood at the threshold as if sensing something dire had transpired.

"Menders, have a valise brought to my room and tell Cline to pack it." He shook his head. "Never mind, I have clothes there."

"Are you going to Huntington House, my lord?"

"Yes, tell the coachman I need to get to Victoria Station."

The butler turned to walk away.

"Menders?"

The servant pivoted around.

"Is my grandmother in the blue drawing room?"

"She is."

Tugging down the sleeves of his shirt, Anthony strode to his desk and picked up his cufflinks.

"Is something wrong?" Olivia asked.

"Yes, the land steward at Huntington House was injured. I need to go there. In my absence, will you continue working on the accounts?"

"Of course. Is he gravely injured?"

"It could have been worse."

"Will you be gone long?"

Would she miss him, or was she just inquiring? "I'll be back before Lord Dayton's ball. Excuse me. I must be off, and I need to inform my grandmother." At the door he turned around. Even if only gone for a few days, he would miss her, and that realization left him even more baffled.

Olivia peered at him. "Safe travels."

"I'm sorry about earlier, Olivia," he said, then quit the room.

Chapter Twenty

A week later, Olivia sat next to the Dowager Marchioness of Huntington in Lord and Lady Dayton's ballroom. Crystal chandeliers cast sparkling light over women dressed in varying shades of colorful fabrics and gentlemen in black evening attire—the starkness of their dark suits relieved by their crisp white shirts and ties.

The dowager glanced at the stairs, leading into the ballroom. She'd done it close to a dozen times while waiting for the arrival of her grandson. "Where is that scoundrel Anthony?" the dowager muttered, her fingers flexing against the gold knob of her cane.

"I'm sure he will be here, my lady," Olivia said, trying to sound reassuring. Anthony had sent a note from Huntington House yesterday assuring his grandmother he would fulfill his part of the bargain and attend. The missive stated that if he was not there when they were ready to depart, he would meet them.

From the corner of her eye, Olivia saw a well-dressed young man approaching them.

"Not another one," the dowager grumbled, her gaze settling on the gentleman. The old woman narrowed her eyes as if she might cause the fellow bodily harm with her cane if he ventured any closer.

The fellow paled slightly and did an about-face.

Since they'd arrived and settled into two of the gilded chairs that circled the perimeter of the grand room, two other fellows besides the last gentleman had started toward them, only to be scared away by the dowager's lethal glower.

Olivia knew why they approached her. After the dowager's lady's maid helped her dress and fashioned her hair, Olivia had felt like a princess, donning the yellow gown of silk that Madame Renault had created. But she was anything but a princess. They didn't have the foggiest notion that she was only her ladyship's companion, not some wealthy relation. It was the elaborate gown, of course. The embellishments at the hem shimmered like finely cut stones under the lights above. It was nothing short of lovely. More expensive looking than most of the other gowns worn tonight, giving the false impression of someone of great means.

What would these highborns think if they realized that she was the Phantom?

"I can see the attention your gown has brought upon you," the dowager said, interrupting Olivia's thoughts. "When you are asked who designed it make sure you inform them Madame Renault. Madame Lefleur will soon regret her chatty disposition."

How was she to tell anyone when the woman didn't allow her to converse with those in attendance? It was like Olivia was a fancy jewel that was set under a glass dome. Something to be looked at, but not touched.

Olivia smiled. In the whole of her life, she had never

thought herself anything closely resembling a jewel, but at this moment she did indeed feel like one. "Yes, madam."

As the first notes of another waltz drifted in the air, another man started toward them. He was handsome, taller than most, with a lean waist and broad shoulders. His dark, wavy hair was a tad too long.

She waited for the dowager to notice and shoot him her don't-come-any-closer glare. Olivia didn't care. She was more pleased than perturbed that the dowager scared them away. She didn't wish to see their disdain on their faces when they learned of her station in life. And she didn't wish to dance. Well, that was not completely true. She had enjoyed dancing with Anthony at the music hall, but he wouldn't ask her. Not here. Not in front of these people. She released a slow breath and recalled how it had felt to be in his arms at the music hall. She'd relived it in her dreams, along with his heated kiss, more than once.

She wasn't sure she wanted Anthony to show up. The idea of watching him dancing with the women his grandmother wished to align him with might cause jealousy to unfurl within her. She didn't like the feeling of such an emotion, especially when she had no right to feel it.

The dowager finally noticed the fellow moving toward them and shot him a fierce don't-take-another-step-toward-us expression.

As if he found humor in the situation, one side of the man's mouth turned upward as he held the old woman's gaze and continued forward.

Who was this bold fellow who ignored the Dowager Marchioness of Huntington's glower?

He stepped before them and his gaze shifted to Olivia.

He flashed a charming smile. His startling blue eyes shifted back to the dowager. “Lady Huntington, how are you?”

“I was doing rather well until you appeared, Lord Talbot,” she replied, her tone sharp.

He set a hand to his chest. “Oh, how cruel you can be, my lady. You’ve wounded my pride.”

“Doubtful. It’s too inflated by the silly twits who flutter around you as if you are the sun.”

It was then that Olivia noticed that several women were staring at the man, their fans fluttering back and forth, while others whispered behind theirs.

He ignored her words, or perhaps he thought them so fitting they did not deserve a response. His gaze returned to Olivia. “Aren’t you going to introduce me to the lovely woman who accompanied you here?”

“I hear your father has disowned you,” the dowager replied, ignoring his question just as he had ignored her jab.

“He has,” he replied as casually as if she’d said it was going to be overcast tomorrow. “But if you know that then you must know the reason? That a man of my father’s nature is displeased that his son has bested him in a business venture and surpassed him in income. So, him disowning me has little financial effect on my life.”

What type of man disowns his son because of a business matter? Lord Talbot’s father sounded like a horrid person.

“He cannot remove the fact that I am his heir,” Lord Talbot continued, “or the fact that one day I will be the Duke of Wharton.”

A thumping started in Olivia’s ears as if she stood too close to a ringing bell in a tower. She studied the man, especially the deep blue of his eyes. How had she not seen the resemblance? She'd only known one other person with such startling blue eyes.

Helen's face flashed in her mind.

This man was her brother. Had he known about Helen? Doubtful. He would have been nothing more than a child himself. And one's father did not flaunt the fact that he'd cornered a maid and forced himself on her, then cast the child his heinous act had produced aside as if she were nothing to him.

The dowager's voice floated back to Olivia, drawing her from her thoughts. "Since that rascal who married my granddaughter is holidaying with her on the Continent, don't you have business that needs to be attended to at that tea company the two of you own?"

"But there is always time for entertainment." His gaze returned to Olivia. "Might I have this dance, Miss Michaels?"

"She is my companion. Not a relation," the dowager informed the future duke as if this would be the trick that finally sent his lordship away in pursuit of other women. Women of his own station.

Olivia waited to see the interest in his eyes dim, but it did not. "And a beautiful one at that."

Did he still wish to dance with her even though he knew she was not his equal in society's eyes? Not even close. She was the woman who intended to rob his father of every bit of blunt she could find in his house.

"Go on dance with him," the dowager snapped, "so I don't have to contend with the rascal's impertinence."

Though Olivia didn't feel like dancing with the gentleman, she could not refuse, and it might prove advantageous to learn more about the man's father. She stood and accepted the arm Lord Talbot offered her.

As they moved to the dance floor, he lowered his head as if to speak conspiratorially to her. "You looked like you needed saving."

"Saving?" she echoed.

"Yes, from Anthony's cantankerous grandmother. And being that you are her companion, I knew you could not."

"You knew my position when you approached us?"

"Yes, Miss Michaels. I thought Anthony would appreciate me saving you."

Her head was spinning with thoughts. Anthony had spoken of her to this gentleman. A gentleman who was obviously a scoundrel but would one day inherit a dukedom. "You are acquainted?"

"We are friends," he said.

Was this who Anthony had gone out with on those nights he'd stayed out late? She clamped her lips tight to stop herself from asking.

"I'm partners with Anthony's brother-in-law Lord Elliot Ralston. Ralston and I own Langford Teas."

She'd drank the tea many times. It shipped far and wide. Even as far as America. She knew his father owned a tea company, as well. Perhaps this is what had caused the strain between father and son. What she needed to know was more about the duke's comings and goings. Though what information would an estranged son have?

"I'm sorry to hear of your strained relationship with your father," she said as they walked toward the dance floor.

His jaw tightened. "Don't feel too distressed over it. I surely don't. The loss of my father's good regard or his place in my life does not worry me overmuch."

She wanted to ask more, but Olivia had a feeling

she'd just poured alcohol over an open wound. He'd acted carefree in front of the dowager, but his façade crumbled a bit for a moment, and she'd seen pain in his eyes. There was more to this story besides the Duke of Wharton disinheriting his son.

They stepped into the swirl of other dancers.

They'd taken several turns around the room when his lighthearted mood seemed to return. The man's smile broadened, and Olivia could understand why women flocked to him. He made her think of Anthony with his carefree ways and handsome looks.

She returned his smile, then glanced toward the stairs. She almost trounced on Lord Talbot's feet when she saw Anthony making his way down the steps into the ballroom. She'd always thought him striking, but tonight he looked the picture of masculine beauty. Dressed in black evening wear and a head taller than most he stood out like a sleek and primal panther in a room of domesticated cats. She swallowed the lump of emotions that climbed up her throat.

Women turned and blatantly stared. Some guests looked startled by the black sheep of the Trent family attending such a tame event. An event where women would be on the prowl, searching for marital compatibility.

Some would think him too wild to tame. Others would look favorable upon the challenge. And Olivia presumed there were those who would just want a dalliance because of his handsome face and glorious body and because they too liked to be a bit wicked behind closed doors.

Two men dashed up the steps to talk to Anthony, but he seemed uninterested in joining them in conversation. Most likely, he was put off by having to attend.

"Ah, Anthony has arrived," Lord Talbot said, pulling her attention back to him.

Like Anthony, Lord Talbot seemed out of place here. Another big cat in a den of tabbies, but she didn't feel the same pull toward her dance partner. Not the burst of excitement she'd experienced while dancing with Anthony. The same desire that made her want to both move to him, yet run from the room.

Anthony had barely set a foot on the steps leading down to the ballroom at Lord and Lady Dayton's Mayfair residence when he was approached by two young bucks from his club.

"Trent," one called out, raising his hand in greeting as he jogged up to meet him. "Tell me who is that ginger-haired goddess who arrived with your grandmother."

There was only one redheaded woman who would have accompanied Grandmother.

The fellow gave him a friendly clap on the back. "Come on. Tell us her name. Your grandmother won't let any of us approach her. It is like she is to be seen but not conversed with."

Anthony narrowed his eyes. Was Grandmother treating Olivia poorly?

"You won't tell us either? A woman of mystery, is she?"

He ignored the young buck and continued into the room. He couldn't recall ever feeling so anxious to see a woman. In truth, he'd missed Olivia the whole time he was at the family's country home in Essex. And when he'd gone down to the local pub, the Hog and Thistle, for a pint of ale, he'd ignored Martha, his curvaceous serving girl, even when she'd offered him something besides his normal pint. He'd drank his tankard and gone home. To a house that was cavernous without the sound of his family milling about.

One by one men approached him, asking about the woman with his grandmother. He ignored their inquiries and searched for Olivia in this bloody crush.

Sir Harry walked up to him. "Who is she?"

"I'd like to know, *where* is she?"

"She's dancing with Talbot. He was the only one brave enough to venture up to her with your grandmother looking as if she'd strike anyone who approached with her cane."

What was his friend about? As he searched the swirl of dancers, a wave of jealousy washed over him.

His gaze settled on Olivia, and it felt as if he'd been punched in the gut.

Everyone's eyes were on her and Talbot. Her lovely red hair was upswept, not in its usual severe way, but loosely, allowing tendrils to fall and frame her face. Her yellow gown fit tightly to her breasts and waist before flaring out into a mass of shimmering silk that reflected the lights from the chandeliers. How could he have not noticed her? It was as if all the lights in the room were drawn solely to her, emphasizing her, like an actor on center stage at the Lyceum.

Talbot leaned close and whispered something, causing her to smile, and Anthony bit back the desire to stomp onto the dance floor and cut in. Such an action would cause a stir and the type of gossip his grandmother abhorred.

Where was Grandmother? Anthony's gaze traveled over the guests. He spotted her. Like him she was staring at

Olivia and Talbot with a face that looked sourer than her usual expression.

He strode over to her. "I'm here, as promised."

"You're late."

He ignored her waspish tone and turned back to the dance floor to watch Olivia in the swirl of dancers. Once again, he questioned why he'd thought her plain. She was lovely. A beacon of light in a dark tunnel. She outshone all the others. It was not the gown, it was her, the sparkle in her eyes, the smile on her face, and that glorious hair he was forever imagining unpinning.

"Anthony, Lord Pendleton's granddaughter is here. I'd like to introduce you."

"Of course," he replied, not paying much attention to what she said. Damn Talbot. The bounder was holding Olivia too close.

"Are you listening to me?" Grandmother growled, thumping her cane.

"What?" The song would end shortly. He needed to save Olivia before the other men who'd approached him asked her to dance. Laughable that he thought he was trying to be noble. The truth was he wanted her all to himself.

"Dash it all, man, get your head out of your—"

"Excuse me, Grandmother." As he headed to the dance floor, he heard his grandmother squawking like an irate goose.

He reached the dance floor as the last strains of the waltz drifted in the air.

Olivia looked at him, her cheeks high in color. Had Talbot said something outlandish to her or was it the dancing that raised the color of her fair cheeks?

Talbot flashed one of his suave smiles as he led her to where Anthony stood.

"Olivia, how lovely you look," Anthony said.

"Thank you, my lord. Your grandmother will be pleased you have arrived."

"Talbot," he said, his tone sharper than he intended as he glanced at his friend.

The man's cocksure smile broadened.

"I didn't expect to see you here. This isn't the type of gathering you normally attend." Anthony forced a smile.

"I decided I wanted to see how the more acceptable members of the *ton* live. I wasn't expecting to see you or your grandmother in attendance, especially with such a lovely companion."

The man was flagrantly flattering Olivia. "I think Sir Harry is expecting you in the cardroom, Talbot."

Lord Talbot offered a sly grin. "If I didn't know better, Anthony, I'd think I was being dismissed." He faced Olivia. "It was a grand pleasure, Miss Michaels. Perhaps after I return from the cardroom, you might grace me with a second waltz."

Looking unsure, Olivia gave a slight bow of her head, without offering a commitment.

The strains of another waltz began.

Anthony held out his arm. "Olivia, might I have this dance?"

She peered over his shoulder to where his grandmother sat. Obviously, she was battling her desire to say yes against the anger she presumed the old woman would clearly make known. "I believe your grandmother would wish you to dance with someone else."

He reached for her hand and set it on his arm. “She’ll get over it. Excuse us, Talbot.”

His friend nodded.

As they walked away, Olivia peered at him. “He said he is your friend. Is that not true?”

“He is. I just do not think . . .”

“What?”

They reached the dance floor, and he twirled her in time to the music. A delicate floral scent reached him. “He is a libertine. He compliments a woman until she . . .” His lips pinched into a tight line.

She smiled. “I have heard the same of you.”

He wasn’t surprised, especially since she’d worked for that gossiping windbag Lady Winton. “Well, Talbot is very good at flattery.”

“Hmmm, a woman does like to be complimented occasionally, but I fear I am immune to sweet words and not so easily swayed.”

She wouldn’t be. She was keen. Smarter than most, but he did want to compliment her. Not to win her favors but because everything he said would be true. That knowledge, along with the fact that he’d missed her a great deal while in Essex, unsettled him.

Chapter Twenty-One

"Your grandmother is shooting daggers at us," Olivia said as Anthony took her into the next turn.

Not surprising. He glanced over Olivia's shoulder to where the dowager sat. The old woman's lips were pinched so tight, she looked like someone was attempting to force her to suck on a salt block. "I told her I would attend. Not who I would dance with."

"She's not pleased."

"She's rarely pleased. What is new?"

A slow, startling smile lifted the corners of Olivia's mouth. He stared at her full lower lip that fascinated him, nearly as much as the raspy texture of her voice.

"Is the land steward at your family's home in Essex doing better?"

He'd found the man in worse shape than he'd expected. For a man used to working alongside his men, the loss of two fingers was devastating. "Physically, yes. Emotionally, he might take longer to heal, but he has insisted on returning to work."

"Were his injuries so severe?"

"Yes, though not life-threatening."

"I wish him a speedy recovery."

The thoughtfulness in the tone of her voice made him realize why he'd missed her. Anthony could not imagine Maria would have given one whit about someone in his family's employ. Olivia was kindhearted. "Will you dance the next song with me as well?"

"Two in a row? I don't think that is wise." Olivia gave a slight shake of her head.

"Why not?" He frowned.

"Because you should be dancing with women of your own station. Not your grandmother's companion." She drew in a deep breath before her gaze shifted away.

The movement caused her breasts to lift, giving him a better view of them in the low décolletage of her gown.

"Are you trying to upset your grandmother by asking me to dance?" Olivia released a slow breath.

The comment and the sadness in her expression was worse than a punch to the gut. "Is that what you truly think? That I'm trying to use you as a pawn in a battle of wills between my grandmother and me?"

Her gaze returned to his face. "I think you know why she insisted you attend. She wants you to find a wife. She wants you to settle down."

"Yes, I'm aware of that. But I do not intend to marry. Ever. And certainly not some simpering miss my grandmother believes will be my perfect match. Anyway, there is only one woman here tonight that I wish to converse or dance with and she is standing in front of me, smelling of flowers and dressed in a lovely yellow gown that complements the color of her red hair. Do you honestly believe I would rather dance with anyone else attending?"

Olivia blinked. Her lips parted as a rosy color mixed

with the dusting of freckles on her face. Her eyes turned glassy.

"Good God, Olivia. What did I say?"

"Things you shouldn't be saying. If you are looking for a new mistress, I will not accept the position."

Mistress? He admitted the idea had crossed his mind more than once. He'd fantasized about having her in his bed, under him, her lovely hair fanned against white sheets like threads of copper, while he buried himself deep into her warmth. After James returned, he'd not need her assistance with the ledgers, and Grandmother would not need her either. The old woman really didn't need her now. What would Olivia do? Where would she go? Wherever it was, he would miss her. He'd not believed she would accept a position as any man's mistress, and now she'd clearly stated she would not.

"Would being *my* mistress be such drudgery? You wouldn't have to contend with my grandmother or be the companion to women as cantankerous as her or deal with harpies like Lady Winton. You could have more gowns such as the one you are wearing. A place of your own. Credit at all the finest stores."

"Do you think that is all I want out of my life? I have never had a family. Perhaps I want that more than anything else."

She averted her gaze, and he felt like a cad. A wretch. Of course she would want a family.

"And is that really all *you* want?" she asked, returning her regard to him. "To grow old without someone who cherishes your company? A woman who loves you? Children to coddle and adore?" She looked away again.

She made it sound so lovely. Briefly, he contemplated

telling her why he didn't wish to marry, exposing the secret he'd kept his whole life—worked diligently not to bare to anyone. Not even revealed to James. Or any of his friends, tutors, or teachers. Instead, he'd taken part in devilish pranks at school and university, so he'd be kicked out. It was easier to let them believe he was ne'er-do-well—lazy and disinterested and a hellion—than reveal the dashed truth. Yet, as he looked at the confusion on Olivia's face, he wanted to pull her onto the terrace and tell her everything he had never revealed to anyone.

What would she think? This brilliant woman who could add sums in her head so easily.

He could not tell her how things that were so simple to others jumbled in his brain. That at times the numbers on a clock confused him. That he'd learned to compensate by memorizing their positions. That he won at cards because he'd discovered the *tells* of the gentleman he played with and had to count the symbols on the cards, one by one, because that was easier than adding the numbers up in his head.

He did not want children who would suffer from the same affliction. He'd always taken precautions so he would not father a child. A mistress understood that. A wife would not. "I don't wish to marry, but I do want *you* in my life. I've come to cherish my time with you."

Her gaze jerked to him so fast, she lost her step and their legs almost tangled. He tightened his hold on her and smoothed out their steps.

"Don't say things you do not mean," she whispered.

He released a heavy gust of breath. "Do you think I admitted that to you to sway you into my bed? That is not the reason, Olivia. I said those words because I meant them."

"Did you say those same words to Signora Campari when you tried to convince her to be your mistress?"

"What? Good Lord, no. What we had was an arrangement." His jaw tightened. "I should not be telling you this."

"You've just implied you want the same arrangement with me. I think you have moved past the point of shocking me."

The song came to an end and they both stood there, staring at each other.

Olivia looked around and realized that nearly everyone had walked off the dance floor. Guests were staring at them as if expecting something. Perhaps something even shocking—salacious gossip they could bandy about in their opulent drawing rooms tomorrow. Something that would have the black sheep of the Trent family's name plastered all over the gossip columns tomorrow. What must it be like to be Anthony? Perhaps similar to what it was like to be the Phantom—everyone waiting for your next move.

"We are being gawked at," she said in a low voice. "Will you escort me back to my chair?"

"We? Perhaps it is you they are staring at. The women in attendance jealous of your beauty. The men jealous, bereft, because they have not just twirled you around in their arms."

His words made the back of her eyes prickle. She blinked to relieve the sensation. Such pretty words. She did not deserve them. These nobs would have no interest in dancing with her if they knew her upbringing. If they knew she was without connections or family. But the way Anthony looked at her, she could almost believe he meant what he'd said. That they were not the seasoned words of a womanizer, but words spoken from his heart.

Anthony thought he knew her, but he didn't know the whole truth. If he did, he would not be staring at her as he was now. He would despise her. No one here would wish to dance with the thief known as the Phantom.

He offered her his arm.

Olivia placed her fingers on his sleeve as they moved toward the dowager. An older gentleman and a young woman stood talking to Anthony's grandmother.

"Who is that gentleman and young woman?" Olivia asked, breaking the wall of silence that had erected itself between them.

"Lord Pendleton and his granddaughter Mary Chester. My grandmother is already up to her matchmaking. And since you won't save me, I fear I shall have to dance with the chit."

A short time later, Olivia watched Anthony twirl Lord Pendleton's granddaughter around the dance floor to the strains of a Viennese waltz. The young woman looked utterly taken by Anthony. Her father, like Anthony, was a second son. The match would be looked upon favorably.

Olivia forced her gaze away and listened as the dowager and Lord Pendleton discussed some political bill. The dowager obviously had the man's ear. He had been the dowager's husband's closest friend.

Farther down the row of chairs sat Lady Pendleton. She

was watching her granddaughter and Anthony with a perturbed expression. Her face reflected she wasn't as pleased about her granddaughter dancing with Anthony as the dowager and the young woman were. Perhaps she'd heard the story about the incident with him and his mistress. If Lady Winton were here and not at home nursing a sprained ankle, the old battle-ax would have taken great pleasure in informing everyone that Olivia was the other woman involved in the fiasco in front of Madame Lefleur's shop—the third player in that disaster. The woman who'd been found in Anthony's carriage, sprawled atop him like marmalade on toast. She'd also have made sure everyone knew where Olivia had grown up.

Through the crush, Olivia noticed a group of gentlemen who kept twisting their heads to peer at her. Was one of them contemplating approaching her? She wished he wouldn't. The man, like all the others, didn't realize she was nothing more than the Dowager Marchioness of Huntington's companion.

Her gaze shifted back to Anthony. He smiled broadly at Lord Pendleton's granddaughter and said something.

The young woman laughed.

Charming her, was he? Even when he didn't wish to, he could not help being a flirt. Or perhaps, he was doing it to draw her regard. To try to vex her. As if he could read her thoughts, his gaze shifted to her. The briefest glance. Yet, it heated her skin as if she stood close to a hot grate.

The devil. She would not accept his offer. After she finished what she'd come to London to do, she would go to America.

She glanced away, wishing she'd never stepped into the

wrong carriage. Oh, who was she kidding? Only herself if she believed that poppycock.

"I think it is time we headed home," the dowager said.

Olivia blinked. She'd not even realized that Lord Pendleton and the dowager had finished talking and the man had returned to his sour-faced wife.

"All the men think you are a mystery," the dowager continued. "The women all envy your gown. Lord Pendleton's granddaughter asked about it while you were dancing with Anthony. I don't doubt by tomorrow she will drag her grandmother to Madame Renault's shop. Soon the seamstress will have a slew of new customers. Customers who were once Madame Lefleur's." A wicked gleam lit the old woman's icy-gray eyes. She leaned her weight on her cane and pulled herself up into a standing position.

As they strode from the ballroom, Olivia couldn't help glancing over her shoulder at Anthony. Lord Pendleton's granddaughter was still staring at him as if he held both the stars and the moon.

If he ever married, she was the type of woman he would wed.

An hour after arriving home from Lord and Lady Dayton's ball, Olivia still couldn't fall asleep. She turned her down-stuffed pillow over, fluffing it, then gave it two hard smacks with the flat of her palm, as if it were the reason sleep evaded her.

It was not.

She attempted to try to convince herself that her restlessness was due to euphoria from having gone to her first ball. Most likely the only one she would ever attend.

Or that her mind dwelled on having worn a lovely gown—lovelier than anything she could have conjured up in her mind, along with the fact that men had looked at her as if she were beautiful. But she knew the truth. The whole evening could be whittled down to a small fraction of time. To the sublime minutes when she'd waltzed with Anthony. To the look in his warm-colored eyes when he'd held her gaze like she was the only woman he really wished to be with and his softly spoken inquiry, *Would being my mistress be such drudgery?*

Drudgery? The word was nothing short of laughable. Just the thought of what being Anthony's mistress would entail made Olivia hot and fidgety. She touched her lips. As if it had only happened a minute ago, she remembered the sensual feel of Anthony's mouth moving against hers. She could also recall the way her heart had beaten, and the physical sensations that had shifted through her body when he'd deepened the kiss and drew his tongue against hers. The memory caused the place between her legs to pulse. She squirmed, attempting to relieve the sensation, but it only caused the pulse to increase.

Hot and more restless than a minute ago, she threw off her bedding and let her arms go akimbo.

Her gaze followed a moonbeam from where it highlighted the ceiling to the slit in the heavy curtains. Perhaps she should dress and make her way outside to the rooftops. To where she would expel the disquiet within her—tire herself to the point of exhaustion, so neither her body nor mind would long for things she should not desire.

Things? She knew what those nameless things were. Wicked things that Vicar Finch would say an unmarried woman should not contemplate unless she wished to go to hell.

She stood and moved to the window to lift the lower sill. Not to venture outside but hoping the night's less balmy air would cool her down. After unlocking the window, she drew the lower sash up. A cool breeze drifted over her body. She turned back, intending to climb into bed but instead lifted her robe from where she'd draped it over a chair and slipped it on.

The dowager was asleep, as were the household staff, and Anthony was probably still twirling Lord Pendleton's starry-eyed granddaughter about. Olivia picked up the book she'd borrowed from the office. She would return the book and find another one to distract her until her eyes grew heavy and sleep overtook her.

On almost silent steps, she made her way down the stairs. As she neared the office, she saw a shaft of light seeping under the door to illuminate the flecks of gold in the corridor's rug. She would have sworn she'd turned off all the lights in the room before getting ready for the ball.

Nibbling her lower lip, she inched the door open. Anthony was seated behind his massive desk, leaning back in his chair with his feet propped on the top corner of the desk, holding a glass of brandy cradled between his fingers. He'd removed his jacket and neckcloth, undone the top buttons of his white shirt, and rolled the sleeves up to his elbows.

Anthony exuded such masculinity that her mouth grew dry.

He glanced up. His gaze drifted over her—from her face, then down over her robe to her bare toes.

Chapter Twenty-Two

Anthony's gaze, which had worked its way down her robe-covered body, slowly traveled back up. As if he'd skimmed his hands over Olivia, scorching heat prickled her skin. Suddenly more aware of her clothing than she'd been a few seconds ago, she pulled the sash tighter around her cotton robe.

"I'm sorry. I thought you were still at Lord and Lady Dayton's ball. I came to get another book." As if needing to prove she spoke the truth, she lifted the novel in her hand. Yet, as she raised it, Olivia wondered if she told the truth. Perhaps she'd hoped he would be in his office as he had been the last time she'd come here to get a book.

Perhaps that was the true reason. She wasn't sure of anything anymore, only her desire to be near him, which caused an odd fluttering in her stomach—a mixture of nervousness and excitement. It didn't help that the top buttons of his shirt were unfastened, leaving his bare skin visible to her.

"Be my guest." With a casual lift of his hand, he motioned to the bookshelves.

Her eyes followed the movement, taking note of how the muscles of his forearm flexed.

She set the book down on the table that was bracketed by two high-backed chairs set on the same wall as the door. "No. I'll get a different book in the morning."

"Why wait?"

She glanced down at herself. "Isn't that obvious? I'm not properly dressed. If someone saw me . . ."

He set his glass down, walked to the door, and closed it. "There. Now no prying eyes can see how lovely you look. Just me."

A flush of heat warmed her cheeks. Absently, she fiddled with the simple ribbon tied to the end of her braided hair.

He moved back to his desk, but instead of sitting in the chair, he half leaned, half sat on the corner next to where she normally worked. "I've always wondered how long your hair is. I bet when loose it is even longer."

The curious tone in his voice made her want to remove the ribbon and unwind the braid. Odd. She'd spent her life self-conscious of the brash color of her hair, but Anthony made her feel as if it was a prized possession—as if he wished to run his hands through it.

Don't think of that, she silently scolded herself. "Your grandmother will not be pleased to hear that you left shortly after we did."

He lifted one shoulder in a casual shrug. "I fulfilled my part of the bargain. I went."

Wondering if he intended to see Lord Pendleton's granddaughter, she nibbled her lower lip. "Miss Mary Chester is lovely."

His expression remained steady. There was no sparkle

in his eyes. No lifting of his lips into a knowing smile. "Was she? I didn't notice."

"I find that difficult to believe."

"My mind was on someone else. The mysterious and beautiful woman in the yellow gown who outshined everyone else in attendance. The woman who every man in the room wished an introduction to."

Only a fool would not comprehend he meant her. Did he really think her beautiful? "I don't think it was my beauty as much as the way your grandmother guarded me that piqued everyone's interest. I was just a curiosity."

"I assure you it was not that."

"Perhaps it was just the lovely gown."

"Men aren't interested in gowns, unless they are taking them off. Believe me, it was not the gown."

The warmth in her body grew with each word he uttered. It was best she left, since her body wanted to stay more than it should, and she had a feeling if Anthony said anything else, the desire within her would overpower any judicious thoughts that remained in her head.

"I really should return to my room." She moved to the door and reached for the handle.

"Are you frightened of what might happen if you stay?"

As if turned to stone, she froze.

Yes. "No," she replied without turning around. "I just realize the impropriety of the situation."

"Is that truly all that makes you want to run away like a scared rabbit?"

"Yes." She lied again. If she told the truth, she would have admitted that she was more frightened by her own desire than his. Anthony was not like the men she had come to London to steal from. He would not force himself on her. But she also knew that if she offered herself to him, he would take her up on her offer. He'd made it quite clear on that account. He wanted her.

The problem was she wanted him just as much.

"I think you're lying. Perhaps it is better you do go back to your room. Regrets can be the devil to contend with, and if anything ever happens between us, I do not wish you to regret a minute of it."

She slowly turned around. "Do you say that from experience?"

"I do. I think everyone has something they regret in their life. Something they wish they could undo. Yet, there are other things in life you fear you will regret, which seem a grand mistake but end up being a decision you cherish."

"Are you trying to imply that if we take our relationship further in a physical way, I will not regret it?"

He chuckled. The sound low. "No. Only you can gauge that. I was thinking how at first, I didn't really wish to hire you, but I will never regret that I did. Even if you left tomorrow, I will always remember you."

Her breath caught in her lungs. Tears pooled in her eyes. No one had ever said they would always remember her. Not true. She had spoken those words to Helen—told her she would never forget her. That she was her sister, even if not truly related. And her dear friend had whispered them back, her voice barely audible, but no man had ever said them. No man had ever made her feel as if she belonged, even when she knew she did not.

Anthony always said the right words. She wondered if he had said something similar to other women, but she didn't care. She moved toward him until only a span of no more than a foot separated them. Close enough to feel the heat radiating off his body and draw in his spicy scent.

His heated gaze slowly drifted over her again. "Olivia, perhaps you should go to bed."

The intensity in his eyes made her both anxious and eager for something she'd never experienced, but desperately desired. Olivia lowered her gaze to where his shirt hung open. She didn't think she could peer at him while telling him what she wanted. "I'm restless. More so, now that I've seen you."

"Which is more reason you should go. Otherwise, I'm going to want to relieve that restlessness."

"I think I might like that."

She heard him draw in a slow breath. "Have you reconsidered my offer?"

"No. I won't be your mistress. I *would* regret that, but whatever happens between us tonight, I will never regret."

"Are you sure?"

"Yes." She took the last step that separated them, knowing what she wanted. It was dangerous to feel the way she did about him, but after she crossed the Duke of Wharton's name off her list, she would leave London. Leave England. She had believed the memory of Anthony would haunt her, but perhaps it would sustain her.

"Olivia," he said, his voice low and raspy. "You really should go back to your room because I have a feeling that once we start something, neither of us will have the fortitude to stop."

"I think you're right, but I still want to stay."

As if her words were a catalyst to the heat burning between them, his hand curled about her nape. His mouth met hers.

There was no soft preamble. It was a kiss that spoke of desire, of need, and unrestrained want. His mouth almost instantly coaxed her mouth open. His tongue tangled with hers.

Olivia wrapped her arms about his neck, answering with the same intensity. Same eagerness. Same passion.

They were incendiary—like scraps of thin paper flung onto hot coals that burst into flames.

She couldn't stop her hands from roaming over his body. As if a sculptor, exploring the planes of her creation, she slid her palms over his chest, gauging every angle that was molded to perfection under the thin cotton of his shirt.

He made a noise that caused a vibration in his chest.

Anthony's mouth moved to her neck to plant tiny kisses against the sensitive skin, while his hands reached to her bum to pull her to him.

The hard length of his manhood pressed against her.

She made a noise. A whimper that spoke of the want that unfurled within her like string on a reel being pulled—unraveling so fast, she thought herself unable to stop it. She didn't care. She just wanted to feel. To explore the sensuality of them together.

He pulled back. His breaths sawed in and out of his lungs, keeping time with her own panting. "Are you sure this is what you want?"

She held his gaze. "Yes."

He took her hand in his and led her from the room, and up the stairs. By the time they reached the door to his bedchamber, her heart was beating a fast staccato from the mixture of anxiousness and anticipation.

Inside, the room was dark except for the moonlight streaming through the bank of windows. Her gaze shifted over the massive mahogany bed with a headboard that soared to the tall ceiling. A brown damask comforter topped it, along with large pillows in a warm brown velvet that made Olivia think of Anthony's eyes.

She released a slow breath, suddenly less confident, but then Anthony pulled her to him and kissed her, and all rational thoughts melted away into a puddle of lust.

His hands traversed her body, as hers drifted over his.

Almost frantically, Olivia tugged on his shirt, pulling it from his trousers.

Anthony's mouth came down on hers again. Demanding, seeking, tasting.

Squawk! "Who's there?"

Olivia froze at the high-pitched sound of Atticus's voice.

Anthony mumbled a curse. "Damn that bird."

She glanced over her shoulder to see the large birdcage covered in the cloth that sometimes draped over it while the parrot slept.

"Let me out!" the bird said before making a sound that seemed to mimic the sound of kissing.

Heat scorched Olivia's cheeks.

"Go to sleep or you'll end up out the window," Anthony said.

The bird replied by making the kissing noise again.

Grumbling, Anthony strode to the birdcage. He picked it up and carried it into what looked like a dressing room. As he stepped back out Atticus squawked. "Dirty landlubber."

Anthony pulled the door closed.

Olivia set her hand over her mouth to stifle a laugh.

"I'm glad you find him funny. I think I'll have him dropped back off at Lord Hamby's."

"He can be very entertaining at times." She smiled.

"Then perhaps I should gift him to you." He grinned and cupped the back of her neck to pull her mouth to his.

Like a match, her cooling desire sparked to life. As he kissed her, Olivia's eager fingers tugged at his shirt again.

He stepped back and lifted the garment over his head. The moonlight in the room seemed to gravitate to him, highlighting the beauty of his male form. Like she imagined the light at an opera would focus on a singer during an aria. Her gaze settled on a long scar near his ribs.

Mouth suddenly dry, she wet her lips. and drew her finger down the length of the raised skin. "What happened?"

"Nothing."

It didn't look like nothing. It looked like it had caused a great deal of pain.

Anthony's hands went to the sash of her robe. "May I?"

Unable to find her voice, she nodded.

He untied it, then pushed the garment off her shoulders.

It fell to the floor.

As he held her gaze, his fingers moved to the buttons that lined the top of her simple nightgown. One by one he slipped them loose. The backs of his fingers brushing lightly against the skin at her collarbone, then at the valley between her breasts.

Her breaths quickened. Not from fear, but from the desire coursing through her, reaching a new height.

Anthony's large hands settled on her hips. He gathered the fabric of her nightgown, lifting it slowly, inch by inch.

Fire ignited in her belly.

Knowing he intended to pull it off her, she raised her arms into the air.

The soft and worn cotton brushed against the sensitized tips of her breasts as he lifted it over her head. Chillier air drifted over her naked body, slightly cooling the heat that had grown within her.

Self-consciously, she lowered her lashes.

Anthony lifted her chin with his thumb and index finger, bringing her gaze to his. "You are too lovely for words."

Heat warmed her cheeks. She knew she was nothing like the voluptuous Signora Campari. But, as before, his heated gaze made her feel as if she were the most beautiful thing he had ever seen.

Olivia reached out and drew her finger over the thin line of hair that ran from his navel to the top edge of his trousers. She clasped the button at his waist. "May I?"

"I won't stop you."

His voice was gravelly, and she knew he was as anxious as her for what they were about to do. She unfastened the top button, then the next, slowly like he had her night-gown. The garment hitched lower on his hips. Her fingers brushed against the hard length beneath the cloth.

She heard the slow intake of his breath.

After she'd slipped the last one loose, Anthony shucked off his trousers and drawers. His manhood sprung free. She thought she shouldn't stare, but it was impossible not to do so. It was thick and long and much smoother looking than she'd expected. Without forethought, she reached out and drew a finger over the length of it from the base to the top.

Anthony sucked in another audible breath through his teeth.

She glanced up at his face, wondering if her touch hurt or pleasured him. The look in his eyes clearly revealed the latter.

He pulled her toward him and, once again, their hands explored each other's body while they kissed. Though the movements of their hands were slow, the kiss held a frenzied quality to it.

Anthony pulled back, took her hand in his, and led her to the bed. He tumbled onto it, dragging her down with him. His mouth was hot as it skimmed over her body. She should have experienced apprehension. She should have questioned everything she was doing, but for a few minutes, she could only center her mind on the pleasure of his mouth skimming a path from her neck down to her breast, but worry settled in.

Olivia cupped his face in her hands and pulled his gaze to hers. "I don't want . . ." She paused, unsure how to voice her concern about getting with child.

As if he understood the few words she'd uttered, he nodded. "I will be very careful." He climbed out of the bed, moved to a tall mahogany dresser, and opened the top drawer. She watched as he removed a folded packet.

When he returned to the bed, she watched him open it, and place the sheath over his erection. She drew her finger down his length.

His manhood stood even prouder.

"What is it?" she asked.

"A French letter." He toppled back onto the bed and whispered into her ear what it was meant to do.

She had not heard of such a thing. Did not even know they existed.

Anthony's lips found hers. He kissed her long and deep until his mouth nibbled a meandering path to one of her breasts.

The gentle, light brushing of his lips made her feel both loose-limbed and eager.

Yet, when his mouth gently nipped at her breast, she tensed slightly, but relaxed as he drew the tip into his mouth. The sensation was warm and wet—almost unsettling in the intensity and want it created within her.

Unable to stop herself she moaned and writhed.

He looked up. The blacks of his eyes so large, they seemed to absorb the brown. "Do you like that?"

The question brought a flood of warmth to her face. Yet, it pleased her that he wished to know how it made her feel. She nodded.

He grinned, then shifted to her other breast and did the same thing.

This time *he* moaned. The sound low.

She had a feeling he was getting as much pleasure from his mouth tasting her as she was from the experience.

He slid his hand over her stomach, then lower until his fingers reached the curly patch of hair between her legs. His fingers touched where she was wet, and another sensation sprung forth. This one even more intense than his mouth on her breasts.

"Spread your legs, love."

Wanting to feel more of his touch, wanting the sensation within her to grow, she did as he asked, allowing him to explore that private place between her legs.

His fingers stroked her, building the unknown sensation within her. She tipped her head back and moaned.

"Wait, love, I want to go there with you."

She didn't know exactly what he meant, but she remembered the wicked pictures she had seen in the naughty book she'd found the girls at the orphanage looking at.

He snatched a pillow from the head of the bed. "Lift your hips."

As she did, he slipped the pillow under her and knelt between her legs. He braced his hands by her shoulders and held her gaze. "Olivia, I have never wanted anyone as desperately as I want you."

Did he speak the truth, or were they the words of a seasoned cad? She didn't care. She longed for his touch.

Anthony slowly lowered his mouth to hers. Her eyes drifted closed, allowing her mind to center on the contact. The kiss was soft, gentle, but when he coaxed her mouth open, it shifted to hungry. Intense. She answered with the same passion.

He lowered his large body to hers.

Skin met skin.

A new flash of warmth shot through her.

Between her legs she felt the tip of his manhood pressing gently against her opening. Impatient, she wrapped her legs about him, attempting to draw him farther into her, to fill the ache that almost consumed her mind as much as her body. She felt a slight pressure, along with a pinch of momentary pain. The sensation felt mildly intrusive, yet she craved it.

Anthony pulled back slightly, causing cool air to travel over her skin.

She opened her eyes.

"Are you uncomfortable?"

"No. Don't stop."

A smile spread across his face. He sheathed himself even farther into her, then withdrew slightly before he pushed forward again. Anthony did it again until it built into a rhythm. With each movement, something within her grew, building toward a culmination.

Anthony whispered her name.

It drifted over her like a soft breeze on a warm night. She squeezed her legs against him as an intense sensation of pleasure spread through her, causing a pulse between her legs. She felt as if she floated before slowly returning to the here and now.

Anthony, who'd stilled, started moving in her again in that perfect rhythm. He made a noise. A low growl of sorts. His body tensed and she realized he experienced a physical pleasure similar to what she'd experienced.

She opened her eyes to see him looking at her.

He gently brushed his lips against hers, then flopped onto his back.

For a long minute, they both stared at the ceiling, as if trying to gather their thoughts.

Anthony pressed a kiss to Olivia's cheek and pulled her into his embrace. He peered at her face. Her eyes were closed, and the moonlight streaming through the bank of windows cast delicate crescent-shaped shadows from her fair lashes onto her cheeks.

What had she thought of their lovemaking? He'd never been with a woman who wasn't experienced, and his vanity, or perhaps insecurity, made him wonder if she'd enjoyed the experience. He certainly had.

"Are you watching me?" she asked, her voice raspier than normal.

He drew his index finger over her cheek. "What did you think?" He couldn't believe he'd given voice to the question that spun in his mind. He'd never asked any lover before. He'd taken his pleasure, hoped he'd fulfilled theirs, and left it at that.

Her eyes fluttered open. "It was . . ."

The muscles in his stomach clenched. "Yes?"

"Like nothing I've ever experienced."

"Is that good or bad?"

She stopped staring at the shadows on the ceiling as if they fascinated her and peered at him. Her kiss-swollen lips formed a slow smile. "Oh, definitely good."

He experienced a flash of relief. Why did it mean so much to him? He didn't believe it solely fell on his vanity. He had wanted to please her—to bring her pleasure. More than any other woman. It was as if his pleasure grew from hers.

"I think I'd like to do it again," she said softly, interrupting his thoughts.

He grinned. "Would you now?"

"Yes, *now* would be fine."

A burst of laughter escaped his mouth. He glanced down at his manhood, which was getting hard again by just the sight of Olivia nude and draped across his bed like an offering from Eros, the god of love. "It takes a man a bit of time to get ready again."

"Then while we wait"—she reached out and trailed her

finger over the scar that ran over his ribs—"tell me more about this?"

"As I said it was nothing."

"It doesn't look like nothing. It looks as if it caused a great deal of pain."

He'd been young and foolish when it happened. Something he didn't like to admit. "Several years ago, I was robbed when some rabble decided they wanted whatever money I carried in my pocket. One of the thieves decided to stick me with a knife."

She gasped. "You could have been killed."

"My own fault. I was in my cups and not as alert as I should have been." It wasn't like him to be self-deprecating, but Olivia made him feel so at ease.

She scooted down and pressed her lips to the scar. Women were fascinated by it. Some thought it a badge of honor instead of the foolishness it represented, but none had ever kissed it as if wishing to soothe any residual pain it might cause.

As she settled back into his embrace and rested her head on his chest, a place close to his heart ached. He pulled her tighter to him as if he wished to sear the memory of them together and leave a mark as indelible as his scar. Maybe that was just as foolish an act. He wasn't sure what would happen between them. For the first time in his life, he thought he might be experiencing the emotion romantic poets wrote of. Not simple infatuation but something much deeper.

Chapter Twenty-Three

The following morning, Olivia sat in the servants' dining hall and stared at the food on her plate. She'd awoken early this morning in her own room, tucked under her covers. Since she didn't remember walking there, Anthony must have carried her.

What would they say to each other? Would he acknowledge what they had done, or would he act like it was all in her head? Her stomach fluttered and feeling someone's gaze on her, she glanced up to see Katie peering at her from across the table.

Did the maid know what she had done? No, of course not. No one knew besides her and Anthony.

"Are you not feeling well?" the maid asked, her gaze dipping to the food still on Olivia's plate.

"My stomach is a bit unsettled."

"Dry toast will help," Katie said. "That was what my mother always gave us when we had the collywobbles."

"Thank you. I think I will try it." Olivia took a piece of toast off the rack and nibbled on it.

"Another grand affair tonight," Cline said.

Olivia's ears perked up.

Menders nodded. “Likely one meant to outshine most of the others.”

“Yes, I heard the Duke of Wharton ordered several cases of champagne. The best money could buy,” Mrs. Parks said.

The dry toast in Olivia’s mouth felt as if it was a sponge, absorbing her breaths. How long had she waited to hear more about Helen’s wretched father? “Tonight?”

“Yes,” several servants said at the same time.

“The Phantom hasn’t robbed anyone since Lord Belington. I wonder if he will try to rob the duke,” Katie said.

The Phantom would definitely pay the last man on her list a call.

“Cline, do you know if they still suspect a nob?” a maid asked.

The footman swallowed the forkful of food he’d shoved into his mouth. “Yes, my uncle says they are still almost positive that the Phantom is a person who has attended all the gatherings. A nob who has gambled too deep. They’ve compiled a list of suspects and will be keeping an eye on those men and following them if they leave the ballroom. Tonight, the commissioner and several detectives will be attending the ball.”

Interesting how they had not even considered it might be a woman, Olivia thought.

The cook stepped into the room and peered at her. “Do you think her ladyship will take her breakfast in the morning room, or should I make up a tray?”

Olivia pushed back her chair. “I shall go see if she is awake and find out.”

* * *

Anthony glanced at the invoice in his hand. He'd read the carpenter's bill nearly as many times as he'd glanced at the door, wondering if Olivia would stop by his office before she went to sit with his grandmother.

Last night after she'd fallen asleep in his arms, he'd carried her into her bedchamber and laid her under her covers. He'd known the foolishness of allowing her to spend the night in his room. Nearly as foolish as having made love to her a second time.

He stared at the invoice again. He was positive he knew the amount of the carpenter's bill, but his fear of making a mistake stopped him from entering the number into the ledger. With a disgusted groan of self-contempt, he flung the invoice aside and snatched up the latest blueprints for Victory Pens. One thing he did know was that the changes he'd implemented would make production more efficient. That knowledge gave him a sense of accomplishment he'd never experienced before.

Yet, the improvements to the pen factory were nearly done. James would return soon. What would that mean for him? What would it mean for Olivia? With Caroline back, Grandmother would insist she didn't need a companion, and in truth, the woman went out so infrequently she didn't need one now.

Someone cleared her throat.

Anthony peered up to see his grandmother's lady's maid standing in the open doorway.

She bobbed a quick curtsey. "Forgive the intrusion, my lord, but Lady Huntington wished me to deliver this." She held up a folded piece of parchment, crossed to his desk, and handed it to him.

He opened it to find Grandmother's summons directing him to visit her in the private sitting room off her bedchamber. He crumpled the missive in his hands and pitched it into the rubbish pail beside his desk.

The young woman's eyes grew round. Her cheeks turned white.

Anthony knew what the old bird wanted. She wanted to question him about Lord and Lady Dayton's ball and Mary Chester. He bit back his desire to tell the maid to inform his grandmother he was busy, but he knew that it would be this poor young woman who would have to deal with Grandmother's anger. "Tell her I'll be there in a minute."

A weak smile settled on the woman's face. She curtseyed and left.

A few minutes later, Anthony stepped into the small sitting room off Grandmother's bedchamber to see her already dressed in her usual black gown that made her fair, papery skin look even paler. She sat on a high-backed wooden chair that resembled a throne. When he was a child, she'd always sat in it when she conversed with her grandchildren. He and his brother James and sister, Nina, would have to peer up at her, causing a measure of intimidation that Grandmother had calculated. But now in her gaunt state, she did not possess the threatening appearance. Now she looked as fragile as a piece of spun glass, except for the determined angles on her lined face.

"Well?" she snapped, her cool gray eyes assessing. "What did you think of Lord Pendleton's granddaughter Mary?"

There were to be no pleasantries. The old woman knew

how to get right to the point. "Miss Chester is a lovely young woman."

His grandmother smiled, further creasing her already wrinkled face.

"But I cannot see a future between us," Anthony added.

Grandmother's smile faded. Her fingers clenched against the gold knob of her cane, turning her knuckles white. "What do you mean? You just called her lovely. She is from one of the oldest and most respected families in England. What more do you want?"

So much more. Olivia's face flashed in his mind. "I have told you on more than one occasion that I have no interest in marriage."

She pounded her cane against the thick carpet, producing a muffled *thump*. "You cannot continue to pine after Caroline. It serves you no purpose. She is married to your brother, for God's sake."

He was quite aware of that. He did not feel the emotions toward Caroline his grandmother accused him of. It was what James and Caroline had together that he envied. Grandmother would not understand that without needing to know why he fought so hard against the idea of marriage if he envied his brother's. "As I've said you are mistaken in your presumption."

"Balderdash! I see it every time you look at Caroline."

He heard a noise and turned to see Olivia standing in the room. How much had she overheard? Too much by the stark look in her eyes.

Anthony fought the urge to move to her. To take her hands in his and explain that his grandmother was wrong.

But doing so in front of the old woman would be a grave mistake.

"Forgive, me. I'm sorry," Olivia said. "I came to see if you wished to eat breakfast in your sitting room or in the dining room?"

Grandmother released a heavy breath. "Here, if I even retain my appetite after talking with my grandson."

Olivia nodded and left the room.

"I need to go, Grandmother. I have work to tend to." He spun on his heel.

"Don't walk away, Anthony!" Grandmother thumped her cane again.

He ignored her and stepped into the hall.

Olivia drew in a deep steadying breath as she walked toward the steps that led belowstairs. When she'd overheard Anthony's grandmother talking about his sister-in-law, Caroline, and the affection he held toward the other woman, she thought her heart might shatter, leaving her a crumpled mess on the Dowager Marchioness of Huntington's costly Turkish rug.

Did his sister-in-law return his affection? An image of the pregnant, green-eyed beauty flashed in Olivia's memory. An ugly question gained purchase in her mind. Whose child did the woman carry? She fisted a hand to her mouth. Could Anthony be that wicked?

She heard a door close behind her and glanced over her shoulder to see Anthony quickly striding toward her.

He was beyond handsome, and she had allowed herself to be sucked in by his almost breathtaking maleness. No.

She could not lay the blame solely on his shoulders. She had wanted to lay with him. She was innately wicked as well. It would explain all she'd done since coming to London. No matter how she tried to spin her actions, she was a thief, and she'd given herself out of wedlock to a man she didn't love. Perhaps the latter sentence was the biggest untruth drifting in her mind, since she feared she did love Anthony. She wasn't sure when it had happened. Surely, she couldn't pinpoint the exact minute or date, but what she felt for him was unique. Strong. Overwhelming in intensity. And didn't that prove she might be losing her mind because loving him was more foolish than anything else and benefited no one?

When Anthony caught up to her, he grasped her upper arm. Not cruelly, but with enough force to stop her from pulling away.

"Olivia. I need to explain what you overheard."

She turned to him and tipped her chin in the air. "There is no need."

"We need to talk," he whispered, his breath a warm puff of air against her ear.

"My lord," she said, holding his direct gaze, willing herself not to look away. "I need to get to the kitchen to tell the cook that your grandmother wishes to dine in her apartment. So, if you will let go of my arm . . ."

"No. Not until I explain what you overheard."

"You do not need to explain anything to me."

"Like hell I don't." He opened the door closest to them and pulled her into the dim room.

Inside, Olivia could see the shadow of a massive bed with long flowing curtains draped in the corners. She'd been in this room before. It was Lord and Lady Huntington's bedchamber. She could almost hear the woman's laughter when talking with Lord Huntington and see the love in their eyes when they had looked at each other. Lady Huntington was either a consummate actress or she truly loved her husband. Olivia believed it the latter.

"Lady Huntington loves her husband," she whispered, more to herself than to Anthony.

"Of course she does. As desperately as my brother loves her." There was such an earnest expression on his face.

"But your grandmother said . . ."

He cupped her face with his warm palms. "I do not love Caroline."

There was something hesitant in his voice. Something not spoken. "Did you at one time?"

He looked taken aback by the question. "No. But if honest, I've envied the relationship she and my brother have. I admire her." He gave a self-deprecating laugh. "Especially her belief that I am innately good, but that only serves to make me feel better about myself. Love makes you want to make the other person feel complete as well. It's not solely about one's own peace of mind. Does that make sense?"

It did. "I also think you are innately good. And your brother must believe in you as well, or he wouldn't have left you such a grave responsibility."

"Yes, I understand that James has a great deal of faith in me." Yet he could not admit to Olivia that his brother was misguided. That if he knew the truth he would not have. And that she was one of the only reasons he'd been able to handle the ledgers and not failed.

He cupped her cheek in his hand.

As their gazes met, she lowered her eyes and her face flushed.

Was she regretting last night? "Olivia, look at me."

She glanced up.

"Please don't regret what happened between us. It was special."

She sunk her front teeth into her lower lip. "I don't regret it. Perhaps that is why I feel so odd."

He smiled. "I need to go to Victory Pens and check on the progress again. Will you go with me this afternoon?"

"But what of your grandmother?"

"I'll send her a missive telling her I need your help. She won't doubt that." He brushed his lips against hers.

She pressed herself to him and opened her mouth, inviting him to deepen the kiss.

He kissed her long and deep.

Footsteps moved down the hall on the other side of the door.

Anthony pulled back. "You better get going. If we get caught in here, together . . ."

She nodded.

He stuck his head out of the door. "The coast is clear."

Later that day, when Olivia walked into the office, light from the bank of windows settled across the threshold to where she stood. The sight of her caused Anthony's chest to tighten. She'd loosened her normally taut chignon, allowing curling tendrils to circle her face. The bright shafts of sunlight highlighted her red hair, while the rich, bronze tones of her new day dress brought out the color of her hazel eyes. Olivia looked almost ethereal. Like a drawing of a redhaired fairy he'd once seen in a children's book.

Goodness, she was beautiful.

She blushed. Could she read his mind? Did she realize how much he wished to remove her clothing and taste every inch of her skin, while tangling his fingers in her fiery hair—all while allowing the sun to touch her skin, so he could see every inch of it?

Shaking his lurid thoughts from his head, he stood. "Are you ready to go?"

"I am."

He picked up a notebook and handed it to her. "I think the project is nearly done, but will you take notes if the foreman has any suggestions?"

"Of course."

A short time later, they sat in his family's closed carriage as it rolled toward Victory Pens. Olivia had taken the seat across from him. He moved to sit next to her. His leg brushed against hers. "Have I told you how lovely you look?"

"You do not need to flatter me, my lord, I've already shared your bed."

He cupped her face in his hands, forcing her gaze to remain steadily on his. "You believe I say these things only to get you to share my bed? Is that what you thought last night when I told you I found you beautiful?"

"I presume most men believe compliments will break a woman's resistance."

"It's not false flattery. You really do not realize how lovely you are. When you walked into my office, I had trouble catching my breath."

"I believe you are in need of glasses." She laughed.

He liked the sound of her laugh. The low, raspy texture of it. "I do not need glasses."

"Really? I thought that was why you asked me to do the ledgers, because of your eyesight."

That was not the reason. He felt the smile on his face flatten out.

She blinked and squeezed his hand. "Forgive me. I was only joking."

He forced a smile—tried to look lighthearted.

They rode in silence as Anthony contemplated telling Olivia the truth.

As the carriage took a turn and swayed sideways, Olivia's shoulder pressed into his. She peered at him with her luminescent eyes.

He dipped his head and pressed a kiss to her mouth.

Without hesitation, she kissed him back.

He coaxed her mouth open and deepened the kiss. For long seconds they enjoyed the feel of their mouths moving against each other. He pulled back. "Have you thought any more about my offer?"

"If you are referring to me becoming your mistress, I have thought about it, but no, I have not changed my mind."

"Olivia, you would not want for anything. I would buy you a house, clothes, a carriage."

"Are you so wealthy, my lord?"

He didn't like the way she'd said *my lord* instead of Anthony.

"I inherited a great deal of money and have invested wisely."

She nodded. "But money, no matter how much, cannot buy me self-respect."

What could he say to that? She would not be allowed into homes that welcomed him. She would be a member of the demimonde. An outcast in good society.

He released a breath as the carriage pulled in front of Victory Pens.

Inside, once again, the construction foreman, Mr. Gibbons, led them around.

When Anthony saw something that he thought could be adjusted or wasn't to his liking, Olivia took notes.

It did not go unnoticed by Anthony that the foreman kept smiling at Olivia. This was the type of man she should marry. A man who would buy her a small house. A man who would gladly give her a brood of children. Children who would inherit their mother's intellect.

The thought of her with Gibbons made Anthony grumpy.

"We made the changes you requested to the loading dock, my lord." The foreman smiled at Olivia again.

"Mr. Gibbons, are you intent on continuing to flirt with my assistant or show me the changes you have implemented?" The censure came out exceedingly sharp.

The man paled. His reputation was all that he had to recommend him. If Anthony or his brother James said something negative, Gibbons's likelihood of future employment with men of means would not flourish in London. It would sink like a ship with a hole in its hull.

"Forgive me, my lord," Gibbons said, his voice solemn.

Guilt assailed Anthony. He had no right to censure this man. He had no hold over Olivia. Anthony felt the heat of Olivia's gaze on him and ignored it as the man continued the tour of the latest improvements.

A short time later, Olivia and he settled back in the carriage. She had been quiet since he'd snapped at Gibbons. He owed her an apology. Sitting across from her, he could not avoid her gaze. He stretched out his legs. "Forgive me."

Her eyes widened. "For?"

"I had no right to bark at the foreman."

She smiled.

Her lighthearted expression wasn't the reaction he had expected. He thought she would chastise him. Her smile revealed one thing. She realized he'd acted out of jealousy. And if he read her reaction correctly, she hadn't minded his interference, even though she knew it boorish and wrong, but he needed to confirm that he wasn't misreading the meaning of the smile on her face.

"I thought perhaps since we are out, I might take you to dinner. Should I ask Mr. Gibbons to join us?"

"If you wish to invite him that is up to you."

"But do you wish it?"

"No." She glanced out the window.

Was she now upset with him? Good Lord, he was an idiot. "I don't want to ask him. I just wanted to make sure I had not overstepped."

She turned back and peered at him. "I have no interest in Mr. Gibbons, but you did overstep."

"Then let me apologize by taking you to dinner. I know a place in Soho with private dining rooms. I think—"

"Could we go to Gunter's?"

"Gunter's?" he echoed.

She looked down at her gloved hands folded in her lap. "I've never had an ice treat."

"Well, we will have to rectify that."

As they stopped and pulled up to an intersection, he knocked on the carriage roof and the coachman slid open the small sliding door that allowed him to converse with the occupants. "Yes, my lord."

"Dawson, take us to Gunter's at Berkeley Square."

Chapter Twenty-Four

As the coachman steered the carriage onto Berkeley Square, Olivia saw people strolling in the park area across from Gunter's. Several carriages were parked under the plane trees. A waiter stepped out of the shop and walked to one of the equipages, holding a tray of glass cups with colorful ices.

A burst of excitement fluttered within her.

"What flavor would you like?" Anthony asked.

"Do they have strawberry?"

"Yes. Strawberry, cherry, pineapple, and more," he replied, grinning.

She was tempted to say one of each. "Strawberry sounds delicious."

As soon as the carriage came to a stop, Anthony set his top hat on his head, jumped down from the carriage, and crossed the street.

He walked like a man who was so assured in every decision he made. But she was starting to realize he wasn't. When she'd made the comment about him needing glasses, she'd seen something flash in his eyes. Regret? Sorrow?

Anthony reached the door of Gunter's at the same time two young women walked out, a maid lagging behind them. Their expensive attire, along with the fancy hats, made it obvious they were members of the upper crust. One of the women started talking to him, while she tipped her head coquettishly.

That ugly spike of jealousy Olivia had experienced watching him dancing with Mary Chester grew within her. She squashed it down.

Tonight, the Duke of Wharton was hosting his ball, and she would be an uninvited guest. After that, she would forget about Lord Anthony and leave this country and him. She needed to do that for her own sake.

Anthony tipped his hat to the two women, and they strolled away.

Olivia's gaze followed them as they walked toward their carriage. One of the women glanced over her shoulder and peered at Anthony, but he didn't glance back as he entered the shop.

Why was it he didn't wish to marry? The question had been spinning in her head for days. She would toss it aside, only for it to return. Perhaps it was nothing more than he didn't wish to be tied down to one woman.

A minute later, Anthony exited Gunter's.

Dawson, who'd returned to his perch, jumped down and opened the door.

Anthony climbed inside. After sitting across from her, he placed his hat onto the space beside him. A lock of his wavy hair fell across his forehead, and she battled the urge to brush it aside, just as she had the time she'd fallen in this very same carriage.

One side of his mouth turned up. "What are you smiling about?"

Had she been smiling? "I was thinking about when I tripped on your foot in your carriage in front of Madame Lefleur's shop and how Lady Winton's drawers landed on your head."

His grin broadened. "I should have realized you were going to change my life then and there."

Not sure exactly what he meant, she drew in a slow breath. She was about to ask him when she noticed the waiter crossing the street, moving toward their carriage. The tray in his hand contained three clear cups with pink-colored ice piled high and shiny silver spoons.

Anthony stepped out and took two, then motioned the waiter to hand the coachman the third one. "Dawson, I hope you like strawberry."

"Why, yes. Of course, my lord. Thank you."

He was so different from her last employer. In the weeks she'd worked for Lady Winton, she'd not seen the woman do anything remotely kind for her staff. The idea of purchasing an ice treat for her coachman, Biddles, would not have even entered her ladyship's mind.

Anthony stepped inside and handed her one of the icy treats. He leaned casually back against the corner, stretched out his legs on the cushion, and crossed them at the ankle. He looked so male, so virile.

She forced her gaze away from him and dipped her spoon into her glass. Bright pieces of chopped strawberries were visible. She made sure to get one on her spoon and brought the frozen treat to her mouth. It was cold, but immediately started melting against her tongue, sending the sweet flavor of the dessert to every corner of her mouth.

She closed her eyes, savoring the sensation, and released a moan of absolute pleasure.

When she opened her eyes, she saw Anthony staring at her. Warmth flooded her cheeks. How gauche he must think her. Those women he'd been talking with would never have acted this way. "Forgive me—"

"No. Don't ever apologize. That was . . ." He shifted as if uncomfortable. "Wonderful to witness."

He always made her feel better about herself. Smiling, she slipped another spoonful into her mouth.

A few minutes later, Olivia gathered up the last dollop of the frozen treat and ate it. She stared at the cup and fought the urge to lick it clean.

Anthony, who'd already finished his, was leaning against the thick velvet cushions, watching her. He smiled. "Would you like another?"

She was tempted. "No, thank you."

He rapped on the roof and the coachman opened the door. "Please return our glasses, Dawson."

"Yes, my lord. And thank you. It was excellent."

He nodded. "Before heading home, I wish you to drive by the British Museum. I want to show Miss Michaels where it is. She'd like to visit the Reading Room next week."

"Of course, my lord."

She knew exactly where the Reading Room was. While employed by Lady Winton, she'd visited the museum.

After Dawson walked away, Olivia tipped her head to the side. "Do you really wish to show me the British Museum's location?"

"That depends."

"On what?" The heated look in his eyes caused her stomach to flutter.

"If you want me to show it to you or do something else."

Was he implying what she thought he was? Surely, he didn't mean for them to do anything in the carriage. Yet, the wicked idea caused excitement to spark within her. "Well, I've seen the museum. In fact, I visited the Elgin Marbles and spent several hours in the Reading Room."

"Then you do not need to learn its location?"

"No," she replied.

"Do you still wish us to drive by the museum?"

They were dancing about each other. Not saying what they both wanted. "Yes, very much so."

The coachman returned from Gunter's and climbed onto his perch. The carriage moved out of Berkeley Square and headed toward Bloomsbury.

Anthony briefly glanced out the window. "The traffic near the museum is rather dense this hour of day. It might take us a great deal of time to get there then back to Mayfair."

"I believe you're right."

"Perhaps we should do something to preoccupy ourselves?"

"Any ideas?" she asked, clearly knowing what he meant.

"A few." Anthony reached over and pulled both the side shades down, making the interior of the compartment dim. "May I kiss you, Olivia?"

Stomach fluttering with anticipation, she nodded.

The next thing she knew, Anthony had pulled her onto his lap and his mouth was on hers.

She twined her hands around his neck.

His tongue entered her mouth to tangle with hers.

That heady feeling his kisses evoked seemed even more

powerful as they drove through the streets of London. The sound of the coachman directing the horses, the clopping of hooves, and the jangling of the harnesses all receded. The only noise that registered was the little sounds of pleasure they made. It was as if they'd fallen into a place where only they remained in the world.

Anthony's hand dipped under the skirt of her dress to skim up the back of her calf. Inch by inch, his palm moved farther up in leisurely exploration, dragging her skirts higher. The inner muscles of her thigh tensed as his fingers flexed against the soft flesh there.

The place between her legs tingled. She moaned her approval as his fingers found the slit in her drawers and moved across her slick folds.

He made a noise, a growl, and then she was not on his lap anymore but propped against the side of the squabs with her dress gathered at her waist, exposing the pale skin of her thighs above her stockings and garters to both him and her.

He glanced up. His gaze was rapacious.

"May I taste you, Olivia?"

Taste me? She wasn't quite sure what he meant, but the already heavy breaths sawing in and out of her lungs grew faster with anticipation.

She nodded, and he dipped his head between her legs. The experience of his tongue touching her made her gasp. But she didn't scoot back or protest. Instead she dug her fingers into his thick, dark hair as his tongue continued to explore her sex.

He slipped his hands under her bum and lifted her ever so slightly, bringing his mouth tighter so his tongue could explore her more fully and delve deeper.

For a minute, she thought she should be mortified, but all her mind could center itself on was the pleasure building within her. It was as if every nerve ending she possessed had shifted to that spot between her legs. Unlike in his bedroom, she now understood the overpowering sensations gathering momentum within her—that an explosion of uncontained pleasure would send her whirling into a vortex so powerful it would make her legs shake and then leave her sated.

The muscles in her thighs tensed and then it hit her. Wave after wave of pulsing sensations. She closed her eyes and bit her lip to stop herself from crying out.

As Olivia's mind settled back to the here and now, she opened her eyes to see Anthony staring at her. She thought she should be embarrassed, but she wasn't. How could she be with the way he was looking at her?

Slowly, the sounds of the outside world came back. The carriage was slowing down. The coachman called to the team of horses.

Anthony peeked out one of the lower shades. "We are nearly home," he said, nuzzling her neck, while lowering her skirts.

She didn't want to move. She wanted to just gather her thoughts and try to enjoy the lingering shocks still throbbing between her legs, but she sat up and smoothed her hands over her dress.

Reluctantly, Anthony lifted the shades. The sky outside was now dusky. Suddenly, everything that had just transpired in the dim carriage seemed to have been a dream. Next to him, Olivia was still straightening her clothes, yet her eyes looked sated and sleepy. He was tempted to tell Dawson to take them to Richmond Park, but he had a feeling any more detours would have the coachman suspicious, which would cause gossip belowstairs.

The carriage pulled in front of his family's Park Lane residence. Anthony stepped out and offered his hand to Olivia to assist her. Both their gazes shifted to a black, shiny carriage in front of the residence with a coachman standing next to the vehicle.

"Was your grandmother expecting company?"

"Not that I'm aware of."

As Olivia and Anthony made their way to the door, the butler opened it. The manservant had a harried look on his face. "Thank goodness you have returned, my lord. Your grandmother is anxiously awaiting you in the receiving room."

"Who's here?" Anthony asked.

"Lord and Lady Pendleton and Miss Mary Chester. They are here for dinner."

A wave of anger moved up Anthony's spine. Meddlesome woman.

They'd no sooner stepped into the entry hall, when the double pocket doors to the receiving room slid open and his grandmother's gaze shifted from him to Olivia. With her back to her guest she scowled. "Anthony, for a minute, I thought you'd forgotten I'd invited Lord and Lady Pendleton and Mary to dine with us."

"Forgotten?" Anthony replied in a low voice, aware of the three people sitting in the room beyond his grandmother. "I believe you forgot to mention it."

"Did I? Oh, how foolish of me."

Balderdash. She hadn't forgotten. The overbearing woman had a memory like a raven and was nearly as ominous.

Grandmother turned back to the three occupants in the room. "Apologies. Anthony's business meeting took longer than expected."

He wanted to ignore the sets of eyes staring at him but could not do that since Lord Pendleton had risen and was walking toward him with his hand outstretched.

"Understandable," his lordship said, pumping his hand. "Your grandmother tells me you're doing a wonderful job overseeing several of the family businesses while your brother is on holiday."

"Did she?" Anthony forced a smile at the old woman. "I have a wonderful assistant. You've met Miss Michaels." He motioned to Olivia.

"Assistant?" Lord Pendleton echoed. "I thought Miss Michaels was your grandmother's companion."

Anthony smiled. "She is both my grandmother's companion and my assistant. I have to admit she has a better head for figures than I do."

"Really?" Lord Pendleton twisted the end of his mustache.

Grandmother turned to Olivia. "You may have the evening off, Olivia."

"Thank you, my lady."

"Miss Michaels," Anthony said. "Why don't you join us?"

The dowager's lips flattened into a straight line. "The poor girl must be exhausted."

"If I'm being honest," Olivia said, "I have a migraine and would appreciate the time to rest."

Anthony knew it was a bold-faced lie. "Very well. I hope you feel better."

"If you'll excuse me." Olivia inclined her head to Lord Pendleton and strode away.

It took a great deal of restraint on Anthony's part not to follow her, but he could feel both Grandmother's and Lord Pendleton's gazes on him. Along with those of Lady Pendleton and Mary Chester, who were still seated in the receiving room.

Several hours later, sitting in the corner chair in her bedchamber, Olivia peered over her book and stared at the door. She was almost positive that after the Pendletons and their granddaughter left, Anthony would wish to speak with her. The look in his eyes conveyed he'd not believed her story about having a megrim.

Had he really wished her to join them and watch Lord Pendleton's young granddaughter make cow eyes at him? Anyway, telling him she had a headache would be the excuse she needed for tonight. Releasing a heavy breath, she glanced at the clock on the mantel. The Duke of Wharton's ball would have already begun, and at midnight, while he and his guests dined on exquisite food and champagne, she would be in his house relieving him of every bit of cash she could pocket. He was the last man on her list. After she robbed him, she would consider her promise to Helen fulfilled.

That thought made her feel as if a huge pile of leaden weights would be lifted off her chest, allowing her to breathe freely once more. It would also mean she was free to leave

England. Free to board a ship to America and start a new life.

Anthony made her want to toss her idea of leaving England aside and stay, but soon the Marquess of Huntington and his wife and children would return, and Olivia's position as both his grandmother's companion and his assistant would not be needed. When that happened, she would be too tempted to take him up on his offer to become his mistress. Nothing could come from such an arrangement but heartache. Plus, it was dangerous. What if she got with child?

It would be wiser if she left before Lord and Lady Huntington returned. She would leave Anthony a note, then board a ship for America. Suddenly feeling melancholy, along with restless, she opened the door and peeked into the corridor. Seeing no one, she moved to the top of the steps to listen. After dinner they would have gone into the blue drawing room, one story below.

Lord Pendleton's voice and hearty laughter drifted upward.

She heard Anthony's voice.

Mary Chester laughed, a light tittering sound.

A minute later, the voices grew louder. Realizing they were leaving, Olivia pushed away from the stairwell so she wouldn't be spotted. She turned to move back to her room and saw Katie stepping off the servants' stairs to the rear of the corridor.

The young maid smiled. "Mrs. Parks asked me to retrieve your dinner tray. Are you feeling better?" The maid followed Olivia into her room and lifted the lid covering the plate. "No. I guess not, since you didn't eat a thing."

Eating was the last thing on her mind. Between thoughts

of Anthony and what she intended to do at the Duke of Wharton's tonight, her stomach was in turmoil.

The maid lifted the tray and moved to the door. At the threshold she turned around. "Do you think he'll marry her?"

She knew who Katie meant. Anthony and Miss Chester. The queasiness in her stomach grew. She forced her expression to remain bland. "I'm not sure. It would make his grandmother happy if he did."

"Yes, that old battle-ax would feed her young to the wolves if it increased her standing in society." The woman peered down at the tray, then looked at Olivia again. "You know they only marry their own kind."

Something in the maid's direct gaze unsettled Olivia. She tried not to fidget. Had the coachman said something? Had he realized what she and Anthony had done in the carriage? Or had members of the staff noticed that she felt something for Anthony?

Katie was warning her to guard her heart.

Too late. "Yes, I know."

The woman pinched her lips together, looking like she wished to say more. "Good night, miss."

"Good night, Katie."

As soon as the woman stepped into the corridor, Olivia closed the door and slumped against it. Suddenly, feeling trapped by her own thoughts, along with the four walls, she moved to the window and threw the sash up. She drew in several large gulps of the night's cool air. If she was sure Anthony would not visit her, she would have dressed and made her way to the rooftops so she might leap from one roof to the other to clear her mind and distract herself.

As the sound of clopping hooves echoed into the night, she leaned farther out the window. A carriage pulled up to the front of the residence. The Pendletons and their granddaughter were leaving. She drew in a few more deep breaths, then closed the window.

Olivia was not startled when a short time later, a knock sounded on her door. Lying to Anthony again would not come easy, but she realized what she needed to do. Wiping her damp palms on the skirt of her dress, she walked to the door and opened it.

"Why didn't you accept my invitation to join us?" Anthony asked.

"As I said, I have a megrim."

He made a face conveying he really didn't believe her, yet he asked, "Is there something I can get you?"

She truly hated lying to him. She shook her head and touched her temple. "No, but thank you. I'm going to retire early. I hope doing so will make it go away."

He glanced up the empty corridor, stepped into the room, and closed the door.

"Anthony, you shouldn't be in here."

"I need to talk to you."

"No. You need to leave."

"I wish to reiterate that I have no interest in Mary Chester."

"Why not? She seems rather lovely."

"I don't love her. I barely know her."

It was a reasonable answer, even though it was not unusual for members of his class to have arranged marriages. "Well, one day you will find a woman you love and have a family with her."

"Family? As I've said, I do not want children." As if

frustrated, he raked both his hands through his hair. It only served to make him look more primal. More male. More desirable. Yet, the expression on his face looked pained. He turned around as if about to walk out of the room, then at the door pivoted back.

She could see the agony in his eyes, and knew he was struggling to tell her something. She stepped up to him and grasped his hand. "Why don't you want children?"

"I don't wish them to suffer the way I have."

"Suffer?" she echoed, confused.

"The truth is that groups of numbers do not make sense to me. I switch their orders and ultimately end up reading them incorrectly. I have struggled with this my whole life and cannot seem to shake the issue. It's the reason I do not like dealing with the ledgers."

Annabelle Green's face flashed in Olivia's mind. The girl had been a student of hers at the orphanage. The child had grappled with reading. She'd told Olivia that the letters got mixed up in her head. It appeared there was such a thing with numbers, too. But Annabelle had been extremely bright, just like Anthony. He needed to realize that.

"This issue does not define you, Anthony. You are enormously intelligent. So this is why you don't wish to marry? To have children?"

"You ask that as if it is something minor. Something I should not fear passing on. But you have not lived it. You look at multi-digit numbers and add them as if they are nothing. I misbehaved in school so I would get tossed out because this"—he tapped at his skull—"doesn't work correctly. I didn't wish people to learn the truth."

Yet, he had told her. And she loved him even more for trusting her to understand and not judge him. The painful expression on his face made her want to weep. She did not want him to see the tears pooling in her eyes. He would misunderstand them. He would think she pitied him. She wished to cry because she could see how this admission hurt him. How this issue made him feel less when he was so much better than any man she'd ever met.

Impulsively, she wrapped her arms about his waist and pressed the side of her face against his chest. "I'm sorry you have found that part of your life a challenge, but it does not detract from the man you are. Kind. Loving. Intelligent. If your children have the same issue, they will be born to a father who understands. Who will not censure them, but love them."

He ran the back of his fingers over her cheek.

The tenderness of it made her want to cry even more. If she was successful at the Duke of Wharton's, she would be leaving London and Anthony. Eventually, hopefully, he would marry, and she wanted that for him. She wanted him to be happy. Feeling as if she could burst into tears, she stepped back and rubbed the heels of her hands against her eyes.

"I should let you rest," he said, misunderstanding the action. "I hope you will feel better in the morning."

She contemplated telling him the truth. Everything. What she had done. All her lies. That she wasn't feeling ill at all. An image of Helen clasping her hand only minutes before she took her last breath appeared in her mind's eye. Wharton, Helen's father, was the last man on the list. She needed to do this. Needed to complete what she'd come to London to do.

He lowered his hand. "I'll see you tomorrow."

She nodded and closed the door.

Down the hall, Anthony's bedroom door clicked closed. Was he getting dressed to go out? She shouldn't be thinking about what he intended to do. Not when the night would be precarious for her. Uncertainty loomed in her future. Tonight, while robbing the Duke of Wharton's house, she could get caught, and there was always the possibility of falling to her death when she leapt from one rooftop to the next.

Yet, she wanted to be with Anthony—one last time.

Before Olivia could think better of it, she slipped out of her room and made her way to his. Lightly she tapped on his door.

As if he'd been standing on the other side, it opened immediately.

She scooted into his bedchamber, closed the door, and on the tips of her toes, wrapped her arms around his neck.

"Olivia, if you stay here—"

Not wanting him to send her away, she kissed him.

The next thing she knew, he'd locked the door, and they were toppling onto the bed.

For long minutes, they just kissed.

The *thump, thump, thump,* of his grandmother's cane, tapping against the rug, forewarned that she was in the hall. The old woman rapped on the door. "Anthony, I wish to talk to you."

Olivia held her breath.

"I've already retired. Tomorrow," Anthony said, his voice firm.

The woman grumbled, but the sound of her cane faded as she moved to her own bedchamber.

Within minutes, they'd shed their clothing and Anthony had put on another French letter. He sat on the bed, leaned back against the headboard, and crooked his finger for her to come to him.

She went to him and, wrapping her fingers around his hard length, stroked him.

"Good Lord." Anthony's breaths quickened.

With his hands on her hips, he lifted her slightly, and she realized what he wanted her to do. She lowered herself onto his hardened flesh, inch by slow inch. She moved awkwardly at first until she found her rhythm.

Anthony tangled his hands in her hair and kissed her with his lips and tongue, absorbing her little moans of pleasure when their climaxes overtook them.

Sated, she slumped against him.

His hand stroked her bare back. After half an hour or so, the movement of his hand stopped, and his breathing fell into the even rhythm of one asleep.

She wanted to stay wrapped in his arms until the end of time, but she needed to leave. She needed to get dressed and make her way to the Duke of Wharton's town house. Quietly, she slipped from the bed, dressed, and tiptoed from the room.

For the last time, the Phantom would pay a call on an unsuspecting wretch.

Chapter Twenty-Five

A bitter wind swept over the roofs as Olivia made her way across them. In the distance thunder rolled in the sky. She hoped the rain would hold off until after she returned to Trent House. The roofs became slippery when wet, increasing the chances of plummeting to one's death.

Today, more than any other day in the past, the fear of getting caught almost overwhelmed Olivia. She reminded herself of what Cline, whose uncle worked at Scotland Yard, had mentioned at breakfast. That they were almost positive that the Phantom was a person who had attended all the gatherings—an invited guest. That the commissioner and his detectives had compiled a list of suspects and would be keeping an eye on those men and following them if they left the ballroom.

The information the footman relayed should have eased Olivia's fears, yet she couldn't shake off the feeling of doom hanging over her.

A cold drop of rain landed on her cheek.

Curses. It appeared her good fortune as far as the weather was concerned would not continue. That knowledge added to her sense of apprehension.

When she reached the roof of the last town house on the street, she carefully grasped the drainpipe. Normally they were already slick from the mist that clung to them from the damp night air, but drizzle made them even more treacherous to climb or descend from. Clasping the pipe, she leaned over the edge of the roof. For a minute, she dangled over the side, until her thighs clamped around the pipe, allowing her to press the heels of her shoes into the cast iron to slow her progress downward.

When her feet touched the ground, Olivia released a gusty breath, then scurried across the terrace to the iron gate that led to the mews. As she lifted the latch, she sent up a silent prayer that the wet hinges wouldn't send a shrill sound into the dark night. Inch by inch, she pulled it open. The hinges were well oiled and didn't make a sound. When she had just enough room for her body to squeeze through, she slipped to the other side of the gate.

Seeing no one, she briskly walked across the street. From here, she would travel mostly by the alleys that ran behind the clusters of stately homes. Though she would need to cross two more streets before reaching the mews that ran behind the duke's residence.

Several carriages rumbled by her as she made her way, but none took much notice. Dressed as she was, while wearing a knit cap, along with her head angled downward, she looked like a young man, perhaps even a groomsman, making his way home after a night at a local pub or after a game of chance played in a back alley.

She reached the square where the duke lived but needed to cross to the other side. Staying in the shadows of the trees in the center garden, she made her way around. Rows of polished black carriages lined the street, looking even shinier with the translucent drops of rain that dusted them.

She'd just started to cross the street when she spotted a uniformed policeman under the portico of the corner town house. Her heart beat double time. Stopping and turning around would draw more attention. She pulled the collar of her sweater up higher on her neck and tipped her face downward.

"Where you off to at this time of night, lad?" the constable asked, stepping out from the shadows and moving toward her.

The sound of her heart beating loud in her chest echoed in her ears. She swallowed the fear that threatened to close her throat. "Just making me way 'ome, sir," she replied, forcing her voice to sound deep.

"Well, get along with you, then. A storm's brewing."

"Yes, sir. I'll do that, sir." As she continued on her way, she felt the bobby's gaze on her and forced her quaking knees to not buckle.

Her heart was still beating fast when she reached the alley behind the square where the duke lived. She glanced behind her to see if the policeman still watched her. Not seeing him, she ducked into the mews. More carriages were lined up there.

Coachmen, wearing oilcloth jackets, gathered around a lit brazier, warming their hands. The fire inside the metal cage sent puffs of gray smoke into the dark sky as the drizzle threatened to douse the flames. A flash of lightning, followed by a rumble, forewarned of the viciousness of the approaching storm. Though frowned upon, Olivia watched as several coachmen took refuge inside their employers' carriages.

Like a mouse trying to avoid the watchful gaze of a cat, she stayed in the shadow of the brick wall that surrounded the gardens of the first town house. At the gate, her fingers curled around the handle and turned it. It swung inward—the sound of the hinges barely audible.

Instead of being relieved, that she'd gained entrance so effortlessly, a frisson moved down her spine. Everything was happening too easily.

For a minute, she thought perhaps Cline had been misinformed. That his cousin at Scotland Yard had given him misinformation. Perhaps Scotland Yard realized it was an uninvited guest.

As she slipped into the yard, closed in by the six-foot brick wall, she peered into the shadows. Though she saw no one, an almost tangible apprehension moved through her body as if any minute a detective would materialize and handcuff her.

Unable to shake her discomfort, she nibbled her lower lip, while she contemplated returning to Trent House.

No. It was only her nerves making her feel this way. And her guilt over lying to Anthony. She was almost at the Duke of Wharton's town house. She needed to see this through. Trying to calm herself, she drew in several slow breaths of the night's cooler air.

On the tips of her toes, she moved to a lean-to off the back of the house. Most likely a storage shed or an old privy. She pulled herself up onto its roof and crawled, almost on her belly, to the drainpipe. She set her foot atop the decorative molding that ran up the corner of the brick home and, holding on to the pipe, hoisted herself up.

By the time she'd shimmied up the pipe and was on the rooftop, the drizzle had turned into a downpour. A bolt of lightning briefly lit the sky like fireworks, followed by the rumble of thunder. Cold drops of rain pelted her face, causing rivulets to stream down it. She pulled her knit cap lower, dashed over to a chimney, and leaned against it, partially shielding herself from the wind that blew the rain sideways.

For a minute, the moon disappeared behind a cloud, sending her into almost complete darkness. When the orb appeared again, she surveyed the roofs. They were only slightly varied in height, making it easier to cross from one to the other, but the heavy rain made the surfaces slick, and her sweater absorbed the water like a sea sponge, making the garment heavy on her shoulders.

Taking extreme care, Olivia jumped from one slick rooftop to the next. When she reached the Duke of Wharton's residence, she moved to the first of the four attic windows. Normally they were open to relieve the oppressive heat that rose inside a town house during gatherings, when hundreds of people crammed into the elegant ballrooms, but because of the weather, Olivia noticed all four attic windows were closed. She tried the first and found it locked. So were the next two. Her fingers felt cold and numb as she pressed against the lower sash of the last window.

Her breath came out in a relieved puff of air as it slid upward.

She poked her head inside and, seeing no one, crawled through the opening.

As usual, it was the maids' quarters. Beds lined the walls. As Olivia surveyed her surroundings, water from her wet clothes created a puddle on the floor. Now the detectives from Scotland Yard would realize that it was not a guest that had committed the crimes but an intruder. They would start watching the rooftops, but after this, she was done. And if she made it back to Trent House, they would be left wondering whatever happened to the Phantom.

Her shoes made a squishing noise as she walked farther into the room. She could not move about the house, leaving a trail of water and shoeprints of rooftop muck. Spotting a tall, white cupboard, Olivia moved toward it. Inside, she found several dark maid's uniforms and white aprons. Quickly, she removed her sopping knit hat, sweater, trousers, and shoes, then put on the uniform. The dress was long enough that she could move around without shoes. She shoved the wet garments under one of the beds and tugged a white cotton mobcap she found in a drawer over her damp hair.

She took the servants' stairs down two flights to where she presumed the Duke of Wharton's bedchamber was, then slipped inside the first door. It took a minute for her eyes to adjust to the dim light, but she could make out the large tester bed with frilly bedcovers and a woman's vanity with perfume bottles.

Not the duke's room.

On the tips of her toes, she crossed to a door on a sidewall and opened it.

Immediately, the odor of tobacco filled her nose. The scent so strong it was as if the furniture had spent years absorbing the smell. A massive four-poster bed with velvet cranberry curtains was centered on the far wall. On the opposite wall was a massive fireplace with an oil painting of a man in almost life-size proportions. Olivia walked up to it.

The opulence of the bedchamber, along with this painting of a gentleman wearing a coronet with eight strawberry leaves, left no doubt that this was the Duke of Wharton's room.

Olivia peered at the painting. She had thought she would see the reflection of evil in his face, but the older, gray-haired gentleman didn't look like the devil's minion. The word *regal* came to mind. His shoulders were broad, his jaw square, and eyes a warm shade of brown.

The man was strikingly handsome. And she could see the resemblance to Helen and the duke's son, whom she'd met at the ball.

How unfair life could be. An evil man should look depraved, so unsuspecting women would not be drawn in, thinking he posed no harm when, in truth, they should be leery. Frightened.

The rain pelting against the window drew her from her thoughts. She should not be contemplating the unfairness of it. She needed to find the man's coin box, then make haste.

She spun around and surveyed the furnishings—a highboy, an armoire nearly as large as a carriage, several dressers, a desk, and a gilded display cabinet with a glass top and sides. Curious what was inside the display cabinet, she strode toward it. Even in the dim light, she could see the antique snuffboxes, some with painted scenes on them, others pewter and silver. One even looked gold. No pawnbroker would want the painted ones, especially after the newspapers reported the robbery. Scotland Yard would send men out to scour the shops. However, the metal ones could be melted down. The stones that encrusted a few of them could be removed and set into new pieces of jewelry if she could find a dishonest jeweler to purchase them. And there were always dishonest people to be found if one looked hard enough.

If she found nothing else, she would take them. She moved to the desk and rifled through the drawers. Finding nothing, she settled her gaze on the armoire. With silent steps, she walked to it. On one side of the massive wardrobe were shelves. The other side contained hooks where clothing hung. She knelt before the armoire and knocked on the bottom of the piece. It sounded solid—not as though it had a hidden compartment or false bottom. She stood and begun rifling through the neatly folded clothes. Once again, finding nothing, she spun around.

The moonlight from the bank of windows highlighted the picture, drawing her to it like a beacon in a dark night. Olivia picked up a small gilded chair and set it in front of the hearth. Then gathering the skirt of the serviceable dress she wore, she stepped onto the chair. Slowly, she ran her fingers over the sides of the massive painting, searching for a set of hinges.

Olivia couldn't help her smile as she touched them on the right side. She grabbed the lower corner of the frame and swung it outward.

Moonlight highlighted the hollowed-out area behind the frame and the ornate silver money box. She removed it, stepped down, and set it on the chair. Of course, it was locked. She removed a hairpin and wiggled it in the keyhole. After five minutes, with no success, she moved to the desk and found a silver letter opener. Quietly, she returned to the box, sat on the floor, and set the box in front of her, determined to pry off the two back hinges. She shoved the pointy edge of the letter opener into the first hinge and twisted. It popped free. The second one was more stubborn. With all her strength, she attempted to pry it off.

She could not have come this far to fail. She jabbed the letter opener under the hinge and twisted it again. The hinge broke loose. The end of the letter opener slid, ripped through the dress, and dug into her thigh. Olivia pinched her lips tight to stifle a scream.

The ache was so intense, for a minute, her vision went black. Sweat prickled her brow, and she prayed she wouldn't swoon. Trying to contend with the pain, she drew several deep, slow breaths into her lungs, while she lifted the skirt of the dress. In the dim light, the blood oozing from the gash on her leg looked almost black against her pale thigh. She gritted her teeth and pressed her palm against her skin, hoping to stem the flow of blood.

A minute later, she tugged off one of her woolen stockings and wrapped it around her wound. She could not afford to dally much longer. She needed to move fast, or she would find herself in Newgate Prison.

With hands that shook, she lifted off the lid of the money box. Her already pounding heart sped when she saw the number of banknotes inside. Olivia stuffed them into the side pockets of the dress, along with the coins. She scrambled back onto her feet and winced at the throbbing pain in her thigh. Hobbling, she returned the broken money box to its hiding spot, then swung the massive painting back against the wall.

As she limped toward the door, she clamped a hand against the pocket holding the coins, so they would not jangle as she moved back into the connecting room. Each step caused the pain in her thigh to ratchet upward. More sweat beaded her forehead. But she could not stop and linger. She'd already spent more time in the house than was wise.

She poked her head into the corridor, and not seeing anyone, stepped into the servants' stairwell, right into a maid, holding a brass coal scuttle.

"Watch where you're going," the woman snapped, steadying the bucket with both hands.

Olivia stared at the woman's face. Her stomach clenched. She knew the maid. Penny had worked at Lady Winton's but left to take another job on Olivia's second day.

"Sorry," Olivia said, trying to scoot by her, while keeping her face cast downward.

"'Ey, I know you. When did you start working here?"

"I'm sorry, I need to get something. Please let me by."

"You were Lady Winton's companion." Her gaze swept over Olivia as her mouth twisted into a sneer. "Working as a maid, are you? What happened? Did that old windbag sack you?"

"I'm sorry, I don't know a Lady Winton." Olivia lifted her hand to push by the woman.

The maid's eyes bulged. "Blimey! What happened to your hand?"

It was then Olivia realized that the hand she'd pressed against her cut thigh had blood on it. "I've cut it and need to bandage it." She scooted by the maid and forced herself not to limp as she made her way up the stairs.

As soon as Olivia stepped into the maids' sleeping quarters, she removed the uniform and dressed in her sopping clothes and shoes. The cold and wet leg of the trousers felt good against the burning sensation in her thigh. Trying to move quickly, she transferred the money to the pockets in her trousers, then, thinking it best to take the damaged maid's uniform with her, she gathered it up and moved to the window.

She needed to get out of there fast.

Chapter Twenty-Six

Breath sawing in and out of her lungs, Olivia made her way over the rooftops. The rain was like a torrent now, pummeling her body with as much force as her thoughts battered her brain.

She had been recognized.

When the Commissioner of Scotland Yard and his detectives discovered the Duke of Wharton had been robbed, would Penny speak up when she realized Olivia *didn't* work there? Surely, they would question the staff. And though she believed that the Phantom had become a kind of hero to many of the lower classes and servants, the duke might even offer a reward. Money could turn any admirer into a bounty of information.

When she returned to Trent House, she needed to gather her belongings and leave. Posthaste.

As she maneuvered the incline of a rooftop, a jolt of pain burrowed into the cut on her thigh. She stumbled and slipped on the slick surface. Both knees hit hard. The air in her lungs exited on an explosive breath. She slid downward. One hand still clutched the maid's uniform, while the other clawed at the roof, trying to stop her downward trajectory.

Her heart pounded against her ribs as she slipped closer and closer toward the edge. Out of the corner of her eye, she saw a pipe protruding from the slate roof and clasped it with her almost numb fingers, stopping her downward descent.

Heart still beating fast, she lay there, allowing the rain to wash over her as if it could remove her sins and wash away the past couple of hours. She wanted to be at Trent House. She wanted to be dry and warm. She wanted to be in Anthony's arms. And she didn't want to leave him.

When her heart stopped thundering inside her, she finally scrambled to her feet and continued over the roofs—the pain in her leg a constant reminder of her torn skin.

By the time she reached Trent House on Park Lane, the intense pain in her thigh burned as if hot coals were pressed against the tender skin. Her gaze traveled up the drainpipe. Climbing it would be almost impossible with the throbbing pain afflicting her leg. Earlier in the day, she'd unclasped the lock in the office window just in case she needed to use it to get back into the house. Staying in the shadows, she kept her back to the wall and moved to the bank of windows. From the outside, they looked as dark as pitch with the curtains drawn closed and not a stitch of light shining outward.

Olivia set her palms to the lower sash and pushed. Silently the bottom pane of glass slid upward. She hoisted herself onto the sill. The hard surface of the wood pressed into her thigh, sending a spike of acute pain down her leg. She bit her lip to stop herself from crying out and slid through the opening.

For a minute, she lay on the floor, biting back her discomfort. When she thought she could move again without bringing tears to her eyes, she bent forward and unlaced her sopping shoes that would squeak as she made her way to her room.

While holding the shoes and maid's uniform, she pressed her free hand to the sill and leveled herself up and onto her feet. A fresh wave of pain caused her already damp brow to prickle with sweat. She closed the window and slipped the lock back into place. After her eyes had fully adjusted to the gloom, her gaze settled on the divan where a woolen blanket lay folded over the back. Teeth chattering, she bundled it around her to absorb the water in her clothes so she wouldn't leave a trail.

The outside corridor was clear. She tiptoed up the servants' steps. Each step made her wince when she settled her weight on her injured leg, but she needed to hurry and pack, then leave.

Leave. The word echoed in her head, making her want to roll into a ball and weep. She had come to like living in this house. For the first time in her life, she felt like she belonged somewhere. She'd even come to like the dowager. As cantankerous as the woman was, she wasn't half as bad as Lady Winton. She'd been kind to her. Bought her gowns, even if her kindness was part of a plot to ruin Madame Lefleur. Olivia would never forget how lovely she'd felt wearing one of the modiste's gowns.

And then there was Anthony. She loved him and truly believed he cared for her. What would he say when he discovered the truth? That she was the Phantom?

As she moved by his bedchamber door, she stopped and placed her hand on the surface. She could imagine him in his massive bed, his large body sprawled out with his dark hair in disarray, adding to his male appeal. She forced her hand away and slipped quietly inside her bedchamber.

The moonlight streaming through the open curtains highlighted a broad-shouldered man sitting in the corner chair. Though his face was shadowed, she would know him anywhere.

Anthony.

The hairs on her neck stood on end. She dropped the maid's uniform and the shoes in her hand. The latter landed with a heavy *thud.*

"When I noticed you'd left my bed, I came to check on you. To see if you were feeling better, but found you gone. Did you have a grand night out, Olivia?"

Anthony's voice reached her as if traveling through a tunnel, along with being muffled by the *swish, swish, swish* of her heart echoing in her ears.

For a moment, she couldn't catch her breath. Couldn't speak. As her eyes fully adjusted, she saw that even though he lounged casually with his legs outstretched and crossed at the ankles, holding a tumbler, his eyes watched her like a nocturnal animal who'd just spotted its prey and would soon lunge for its throat.

He brought the glass to his lips and took a slow draw as if he had all the time in the world to await her answer.

The shivering within her intensified. She wet her dry lips and searched her mind for a response. Anything she told him he would know was a lie. She was sopping wet and dressed in men's clothing and a knit hat. The soles of her shoes were filthy. Saying she had gone out for a bit of fresh air would be as believable as saying she'd snuck out by way of a window because she knew it wasn't proper to go out at all.

"Cat got your tongue, darling?"

"No, I . . ." She swallowed the thickness in her throat.

"Yes?"

"Anything I tell you, I doubt you'd believe."

He took another sip of his drink. "Unless it's the truth."

"Even the truth might sound unbelievable." She tugged the wet knit hat off her head.

"Why don't you try it?" He set his glass down on the adjacent table and crossed his arms over his chest.

Briefly, she contemplated throwing the window open and darting out of it. But her leg throbbed, and he was no weakling. He was quick and strong, and she had a feeling he would just drag her back inside if she was even capable of getting out of it before he reached her.

As if Anthony realized what she contemplated, he stood and strode toward her. He wore no jacket or waistcoat—only a white shirt and dark trousers. He stopped directly in front of her.

So close, she could see the taut angle of his jaw.

His gaze drifted from her face and down the length of her body, then back. His normally warm eyes looked hard. Distrusting.

She held his gaze, then bravado fading, lowered it to where the top buttons of his shirt were unfastened, exposing the scattering of dark hair on his chest. She remembered the texture of it on her fingers and the comfort of his warm skin against hers. It all seemed like a dream now. Or more like a cherished memory that would never be repeated.

"I'm waiting."

The sharpness of his voice drew her away from her thoughts. "Would you believe I went out for a midnight walk?"

He didn't respond, just held her gaze.

"I guess that's a no."

"Oh, that was a serious response? I thought you were trying to be a wit."

She suddenly felt so small with him peering down at her.

"Tell me, Olivia, how long have you been in London?"

Her heart stuttered in her chest. Anthony was no fool. She didn't need to tell him the truth. He'd already figured it out. "A couple of months."

"Isn't it odd. If I recall correctly that's about when the robberies in Mayfair began."

The room around her had begun to spin. She briefly closed her eyes and tried to gain her equilibrium. "Really? What a coincidence."

"Is it?" His voice sounded rough as if his throat burned and the words were hard to get out. "Don't you think it's time we stop playing this game?"

"You think I'm the Phantom? How absurd." She forced a laugh, but instead of it sounding cheerful, it came out sounding shrill. She glanced over her shoulder. She was much closer to the door than the window. Could she get it opened and make her way out of the house before he caught her? As if her body wished to remind her of the cut on her leg, intense pain shot up her thigh. She clamped her teeth, fighting against the bone-deep ache.

If Anthony noticed the way she flinched and tensed, he said nothing.

Yet, as if once again sensing her desire to flee, he shifted even closer. "You won't make it."

She realized she wouldn't. Not with her injured leg. Not with him so close.

Suddenly, his hand snaked out so fast she flinched and stepped back. She'd thought him about to strike her, but his hand caught the edge of the blanket to pull it off her shoulders. It fell to the floor.

Once again, his hard gaze traveled over her length from the man's sweater she wore, then down the length of her trousers. "Now deny it."

"If I say yes what will happen?"

For a long moment, he just stared at her with eyes that looked so dark, so cold, a shiver moved down her spine, which had nothing to do with her chilled body.

"How many lies have you told me, Olivia? Have I just been a pawn in your scheme?" He gave a bitter laugh. "Here I worried I'd caused you to be frightened when the police raided Finley's Music Hall. How foolish you must have thought me."

"No. I never thought that."

He cocked a brow. "You played the innocent maiden as well as any actress who treads the boards."

"I never set out to deceive you. I swear. I only came here to ask for your help with Lady Winton. You offered me the job."

"More reason to see me as a fool. What do you think my family will say when they realize who you are? When they realize who I welcomed into this house. I've botched up plenty of things in my life, but you are the biggest mistake I've ever made."

The utter look of disgust on his face, along with his words, made tears burn the backs of her eyes. She wet her dry lips. "Do you intend to turn me over to Scotland Yard?"

"No. Just gather your things and get out." His arm brushed against hers as he moved past her.

"Anthony."

He spun back around. "What?"

"I should warn you. Detectives from Scotland Yard might come around and ask questions."

A nerve twitched in his jaw.

She wet her dry lips again. "A maid who used to work at Lady Winton's saw me at the Duke of Wharton's. As soon as it is discovered he's been robbed, and they question the staff . . ."

"Christ," he mumbled. "Is that where you were at? The Duke of Wharton's?"

She swallowed. "Yes."

"Then you better leave. Now." Without giving her a backward glance, he slipped from the room.

As if frozen by Medusa, Olivia stared at the door. She wanted to go after him. She wanted to tell him how she felt about him, but what difference would that make?

He hated her.

She clasped her hand over her mouth, muffling the way her breaths kept catching as she started to cry. Waking the dowager would bring on even more scorn. She needed to leave. Any minute the detectives from Scotland Yard might knock on the door. Anthony was right, she'd brought shame onto his family. They'd harbored the Phantom. Brought her to a ball and dressed her in finery. The dowager would most likely keel over when she learned the truth.

If she left before the police arrived, perhaps the scandal

wouldn't be so horrible. Why had she not thought of what her actions would do to them? Because she'd thought she would never get caught, or at least prayed for that and hoped God would shield her because the men she took from were not deserving of His benevolence.

Anthony was not the fool. She was. With the backs of her hands, she brushed away the tears trailing down her cheeks.

Wincing from the pain in her leg, she made her way to the armoire and pulled out her valise. Her gaze traveled over the lovely gowns from Madame Renault's shop. She would not—could not take them. It would be like rubbing salt on the family's wounds.

She peeled off her wet sweater and trousers. After removing the latter, she looked at where she'd wrapped her woolen stocking around the gash on her leg. Blood had seeped through it. Once she found a place to lodge for the night, she would wash it and wrap a fresh bandage around it. There was no time for that now.

As quickly as she could, she removed the rest of her wet clothes and put on the old, serviceable dress she'd arrived here wearing.

The bang of the front door slamming made her jump.

Anthony. She fought the urge to run after him. Such a foolish idea. He was done with her, and with the pain plaguing her thigh, she would probably fall flat on her face. She shoved her wet garments and the maid's uniform into the bottom of her valise and gathered the few items she'd arrived with, including her small notebook, then snapped the clasp closed.

Odd while Anthony had stared at her, she'd almost forgotten the pain in her thigh. Almost. But it was coming back with a vengeance—so intense, she wanted to retch. She stepped into the corridor at the same time the dowager's door flew open.

"What the devil is going on? What is all this noise about?" The woman's regard dipped from Olivia's face to the suitcase she held. "Where are you going?"

"I've decided to leave, since Lord and Lady Huntington will be returning shortly, and my services will no longer be required." Olivia bit her lip to stop it from trembling.

With a questioning expression that further deepened the wrinkles on the dowager's face, the elderly woman tipped her head to the side. "It's the middle of the night. Where will you go?"

There appeared to be actual concern in the woman's voice. However, when she found out what Olivia had done, the dowager would wish her to the devil.

Impulsively, Olivia hugged the old woman, then ran down the corridor.

"Olivia, what is going on?" the woman called out after her.

She ignored the question. As she made her way down the flight of stairs, she found it much harder to ignore the pain. By the time she reached the entry hall, it felt as though someone was trying to peel off the skin on her thigh. She took several deep breaths, opened the door, and stepped outside.

The rain had stopped.

Cold sweat prickled her forehead. She swiped her palm against it and glanced around. Where did a woman alone go to find lodging in London during the small hours? Her gaze shifted toward the direction of Hyde Park. So close, she could see the tops of the trees. Perhaps she could find a bench and sleep there for the night. She stepped out from under the portico and the pain in her thigh shot up to her hip—an intense strike, so fast it was like lightning. She doubled over and cupped her mouth to stifle a scream.

Straightening, she glanced at the park. It suddenly looked miles away. She took another step and whimpered. A bead of sweat trailed down her spine. The pain in her leg was intensifying as if someone prodded the gash with their finger, attempting to reach for her bone.

She needed to sit. Just for a moment. Just until the pain subsided. Sucking in a ragged breath, she shuffled toward the steps that led belowstairs—to the kitchen. She lifted the latch on the gate and the wrought iron swung open on quiet hinges. Cautiously, she took the first few steps, then two more before sitting. The dampness on the stair was inconsequential to the pain in her thigh. Drawing in a deep breath, she lifted the skirt of her dress.

The blood from her gash had further darkened the woolen stocking she'd used as a makeshift bandage. As soon as she untied it, fresh blood oozed from the red gash, causing narrow rivulets of blood to run down her leg.

She opened her valise, ripped a strip of fabric from the bottom of one of her old dresses, and tied the material around her thigh.

The task completed, she leaned sideways against the damp concrete in the stairwell. Normally, the wet surface would have bothered her, but the cold felt like a balm against her hot skin.

She would rest just for a minute, then make her way to Hyde Park.

Just a minute.

Chapter Twenty-Seven

As he walked aimlessly about London, Anthony's shoes struck heavily against the flagstones, echoing into the quiet night. Earlier the rain had stopped, but now a fine drizzle fell from the sky. He raked his hands through his wet hair and cursed himself for not having the forethought to grab his hat before decamping from the town house.

He'd only grabbed his coat, since an overwhelming desire to shake some sense into Olivia had come over him. She risked her life, and if caught she'd rot in Newgate for the rest of her days. The powerful men she'd stolen from would see to it.

Hopefully, when he returned, she would be gone.

Gone. Was that what he really wanted? Of course it was. She'd made a fool out of him. He felt as if he'd been kicked in the bollocks, knocking the air out of his lungs.

Yet . . . He mumbled a curse as he remembered the sound of her breath catching when he'd told her to leave. What had she expected?

Once in the corridor, he'd contemplated returning to her room and telling her to stay. He'd even set his palm on the door handle, then released the metal as if it singed his skin. Olivia played a dangerous game and if someone had seen her at the Duke of Wharton's residence, her leaving would be for the best. She needed to not only leave London, but the country.

Ahead, a man stumbled out of a corner building and onto the pavement.

A slight breeze caused a wooden sign protruding from a brick façade to sway back and forth on damp, rusty hinges.

THE FOX AND HEN TAVERN

It looked as good a place as any to get pissing drunk. And that's what he intended to do—wipe all thoughts of Olivia from his mind. All thoughts of the Phantom from his mind. Hard to believe they were one and the same.

Anthony stepped into the dim establishment with its low, beamed ceiling, worn tables, and sooty walls. Several blokes seated at round tables, drinking and laughing, turned and stared at him, and Anthony realized, though wet, his bespoke garments and costly polished shoes made him look out of place.

Ignoring the other patrons' whispers, he strode to the bar that had only three stools, all empty, and settled onto the middle one.

A gray-haired bartender with bushy whiskers arched a thick caterpillar-like eyebrow at him. "What can I get you?"

He ordered a pint and set a coin from his pocket onto the wooden-topped bar. Anthony had downed half of his drink when the hairs on his neck stood on end. He glanced over his shoulder to see two bulky men whispering to each other as they approached.

Each one slipped onto the worn stools on either side of him.

"What's a toff like you doing here?" The one on his left asked, knocking Anthony's elbow so his ale sloshed against his tankard.

"Lost are ye?" the one on his right inquired.

"No. I'm just enjoying a pint." He took a hearty swallow of the bitter ale.

The fellow to his right leaned in as close as the other bloke, crowding Anthony between their bodies.

"Why don't the two of you go back to your table? I'm not looking for trouble."

The man to his left grinned, showing a front tooth that was chipped. "You hear that, Martin, this bloke wants us to go away."

The fellow named Martin narrowed his eyes. "Don't seem too hospitable, does he, Henry?"

"No, he don't, but I reckon we will forgive him if-in he buys us each a pint."

"Go away." Anthony took another swig of his ale.

The grin on Henry's lips disappeared.

"You ain't going to buy us a drink?" Martin blinked.

Maybe on another day, Anthony might have excused their bad behavior, but not today. Not now when he was in such a foul mood. "Sod off."

The bartender, obviously sensing nothing good would come from this exchange, backed away, moving several feet toward the end of the bar.

Anthony knew he was pouring kerosene on an already combustible situation, but he didn't bloody well care. If they wanted a fight, he was in the right mood to give it to them. He was primed and ready. As angry as a badger who is set upon with his nose to the ground.

Henry slipped off the stool and ground his right fist into his left palm.

Anthony jerked back as the bloke's fist came at him. Instead of hitting Anthony, Henry's fist struck Martin in the jaw.

The impact knocked Martin from his stool. With an *oof*, the man landed on his back.

It only took a second for Anthony to stand and swing an uppercut at Henry, striking him squarely in the jaw.

The man stumbled backward but stayed on his feet. Several other men got up as if intending to become part of the fray, but when Anthony hit Henry again with a combination punch to the gut and jaw, sending the man onto the floor, the men approaching stood still.

He turned just in time to see Martin with his stool lifted, ready to smash it down on Anthony's head.

With his left foot Anthony kicked out, hitting the man in the shin, sending him crashing into a table.

"You want a round of fisticuffs?" Anthony motioned with his hands for the other men in the bar to approach him.

"Blimey, he's mad," several men in the group said as they returned to their seats.

Martin stood and helped Henry to his feet. Both looked unsure whether they should come after him again.

"Damn fool's mad as a hatter," Henry grumbled.

Martin nodded and they both sat at a table, casting him leery glances.

After Anthony finished his ale, he stood and tossed a few more coins onto the bar top. The alcohol had done nothing to prevent his mind from thinking of Olivia. He stepped out of the pub. The rain had stopped, but lightning flickered in the distance.

The memory of how he'd been robbed and stabbed when younger flashed in his mind. He glanced over his shoulder to see if any of the men were following him. He pressed his palm over his shirt, above the scar. Unbidden, his mind drifted back to how Olivia had run her finger over the raised skin before pressing her lips to it. He shook his head to disperse the memory. In this part of town, a man needed to stay alert.

An hour later, he strode up to the front door of Trent House.

Was Olivia still here?

Part of him desperately wanted her to be. The other part wanted to rail at her and wished she was gone, since she might be arrested if she remained. As he set his hand on the door handle, he heard a noise. Concerned the men from the pub might have followed him, he spun around.

He saw no one. Just the fog drifting up from the damp pavement and ground.

A low groan whispered in the air, causing the hairs on the back of Anthony's neck to stand on end. His gaze shot to the basement stairwell where low fog hovered. He stepped closer.

A woman sat on the steps—her body slumped. Her head lolled to the side as if she were a rag doll. Ginger hair, wet and darkened by the rain, trailed down her back.

Olivia! Good God, what was wrong with her? Terror spiked through Anthony, making his heart pound in his chest. He opened the gate, moved down several steps, and crouched beside her. Her eyes were closed. The coloring of her face resembled Wiltshire chalk, while her lips looked tinged with blue. Her wet clothes clung to her skin, and she visibly trembled.

Damnation. "Olivia?"

In response, she moaned.

He cupped her face. Though she shivered, her cheeks felt hot. He pressed a hand to her forehead. It was as if she sat close to a balefire and her skin could do nothing more than absorb the heat. Anthony scooped her up into his arms and swallowed against the panic rising within him.

As he moved toward the front door, she moaned and started rambling—incoherent words that were mostly indecipherable, but he comprehended, "Need to leave."

She couldn't go anywhere in this state.

Once inside the house, Anthony took the steps two at a time. He couldn't pull his gaze away from Olivia's face. So pale. Her lips now looked bloodless.

With his shoulder, he pushed Olivia's bedchamber door open, then laid her on the bed. After closing the door, he lit the gas lamp and turned the wick up. A yellow arc of light lifted the gloom. The glow made her look even paler. Ashen. Like a corpse.

Anthony's hands trembled as he worked the buttons lining the front of her gown from the collar to the waist. Hopefully, once he removed her damp clothing and piled blankets on top of her, she would stop shivering and gain her color back.

Eyes still closed, she moaned and swatted at his hands. "I need to go."

"You need to get warm."

She started rambling again. "Police will come. So sorry."

"Shhh," he crooned, unfastening the last button that

lined the front of her dress. He tugged her arms out of the sleeves and slipped the garment down her hips and legs. He flung it aside. It landed on the rug with a heavy, wet sound. His gaze narrowed on a bright crimson stain bleeding through her white slip.

Christ. Not just cold but injured. Heart thundering with such force he thought it might leap from his chest, he untied the ribbon holding the slip at her waist and carefully removed the damp garment. A blood-soaked scrap of cloth was tied around her thigh.

"Why didn't you tell me you were hurt?" he asked, as he unbound the fabric.

Her lashes fluttered, but she didn't answer.

The gash was a good four inches long. Though it didn't appear to be bleeding heavily now, the blood on her clothing and the strip of fabric indicated she lost a good deal of blood before she'd stanched the flow.

Had someone done this to her, or had she cut herself climbing in or out of a window? With no time to think about that now, he moved to the pitcher and bowl set on the low dresser. A slight tremble shook his hand as he poured cold water on a clean flannel.

When he gingerly set it to her thigh, Olivia whimpered. Yet, her eyes remained closed. Carefully, he washed the skin around the gash, which was red and hot. Anthony knew from the time he'd been stabbed that infection could be deadly. If she was not better in a few hours, Dr. Trimble would need to be called, but could the physician be trusted? The man tended to ask questions.

Anthony raked his hands through his hair. If Olivia was not better by daybreak, he would need to send for the physician. He removed the rest of her clothes. As he lifted her to help settle her under the bedcovers, she let out a cry.

"Shhh, you'll be fine," he said. Yet, as he looked at her pale complexion, the muscles in the back of his neck tightened. He rubbed at them. Perhaps it wouldn't be wise to wait until morning to fetch Dr. Trimble. Trying to rein in his worry, he strode to the door. He'd send someone to the physician's residence now. He jerked open the door and almost slammed into his grandmother dressed in a green velvet robe.

"I heard a scream. Has Olivia returned?"

Returned?

Sensing his confusion, she said, "I got up earlier and found her in the corridor, suitcase in hand. She said she was leaving. I demand to know what is going on."

He couldn't tell her the truth. Not now, but if detectives showed up . . . "She said she was no longer needed here and wished to find a new position. Outside, I believe she slipped on the wet ground and hurt herself."

"During the night?" Grandmother pinned him with a hard stare. "Did you do something to the girl to make her leave so suddenly?"

Normally the accusation would have upset him, but right now all he could think about was Olivia's well-being. "No. Of course not."

Grandmother pushed past him and stepped into the room. "Good Lord!"

Even from the doorway, Anthony could see how Olivia's body trembled. "I need to send for Dr. Trimble."

"You better hurry!" Grandmother said, striding toward the bed.

Anthony left the room and took the steps three at a

time. Once outside, he made his way to the carriage house, then up the stairs to where the groomsmen and their coachman quartered.

He stepped into Dawson's dim room and grabbed the man's shoulder and gave it a hearty shake. "Wake up, Dawson."

Startled, the man bolted upright. He blinked a few times as if trying to ground himself in his surroundings. "My lord?"

"Get dressed. I need you to fetch Dr. Trimble on Harley Street. Now."

"Yes, right away, sir." The man scrambled out of his bed and moved to the hooks where his clothes hung.

Anthony took several deep breaths as he dashed back into the house and up the stairs. He walked in to find Grandmother pressing a wet flannel to Olivia's cheeks.

She glanced over her shoulder. "You going to tell me what really happened?"

"I don't know." It wasn't a complete lie. He honestly didn't know how Olivia had injured herself.

After examining Olivia and suturing the cut on her leg, then treating it with linen dipped in carbolic acid to help stave off infection, Dr. Trimble closed his medical bag. He clasped Anthony's shoulder. "She should be fine. I'll check on her tomorrow. As you know, it is infection that is the greatest danger to her recovery."

Anthony nodded and looked at Olivia lying in bed.

The physician pointed to the brown medicinal bottle on the low dresser. "The opiates I gave her should help her sleep for a while. If she wakes and is in a great deal of pain, give her a teaspoon. Use care in administering it, my lord. Opiates can be very addictive."

"I will. Thank you, Doctor."

Looking as if he wanted to ask several questions, the physician opened his mouth, then clamped it closed. Anthony had been rather evasive about how Olivia had injured herself, telling the doctor he wasn't quite sure, and that she'd been unresponsive when he'd found her. "I will see you tomorrow."

As soon as the physician stepped out of the room, Grandmother walked in. She still wore her velvet robe. He didn't think he'd ever seen Grandmother in any color except black.

Her fingers flexed against her cane. "I want answers."

God knows, the old woman wouldn't like them. If he told Grandmother the truth—that all along they'd been harboring the thief London called the Phantom—she might suffer some type of apoplexy. Worse, Grandmother had bought Olivia gowns and brought her to Lord and Lady Dayton's ball. It was best he didn't reveal the truth. Better for the old woman and Olivia. But if Olivia had been seen, everything might be revealed in only a matter of time.

Anthony released a heavy breath. "I cannot tell you what I do not know."

"Do you think she was robbed while leaving?"

If things weren't so dire, the question might have been laughable. Olivia *was* the robber. Most likely she'd been injured leaping from the roofs or scurrying off one of them.

"London is full of rabble. It's possible. There is nothing you can do. Go to bed."

Grandmother nodded and left the room.

Anthony strode to the basin and pitcher and poured cool water into the bowl. After dipping a clean flannel into it and wringing it out, he stepped up to Olivia and removed the one folded over her brow. She didn't even stir when he set the new compress against her forehead.

As the sky turned from dark gray to a lighter shade, Anthony settled into the corner chair and leaned his forearms on his thighs, while he peered at Olivia. For the most part, she'd slept soundly. A few times she'd restlessly tossed and turned, but never fully awakened.

While tending to her, he'd tried to make sense of her actions. They didn't add up. When he'd gone through her valise, looking for a nightgown to put on her before Dr. Trimble arrived, he'd found nothing of great value, only the money in the pockets of her wet trousers. Money he presumed she'd taken from the Duke of Wharton. But she'd robbed several other men. What had she done with *that* money? And when she'd left, she'd not taken a single item that had been purchased for her from Madame Renault's shop. All the expensive gowns still hung in the armoire.

Even the garments she possessed in her suitcase were old. Obviously, a servant who is trying to deceive those around her would not wear costly gowns, but he'd found stockings that had been mended several times. So, where had the money she'd stolen gone?

He'd also found the pocket-sized notebook with the names of all the men she'd robbed. All with a checkmark beside their name except the Duke of Wharton. She'd not been afforded the time to mark his name off her list. All the evidence pointed to a plan. She'd not robbed randomly but had set out to only steal from these men. Why?

Most were not men he associated with. He'd heard terrible things about a few of them. Lord Hamby was a letch. A man who gave a bad name to other members of the nobility. Talbot's father, the Duke of Wharton, was a cold bastard. What was the connection between these men?

He wondered if his grandmother could shed some light on that question. The woman seemed to have a direct link to every scandal, whether common knowledge or not. Grandmother would grow suspicious if he started asking questions about the men the Phantom had robbed, but he doubted she would ever draw the connection between Olivia and the thief. If he hadn't seen Olivia dressed like a man, he would never have believed it.

Anthony rubbed at his tired eyes. A voice in his head told him he should sleep while Olivia did, but restlessness coursed through him.

He released a heavy sigh and glanced out the window. The rising sun had almost obliterated the night's shadows. Would detectives from Scotland Yard show up in a few hours?

He prayed to God the answer would be no.

Chapter Twenty-Eight

Olivia's lips felt dry and cracked. Her mouth felt as if someone had stuffed wads of cotton into it. And her head felt as if it were submerged under water.

Muffled voices came to her ears.

She tried to force her eyelids open, but as if weighted down, they wouldn't lift.

A man she didn't know spoke.

Has he come to take me to prison? She tried to move. A sharp pain stabbed at her thigh, and she heard her own whimper, louder than the voices.

Perhaps she was already in prison.

Oppressive fear settled within her. Ignoring the pain in her thigh, she thrashed about, trying to release herself from the dreamlike state that clasped onto her.

A cool hand pushed the damp hair off her brow. "Shhh," a softer, gentler voice said.

Anthony? Yes, she knew his touch. She stilled. Relaxed.

Warm liquid touched her lips, then surrounded her tongue. She swallowed it, then drifted back into a state of mindless oblivion.

* * *

Sunlight filtered through Olivia's eyelids. She forced them open.

This time they lifted.

She blinked against the sun streaming through the open windows in the bedchamber she'd occupied at Trent House. She glanced around the room. The under curtains billowed inward, lifted by a breeze. How had she gotten here? Perhaps she'd been dreaming about robbing the Duke of Wharton and hurting her thigh. A nightmare of sorts.

She tried to push herself up into a sitting position. Pain shot through her thigh.

Not a dream.

She *had* robbed the Duke of Wharton.

She *had* cut her leg with the letter opener.

She *had* been seen, and Anthony knew the truth and hated her.

The latter realization made her want to weep. She bit her lip to stop it from trembling. How had she ended up back here? She remembered leaving, but little else.

A noise caused her to jerk her gaze to the other side of the room.

Anthony sat in a chair. Sleeping. His legs stretched out. The white shirt he wore looked wrinkled as if he'd slept in it for days.

His eyes opened. "You're awake."

He stood, strode to the bed, and pressed his cool hand to her forehead. "Your fever has broken."

"How did I get here?"

"I found you in the stairwell outside. You were slumped over."

She remembered that now. Remembered how the cool concrete had felt like a soothing balm against her warm cheek.

Anthony walked over to the low dresser, lifted a pitcher off a tray, and poured water into a glass.

The sight of the crystalline liquid caused her mouth to salivate.

He handed her the tumbler. "Don't drink it too fast. Dr. Trimble said you should only take small sips at first."

A physician had tended to her? She didn't remember that.

Even as angry as Anthony was with her, he'd brought her back inside and called a doctor to tend to her. She swallowed the lump forming in her throat. "How long have I been sleeping?"

"Two days."

Had he stayed with her the whole time? The wrinkles on his clothing implied the idea wasn't so far-fetched.

He picked up a wooden chair and set it next to the bedside. As he sat, she noticed the dark smudges under his eyes. "You've been on opiates to help you sleep."

That explained a lot. "Has anyone from Scotland Yard inquired about me?"

"Not yet." Anthony craned his head to the side and rubbed the back of his neck.

It was only a matter of time till they tracked her down. She needed to go. Anthony had been good to her. She tossed the blankets off and winced when she tried to swing her legs over the side of the bed.

"Where do you think you're going?" He stood.

"I need to get to Southampton or the docklands and find a ship."

"Yes. I agree. But not today. Perhaps tomorrow."

Somehow, her foolish heart had hoped he'd say stay. But that was impossible. He might have helped tend to her, but he wanted her gone. Understandable. Having the Phantom arrested at the Trent family's home would cause a scandal.

"But what if they come today looking for me? It's better I leave now."

"You're too weak." He strode to the door and grasped the handle and hesitated. He pivoted around and removed a small notebook from his trouser pocket. She recognized it right away as hers. It listed the men she had robbed and all the information she'd gathered while here and at Lady Winton's house. Times. Dates. "Why did you do it?"

"I didn't do it to line my pockets."

He raked his fingers through his hair. "Damnation, Olivia, then why? Why these men?"

"Because they are monsters. They deserve worse than losing money."

The smooth skin on his brow creased. "I don't understand."

"I think of myself as a benefactor trying to right several wrongs. Each one of the men I've stolen from fathered a child with an unwilling servant in their household. They did not think of what would befall their offspring or the women they had wronged. What is a poor maid to do when her belly grows round with a child and she is sacked by the monster who placed her in such a situation? These men see what they have done and feel no remorse. They toss these women out. Pregnant. Their families shun them for immorality. The child is placed in an orphanage or *worse*. Do you know what it is like growing up in an orphanage? Of course not. You were raised in this house." With a wide sweep of her hand, she motioned to the opulence of the bedchamber. A guest room that was like nothing she'd ever seen before, not even in Lady Winton's residence. "You do not know what it is to be cold and hungry. To have lice scratching at your head. To be struck with a birch rod for the most inconsequential things."

Olivia could feel the tears pooling in her eyes. She blinked them back. She would not cry now. She would not let the circumstances of her birth, or those wretched men, bring her to tears.

"You're right, Olivia. I don't know what it feels like, but you risk your life. For what?"

"The money I steal I send to the orphanage. I've also sent some to the young women who have been wronged. All anonymously."

"But if caught these powerful men that you have robbed will see you sent to jail." He strode to the bed and cupped her face in his hands. "They will do everything in their power to see you never leave Newgate Prison."

"You don't understand. I had to. I promised Helen."

He straightened, leaving her longing for the warmth of his palms on her face. "Helen?"

"She was my dearest friend. She was also the Duke of Wharton's illegitimate daughter. He forced himself on her mother, a maid in his house, and when her belly started to swell, he cast the woman out. What choice did Helen's mother have but to leave her infant at the orphanage? No one would hire a maid with child."

"How do you know all this?"

"Mrs. Garson knew the reasons. The women would tell her when they asked her to take their children into the orphanage."

"And she told you?"

She peered into the shadows of the room, then back to him. "When younger, both Helen and I were tasked with cleaning Mrs. Garson's office. It was there Helen came across a book in a hidden compartment in the wall. Curious as to why it was hidden, she opened it, and found out the truth about her parentage. Mrs. Garson had written everything she'd been told.

"Helen said when she grew up, she would make her father pay, along with all the other wretched men who were named in the journal. But Helen got sick and died. The doctor said she had weak lungs, and the orphanage was cold. So, while her father lived in opulence . . ." Olivia blinked at the tears blurring her vision. "On her deathbed, she made me promise to avenge all the girls. Stealing from these men who valued their wealth was the only thing I could think of doing."

Anthony slumped into the chair by the bed. "Good Lord."

"Forgive me for deceiving you, Anthony. I want you to know I took no pleasure in doing so."

The following day, Anthony used paperweights to pin down the corners of the revised blueprint for Victory Pens. After James and his family arrived home today and settled in, he was sure his brother would want an update.

He stared blindly at the drawing—his mind returning to the thought that had taken over his brain last night as he'd lain in bed. Should he tell James about Olivia and what she'd done? Perhaps it was best not to say anything. Olivia would be well enough to leave in a day or two. And though he knew for certain his brother would not tell Scotland Yard after he explained why Olivia had robbed those men, he didn't want her to feel uncomfortable during her remaining days in this house. Olivia's secret would be known by only Olivia and himself—if the police didn't figure it out.

His stomach clenched, and to distract himself, Anthony smoothed his hands over the blueprint. When he'd first started making changes, he'd worried about what James would say. Now he felt confident in every change he'd made. He'd come to realize how much he enjoyed architecture, more specifically, the design of production lines in manufacturing. He could see himself engaging in this type of business. He felt better about himself and his abilities than he had in a very long time.

A knock sounded on the door.

"Yes, come in."

The butler entered the room. "My lord, there is a Detective Linden here from Scotland Yard."

Just as quick as the snap of one's fingers, cold dread exploded in his belly. "Show him into the receiving room, Menders."

"Yes, my lord."

As soon as Menders walked away, Anthony's mind spun. Should he lie and say Olivia had left their employment several days ago? No. The servants knew she was here. They thought her sick. He could just deny it could be her since she'd been ill. It would be his word against the maid who'd seen Olivia.

The *thump, thump, thump* of Grandmother's cane moving at a faster speed than normal indicated she'd heard about their guest.

She stepped into the room. The lines around her mouth appeared deeper. "Why is a detective from Scotland Yard here?"

He shrugged with a casualness he did not feel. His grandmother was beyond keen, but he doubted she would figure it out. The fact that Olivia was the Phantom was almost incomprehensible. "Excuse me, Grandmother. I need to see what the man wants."

As Anthony made his way to the receiving room, his mind swirled. Dr. Trimble knew Olivia was not sick but injured, but he doubted the physician would volunteer the information. More doubtful that he even suspected how she'd hurt herself. Had the maid at the Duke of Wharton's realized Olivia was injured? Damnation, he should have asked Olivia.

Chapter Twenty-Nine

Anthony entered the receiving room to find Detective Linden examining the blue-and-gold ormolu clock on the mantel shelf. The man looked to be in his late forties, short, with a sizable paunch, and thinning hair combed over to one side to hide the bald spot on the top of his head. As Linden examined the clock, he seemed oblivious to the fact Anthony had entered the room.

Anthony cleared his throat.

The detective's gaze jerked to him. The man's keen gray eyes seemed to take in everything about Anthony. "Forgive me, my lord, I'm a collector of clocks and this one is most impressive. I've never laid eyes on such a fine piece of workmanship. Chinese in origin?"

"Yes. Late eighteenth century. What might I help you with, Detective Linden?"

"Oh, yes, forgive me, my lord, I'm sure you're a busy man." Something in the man's tone conveyed he thought nothing of the kind—that Anthony was an idle man, or worse, a complete scapegrace.

Anthony realized that sadly that had been true a month ago.

"I thank you for seeing me. This should only take a few minutes." Linden reached into the inside pocket of his dark coat and pulled out a small notebook and pencil.

Seeing as he couldn't avoid what he presumed was an inquisition about Olivia, Anthony motioned to the two upholstered chairs that flanked the fireplace.

Linden flashed him a smile. As the man sat, his gaze briefly returned to the clock.

For a few seconds, Anthony wondered if he offered the costly timepiece to the detective, the man would go away. But if Linden didn't accept what would clearly be conceived as a bribe, Anthony's offer would surely confirm that Olivia had something to hide and possibly seal her fate. As it stood now, it was only the maid's word that she'd seen Olivia inside the Duke of Wharton's home on the night of the robbery. He didn't believe that would be enough to convict Olivia, especially if he remained adamant that Olivia was here on that night. And he'd burned Olivia's knit hat, trousers, and sweater in his bedchamber's grate, along with the maid's uniform from the Duke of Wharton's, reducing the items to ashes. Though her injury could not be so easily explained, especially if the maid had noticed it.

Linden flipped to a page in his notebook, then zeroed in on Anthony with his intelligent eyes. "I'm sure you're aware, my lord, that the Duke of Wharton was recently robbed."

Anthony forced his expression to remain bland. "Of

course. It was in all the papers. What's this have to do with me, sir?"

The man's eyes grew round. "Nothing to do with you, specifically, my lord. However, there was a witness."

"To the robbery? Well, that's wonderful," Anthony said. "That still doesn't answer why you are here, Detective Linden."

The man pulled on his chin. "Not an actual witness to the robbery itself. A maid who works at His Grace's residence said she saw a woman dressed as a maid that night. A woman that is not employed by the Duke of Wharton."

"I still don't understand." Oh, but he did, and a sinking feeling as if he'd ingested lead settled in his stomach.

"Well, the woman used to work as Lady Winton's companion, but when I called on Lady Winton, she informed me that the woman in question now works for the elder Lady Huntington. If she was there, she is a suspect in the robbery."

"Good God, man. You think that my grandmother's companion, Miss Michaels, is the Phantom." Anthony forced a laugh. "That's preposterous."

"It does sound so, sir. Her being a woman and all, but I need to check out every lead."

"Yes, understandable, but Miss Michaels has been sick. I can vouch that she hasn't left this house."

The man peered at Anthony for several long seconds, then jotted something in his notebook before looking at him again with his keen gray eyes. "These robberies take place during the night, my lord. It is possible you are unaware she is leaving."

Linden had him there. "That is true, Detective, but her

room is on the third story, across from my grandmother's suite of rooms, and contrary to her age, the elder Lady Huntington's hearing is keen. Along with the fact that we have a sizable staff here. I do not see how the woman could leave without being detected."

Tapping his pencil against the notebook, Linden seemed to mull over this information. "True, but we now have new evidence that points to the belief that the Phantom enters homes through an attic window after moving across the rooftops. It seems reasonable that this thief would exit wherever he or she lives by using the same method."

Anthony forced a broad smile. "Miss Michaels leaping from one roof to the other seems as likely as my elderly grandmother doing so. Might I tell you something about the woman in confidence?"

This got the detective's attention. Eyes wide, he leaned slightly forward. "Of course."

"I met Miss Michaels when she mistakenly entered my carriage. She also tripped upon entering." Anthony glanced around the room as if he didn't wish to be overheard. "The woman is clumsy. She'd probably tumble to her death if on a rooftop."

The detective shifted backward and pulled on his chin again. "I'll still need to question her."

Damnation. "Yes. But as I said, she is rather ill."

"I will only take a minute, my lord. You see, the maid at the Duke of Wharton's residence said the woman was injured."

For a minute, Anthony thought his heart stopped beating before it accelerated.

"I've concluded it happened while prying open His Grace's money box," Linden continued. "If Miss Michaels is not injured, she will be cleared, and we will conclude that the maid was mistaken and identified someone who resembled her." The man arched a brow in challenge.

Anthony's heart hammered in his chest, so loud he feared the detective might hear it. If he refused to let him see Olivia, Linden would grow suspicious. "Yes, of course. Let me send a member of my staff to ask her to join us."

The man smiled like a barnyard cat who'd spotted a mouse.

Anthony strode to the bell rope, then stopped. He needed to get Olivia out of the house, or she would spend the remainder of her life rotting in a dank cell. "Oh, I forgot. The dashed thing is in need of repair. I'll just go and get her."

Mind racing with how he could accomplish getting Olivia out with Linden downstairs, Anthony took the stairs two at a time. He'd simply tell Detective Linden that Olivia was not in her room. That she'd disappeared. Then tonight, he'd take her to Southampton and sneak her onto a ship heading to America. He was sure he could find a captain more than willing to take her on board for a hefty sum.

He reached her bedchamber door and knocked lightly on the surface. "Olivia?"

She opened it, and Anthony was startled to see her up and wearing one of her old navy serviceable gowns.

"What are you doing dressed?" He stepped into the room and closed the door.

"Katie brought me a fresh pitcher of water. She told me

that a detective from Scotland Yard is here. The maid at the Duke of Wharton's residence told him about seeing me, didn't she?"

"Yes, he wishes to speak with you, but I have a plan. I'll tell him you're not here. That you must have left. That you once mentioned to me that you wanted to go to Scotland. While he's at Victoria Station trying to find out if you've boarded a train, tonight we'll travel by carriage to Southampton, and I'll get you on a ship."

"I cannot have you lie for me. I will let him interview me. As you said, they only have the maid's word. And it was dim in the stairwell."

He grasped her shoulders. "You don't understand. The maid told him you were injured."

Olivia drew in a sharp breath.

"While I'm telling him you've disappeared, you need to gather your things, then go hide in my bedchamber. He might request to see this room. Do you understand?"

She nodded.

"Hurry," he whispered.

Trying to garner Olivia more time to gather her belongings and sneak into his room, Anthony moved down the stairs at a turtle's pace. He stepped into the receiving room to find Detective Linden once again ogling the ormolu clock like a naked woman's breasts.

He could offer it to the man. No, something within Anthony, a gut feeling, told him not to venture there. He shoved the idea from his mind.

"It really is a magnificent piece." The man's regard shifted to Anthony, then moved past him, obviously searching for Olivia. "Am I to question Miss Michaels upstairs?"

Anthony forced a concerned expression. "Miss Michaels appears to be gone."

"Gone?" The detective's eyes narrowed.

"Yes. She's not in her bedchamber. I thought her too sick to get up. I don't understand where she could have gone."

"Might I examine her room?"

"Of course. Follow me."

As quickly as Olivia could move with her thigh still plaguing her, she strode to the armoire and flung the doors wide. With hands that shook slightly, she bent to withdraw her suitcase and winced when a lightning-fast pain shot through her thigh. A bead of sweat trailed down her spine. Ignoring her pain, she pulled out her suitcase. She glanced around the room to see if there was anything else that she'd forgotten and realized how little she possessed. Her gaze shifted back to the armoire and the lovely dresses from Madame Renault's shop.

Would it be so wrong to take one of the day dresses? Yes.

She closed the armoire, then opening her bedroom door, she peered down the corridor. Seeing no one, she moved down the hall and slipped into Anthony's room.

The exertion of moving after being in bed, and the ache in her thigh, along with fear, caused her knees to quake under her skirt.

Breath sawing in and out of her lungs, she slumped against the door and tried to slow her breathing to a normal rhythm, while glancing around the room. It was imperative that she find a place to hide in case the detective decided to carry out an extensive search of Trent House. Olivia's gaze settled on the massive bed where she and Anthony had made love. What she would give to join him in that bed again—to feel his warm palms skimming over her skin and experience his mouth pressed to hers as he buried himself deep within her—until they had almost become one body, one soul.

Tears blurred her vision. She blinked them away.

There was no time to become melancholy.

No time to live in the past.

No turning back.

Penny had seen her. Her mind drifted back to that moment when the maid had stared at the blood on Olivia's hand. The shock on her face, along with her words, replayed in Olivia's mind. *Blimey! What happened to your hand?*

Olivia straightened. Penny had thought she'd cut her hand, not her thigh. Is that the injury she'd told the detective about? If so . . .

Without further thought, Olivia opened the door and hobbled back to her room. Quickly, she removed her hairbrush and several hairpins from her suitcase, then set the luggage back into the armoire. As she sat at the vanity table, fixing her hair into a severe bun, she silently prayed that Penny had said that Olivia's hand was cut. If not, Olivia's gamble would land her in prison for the rest of her life.

When done setting her hair, she stood and moved to the door. She would go and see the detective. It was a gamble, but one she needed to take, or else she'd spend the remainder of her life looking over her shoulder, fearing these noblemen had sent someone to find her. She just hoped she could walk down the stairs and not collapse from the pain.

She opened her bedchamber door and almost bumped into Anthony and the detective.

Chapter Thirty

"Miss Michaels?" Anthony's voice conveyed his surprise. His eyes conveyed his fear at seeing her still in her bedchamber.

"My lord," she replied, forcing her voice to sound carefree, even though she felt as if the devil waited for her on the other side of a tightrope. Her gaze traveled past Anthony to the short man standing behind him. The detective's gray eyes drifted over her. His brow creased. She wasn't sure if that was a good sign or not, but she hoped she looked insipid enough for the man to question every presumption he had about her.

"You're Miss Michaels?" The man scratched at his jaw.

"I am." She tipped her head to the side, hoping it added to her forced look of bewilderment.

"The elder Lady Huntington's companion?" The detective's gaze drifted from her face to her hands clasped piously in front of her.

"Yes."

"My lord, I thought you said she wasn't in her room." The man brushed past Anthony.

"She wasn't." Anthony's jaw tensed.

"Were you looking for me, my lord?" She lowered her lashes and tried to look demure and uncomfortable with conveying where she was. "Forgive me. I was attending to my toilette. I've neglected my duties for far too long, but I'm feeling much improved. Her ladyship, along with you, my lord, have been exceedingly kind allowing me to rest while I suffered with catarrh, but I am breathing much better now." She covered her mouth and forced a delicate cough.

Standing behind the detective, Anthony mouthed, *Are you mad?*

Ignoring him, she shifted her attention to the detective. "You have me at a disadvantage, sir. Might I ask who you are?"

"Of course. Forgive me. I'm Detective Linden from Scotland Yard."

"From Scotland Yard?" She innocently blinked.

Anthony picked up a blue and white chinoiserie vase from the hall table and lifted it over the man's head as if about to knock the man senseless, so she could make a quick escape.

She gave a small, almost indiscernible, shake of her head, hoping Anthony would pick up on the signal.

Brows pinched together, he set the vase down.

"Might I ask what this is about?" She folded her hands primly in front of her.

"Detective Linden wishes to ask you a few questions," Anthony said.

"Me? I cannot imagine . . . Oh, I know why."

"You do?" both Anthony and Linden said in unison.

"Yes, last week I stepped in front of a carriage with a crest emblazoned on the door. The horses had to quickly veer, and the driver said some rather harsh words. Words I didn't quite know the meaning of. I fear the nobleman inside must have written a complaint against me." She cast a solemn expression at the detective. "Is that it?"

This time Linden blinked as if unsure what to make of her.

"Detective Linden, I must insist you question Miss Michaels on another day. I think she might be delirious."

"Perhaps that would be for the best." The detective outstretched his hand for her to shake.

Was he attempting to discern if her hand was injured? As she reached out, she sent up a silent prayer that indeed that was his intention.

His fingers curled around hers. His palm was dry and warm. Hers was a bit clammy, but hopefully, he would think that was due to her illness.

Before releasing her hand, he turned it over and examined her palm. He turned to Anthony. "I think there has been a mistake, my lord. Forgive me for the intrusion."

The tension within her eased. Once again, she tipped her head to the side and forced a bewildered expression. "Mistake?" she echoed.

Even though Anthony appeared confused, the tautness in his body visibly dissipated. "I suggest you return to your bed, Miss Michaels. You're still looking rather pale, and I don't wish my grandmother to catch whatever you have."

"I had not thought of that, my lord. Yes, you are right. I might still be contagious." Olivia closed the door and slumped against it. Like an underwater swimmer who has just resurfaced after a great distance, she dragged several deep breaths into her lungs. Beneath her skirts her thigh ached, and her knees felt ready to give out. The past few minutes had been as terrifying as when she'd almost slipped off the roof after leaving the Duke of Wharton's residence.

Five minutes later, Olivia was still leaning against the door when someone knocked on it.

She opened it to find Anthony.

He slipped inside the room and closed the door behind him. "I thought you had gone mad. What was that all about?"

She explained to him how Penny had seen the blood on her hand and believed she had cut her palm. "I took a gamble that Detective Linden was looking for someone with an injured hand."

"Good Lord," he mumbled.

"Do you think he will return?"

Anthony scrubbed a hand over his face. "I don't believe so. He seemed convinced the maid was mistaken."

"Did he say anything to you before he left?"

"A few pleasantries, nothing more." He cupped her face in his palms. His warm-colored eyes held her gaze as if he could see into her soul. "I truly thought you'd gone mad."

"Yes. I know. And I thought you were going to crack that vase over his head."

"I was." His lips moved closer to hers.

A loud *bang, bang, bang* on the door froze them.

Anthony flung the door open and almost got knocked in the chest with the gold handle of his grandmother's cane as she lifted it to rap it against the door again.

"Stand back, Anthony! I demand to know what is going on."

Laughing, Anthony picked up his grandmother and swung her around.

"You big ape. Let me down." She tried to hit him with her cane. "Are you deranged?"

She got one good conk on his head before he set the old woman back on her feet. Yet, a wide grin remained on his face.

Olivia found herself grinning as well.

"Are you going to tell me why a detective from Scotland Yard was here?" the dowager asked again.

"I didn't wish to make you nervous, so I told you I believed Olivia fell, but she was set upon. He came to inform us that the man who attacked Olivia has been found."

Grandmother's mouth gaped. "You were attacked?"

Olivia wanted to be done with lying. Done with robbing. She'd had enough excitement to last her the rest of her life, but she needed to lie one more time. "Yes."

The dowager's head tipped to the side. "Then you will be leaving soon?"

Olivia presumed she probably should. It was time to start a new life. She fought the urge to glance at Anthony's face and see his expression. "Yes."

"Well, I hope you are not foolish enough to do it during the night again," the woman said, then walked out of the room.

As soon as the door closed, Anthony peered at her. "You should wait a few days to gather all your strength back."

Deep down she'd hoped he would ask her to stay. She was a fool.

Anthony peered at her. "How does your leg feel?"

"It hurts, but the pain is much more bearable now."

Anthony offered a weak smile. “Rest, Olivia. The journey to America is long. You’ll need your energy.”

And then he left, pulling the door closed behind him, leaving her feeling as if the Fates had set her back on that tightrope. Alone.

For most of the day, Anthony had stayed away from Olivia. He told himself he did so because she needed to rest, but he doubted that was the true reason. Part of him wanted her to go. The other part of him thought he was mad for already missing her before she left.

He leaned back in his office chair and tipped his glass of rum to his mouth and downed a sizable swig. Brandy was his usual drink of choice, but today he wanted something more potent, and the decanter of rum was doing a dashed good job of numbing his brain. But if he didn’t stop drinking, he’d be soused before his brother arrived home, and end up under the table during dinner.

He glanced at the clock on the mantel and blinked his eyes a few times to try to draw the timepiece into focus. Four o’clock. Standing, he tipped the glass to his lips and drained it dry. He really should check on Olivia and see how she was doing.

A minute later, in the corridor outside of Olivia’s room, Anthony stared at the door. She was probably fine. He should go back downstairs. Yet, he lifted his hand and rapped his knuckles against the surface.

Silence.

“Olivia, may I come in?”

No reply.

An unsettling sensation crept up Anthony's spine. He grasped the handle and flung the door open. The room looked as if no one had ever occupied it. As if he'd dreamt all the events of the past weeks.

He marched to the armoire. The hinges squeaked slightly as he opened both doors. Inside were the yellow evening gown and the day dresses from Madame Renault's establishment, but nothing else.

He moved to one of the dressers and pulled the drawer out with such force, he heard the wooden rail snap.

Empty.

He tried the next and the next. All empty, except the last one that held a pair of silk stockings and the lovely corset he'd seen on Olivia the day Madame Renault had come for Olivia's fittings.

Good Lord. Olivia was gone. Vanished like a shadow. Or better yet, the Phantom—without anyone knowing the wiser.

Uttering a curse, he took the stairs three at a time. The butler stood in the entry hall awaiting the arrival of James and his family.

"Is something amiss, my lord?" Menders's brows lifted slightly.

"Did you see Olivia?"

"Olivia? Oh, Miss Michaels. No, sir."

Damnation. He dashed out the front door and glanced up both sides of Park Lane. Not seeing her, he darted between two carriages and moved to the other side of the street.

One of the drivers shook his fist at him. "Bloody fool."

He peered toward the entrance to Hyde Park. His gaze

brought him to a hackney that looked to have just picked up a customer.

Heart beating fast, he ran toward it.

The carriage merged into the stream of moving vehicles on Park Lane. If it was Olivia and she left, he'd not know where to find her. Why did that matter to him? He'd told her she needed to leave, but the thought of her actually stepping away from his life . . . of never seeing her again made his already pounding heart hammer inside his chest with an intensity that seemed capable of snapping a rib.

He should have told Olivia how he felt.

How did he feel?

Was he in love?

Damnation. It appeared so.

"Wait," he called out, lifting his hand in the air. "Stop."

The sound of the traffic—of horses moving up the street, their shoes striking the pavement, harnesses rattling—drowned out his words.

The vehicle kept moving, picking up speed, until it turned out of sight.

Breathing heavily, Anthony braced his hands on his thighs and tried to slow the breaths sawing in and out of his lungs.

A carriage slowed as it moved up the street. "Anthony?" his brother James called out, above the din of traffic. "What the deuces are you about?"

Anthony straightened and raked his fingers through his hair. He wasn't sure. All he knew was that a dark emptiness had settled over him.

* * *

After returning to the house and greeting James, Caroline, and the rest of the family, Anthony walked back into the office and slumped into his chair behind the desk. Well, he supposed now that James had returned it was once again his brother's chair.

He set his elbows on the blotter and cradled his head in his hands.

Squawk. Atticus bounced up and down on his perch. *Squawk.* "Chowder head."

He narrowed his eyes at the bird. He deserved the insult, but he wasn't in the mood for a lecture from the damn parrot. "One more word from you, and I'm going to toss you out of the window."

Someone cleared his throat.

Anthony glanced up to see James staring at him, a concerned expression on his face. He probably wondered why he'd been chasing a carriage down the street like a madman and smelled like a sailor on a two-day drinking binge, along with why he was threatening the parrot. No, the latter he probably understood.

"Would you have an issue with me gifting Atticus to your eldest son?" Anthony asked.

James blinked. "You're not serious, are you? I don't need that foul-mouthed bird expanding on my son's vocabulary. He hears enough unfavorable words from our grandmother."

"True."

James peered at him for a long moment.

He knew the way his brother's mind worked. He was deciding whether to ask Anthony about his sullen mood, along with why he'd been running after the carriage.

James expelled a slow breath. "So, what are these changes you wrote me about?"

"Changes?" Anthony echoed.

"Victory Pens. The blueprints."

It appeared James had decided to skip the inquisition about more personal matters. Perhaps that was for the best. He needed a distraction. Anthony stood and pointed to where he'd spread the drawings across the desk. "The changes I've implemented to the architect's blueprints are rather substantial."

James braced his hands on the desk and leaned over the drawings. "I see."

Anthony had thought he would be energized when he spoke to James about the changes, but he felt distracted and unable to pull his mind away from how he could track Olivia down.

"The layout is completely different," James said, drawing Anthony from his thoughts.

"The reorganization of the manufacturing stations should make the flow of production easier. Quicker. You see that the packing station is now closer to the loading dock. And the materials are closer to the first production line."

Brows pinched together, James glanced at Anthony. "I would never have thought of questioning the layout. You've done a remarkable job."

Anthony nodded. The accomplishment, along with his brother's approval, felt empty without Olivia there to share in it. She had been such an integral part. He'd bounced ideas off her, and she'd helped tremendously, along with handling the ledgers.

"I think you might have found your calling." James

clapped him on the shoulder. "I think a few more of the family's manufacturing facilities could use your help."

"I thought the same thing, but first I have to go somewhere."

"Does this have to do with what I witnessed outside?"

"Yes. I think I might have just allowed the biggest mistake of my life to happen." Anthony rubbed at the knotted muscles in his neck.

A concerned expression settled on James's face.

Anthony feared, at this moment, his brother was trying to comprehend what mistake surpassed some of the outlandish and foolish things Anthony had partaken in over the years.

James squeezed Anthony's shoulder. "Whatever has happened we will handle it together."

There had been times in his life when James had railed at him. Times he'd deserved his brother's ire, but now James sensed this mistake was something else—that he simply hadn't gotten drunk or gambled too deep. This was the reason Anthony realized how fortunate he was to have his older brother.

"James, I've fallen in love."

"You're in love?" His brother gave a slight shake of his head as if he hadn't heard him correctly.

Anthony gave a humorless laugh. "Yes, but I might have botched everything up."

"To have captured your heart she must be special."

"Oh, yes, she's special, all right. She's a thief."

"A thief?" His brother's brows pinched together.

"Yes. She's stolen my heart."

"Ah, that serious, is it? Might I ask whom we are speaking about?" James asked.

"Miss Michaels."

"Miss Michaels? The woman you hired to be Grandmother's companion?"

"Yes." He waited to see what his brother would say to that.

"Go after her. Tell her how you feel."

Startled, Anthony blinked. He should have known James would not talk about social standing. His brother believed in true love. He would have married Caroline if she'd been nothing more than a flower seller.

"I was intending to, but I don't know where to start. She wishes to go to America. She could have gone to the London docks or Southampton. I'm not sure."

"I'll go to the London docks. You go to Southampton. Hopefully, one of us will find her."

"You'd do that?"

"Of course. If I find her, what should I say?"

"Tell her I love her. Desperately."

His brother smiled. "If I find her, I think I'll just tell her to come back here so you can tell her that in person."

"Thank you." Anthony hugged his brother.

Caroline poked her head into the room. "Is everything fine?"

"Yes. It will be. Once I find Olivia," Anthony said, dashing from the room.

Chapter Thirty-One

Ignoring the dull ache in her thigh, Olivia climbed the winding path that led to the simple graveyard where the girls from All Saints Orphanage were buried. Before leaving for America, she had two things she needed to do. She opened the creaking iron gate to the cemetery and made her way to the three moss-covered stones that stood guard over Helen's grave.

There was no tombstone.

No sentimental engraving.

No wreath that marked that Helen lived an eternal life.

A chill moved through Olivia's body, and she pulled her shawl tighter around her shoulders.

With the back of her hand, she brushed at the tears seeping from the corners of her eyes. "Though I am traveling halfway around the world, I will never forget you, Helen." She pressed her hand to her heart. "You will remain here, along with Anthony."

"Olivia?" a woman called out. The voice as familiar to her as her own.

She turned to see Mrs. Garson walking toward her.

The breeze caused wisps of the woman's gray hair to fly free of her chignon.

"The groundskeeper told me he thought he saw you making your way to the graveyard."

"Yes, I came to say goodbye to both you and Helen."

"Goodbye?" The older woman clutched Olivia's hand as she glanced at the suitcase set by Olivia's feet. "Where are you going, child?"

"I've decided to go to America. Perhaps New York." She'd heard though the city wasn't as populated as London, one could start anew there.

The woman's grasp on Olivia's fingers tightened. "Why so far away, dear? You didn't like working for Lady Winton?"

"Not particularly. But I ended up working for Lord Anthony Trent and his grandmother, the Dowager Marchioness of Huntington. I loved it there, but it was only a temporary position." She heard the tremble in her voice.

"If they were pleased with your work, I'm sure they will give you a letter of reference, so you may find another position in London."

Olivia doubted they would, but she smiled. "It is just time for me to move on. Go someplace else."

The woman nodded.

Olivia reached into the side pocket in her simple dress and removed two envelopes. "Mrs. Garson, will you do me a favor?"

"Yes, of course, dear."

She handed her the first envelope tied with a green ribbon. Helen's favorite color. "I wish you to take the money in here and buy Helen a stone with her name on it."

The woman blinked at the envelope as Olivia placed it in her hand. "Of course, I will go to the mason in Leeman tomorrow and order one."

"Thank you. Will you have him carve a wreath and etch 'beloved sister' on it?"

As she nodded, Mrs. Garson's lower lip slightly trembled.

Olivia handed her the second envelope. "And this is for coal to help heat the orphanage this winter and to buy the children a special treat of oranges."

The woman took the envelope and peeked inside. She gasped. "Where did you get this? Are you the secret benefactor who has been sending the orphanage money?"

Without answering, she wrapped Mrs. Garson in her arms. The woman's thick arms embraced her in a tight squeeze, just like they had the morning they'd buried Helen.

The matron's warm breath touched Olivia's ear. "Every time I heard one of those wretched men had been robbed, I thought God was punishing them. Now, I think I know the truth, but they will still have to answer to their maker when death comes. God bless you, child, and safe travels." The woman kissed her cheek, bringing a fresh rush of tears to Olivia's eyes.

She picked up her suitcase and walked away.

As dusk settled over the sky, the steamship grew smaller and smaller as it sailed away from the dock at Southampton. Before departing, Anthony had slipped the captain a sizable sum to see the ship's passenger list.

Olivia's name wasn't on it, but he'd stood on the dock and watched the passengers board in case she'd used an alias.

Over the last several hours, Anthony had checked every ship leaving the port and come up with nothing. He presumed James hadn't found her either or he would have sent word.

Where are you, Olivia?

Feeling almost hopeless, he pulled his gaze away from the steamship to where several stevedores unloaded crates from an American vessel named the *Charleston*. The ship had docked this morning. The captain had said he would not be leaving port to sail back to America until next week.

His gaze drifted over the other ships in port. None would be leaving tonight. Maybe tomorrow Olivia would show up. He would take lodging at the Sail and Anchor and return to the docks before daybreak.

Anthony rolled over on the lumpy mattress, then gave the flat pillow a thump with his fist before setting his head back onto it. He couldn't sleep. His mind wouldn't stop spinning with the possibility that he would never find Olivia. That he'd let the one woman he truly loved slip through his fingers. He'd made a bollock of so many things in his life, but not telling Olivia that he loved her was far greater than any other blunder.

Could Olivia have changed her mind about going across the pond? Perhaps she'd decided to go to France and crossed the Channel at Dover. He couldn't discount the possibility that she might have taken lodging for a day or two, so she might rest before journeying across the Atlantic. Even on a steamship it would most likely take over a week. And if she booked third-class passage, she would be subjected to a diet that might consist of nothing more than reground bread and rancid-smelling water from old casks. The thought of her drinking putrid water in her weakened state made his hands clench.

Anthony scrubbed a hand down his weary face and his eyes drifted closed.

The sound of the taproom and boisterous voices pulled Anthony from sleep. His gaze pivoted to the window where muted light peered through the dirty panes of glass.

Damnation. He'd meant to be on the dock before daybreak. He threw off the bedding and stood so fast, he cracked his head on the low ceiling.

Bugger it. Keeping himself stooped so he wouldn't bang his skull again, Anthony made his way to the lone chair, snatched his trousers off it, and tugged them on.

A minute later, he was making his way through the already crowded taproom that smelled like a mixture of tobacco smoke, strong ale, and bacon. Sailors were already at the bar and tables downing tankards of ale.

He weaved through the crammed room.

"You wish for breakfast, sir?" a serving girl, carrying two platters of food, asked as she strode by him.

"No, thank you." Anthony stepped outside into the salty air and hurried toward the ships.

In front of him, two sailors chatted as they entered the docks.

"I'm not looking forward to the long journey home today. The eel I ate last night at the Sail and Anchor has left me queasy." The man's accent clearly indicated he was American.

"I told you it smelled off." The older, more grizzled sailor shook his head as if he couldn't believe the other fellow had foolishly eaten it.

"Are you journeying to America?" Anthony asked.

Both men turned to stare at him.

"Yes," the American who looked a bit green replied.

"You looking for passage? I think the captain has a few bunks left?" The older sailor arched a bushy gray brow.

"Which ship?" Anthony asked.

"The *Albany*," the younger seaman replied.

"Where is it docked?"

The older sailor pointed to a sailboat with a wooden hull. When he'd asked about the vessel, he'd been told it was having one of its masts repaired and wouldn't be sailing for several days.

"It's now ready to sail?"

"Sadly." The younger sailor clutched at his stomach.

"Did a woman board?" Anthony held his breath.

"Yes, the captain took on several female passengers."

"Damn foolish if you ask me." The older seaman scowled. "Women are bad luck."

"Cap don't believe in that nonsense," the younger seaman said.

"Thank you!" With ground-eating strides Anthony moved toward the ship, experiencing a glimmer of hope.

* * *

As Olivia and the two other female passengers settled into their tiny cabin, Ella Smythe grumbled. "I don't see why we must remain cooped up in this tiny room for the whole trip."

"The captain said some of the older sailors are suspicious about having a woman on board." Mrs. Finnigan, a middle-aged woman, who wished to join her family in New York, slipped her suitcase under one of the bunks.

Ella Smythe peered at Olivia. "You're awful quiet, duckie. Leaving your family behind, are you?"

Family? The word seemed as foreign and distant to her as the Orient. "No. I'm hoping to find a job in New York City."

"A job? Ha! I'm hoping to find me a husband who lives on Fifth Avenue." Ella grinned.

Mrs. Finnigan clucked her tongue. "Not all Americans are rich like you read in the newspapers. My daughter, her husband, and their three bairns live in a two-room flat."

"I ain't intending to live in no tiny flat." Ella wrinkled her nose and patted the blond bun at the back of her head.

"Well, I wish you luck." Mrs. Finnigan's gaze drifted over Ella, who was quite pretty, but Olivia had a feeling that the pink on the blond woman's cheeks and lips had been enhanced with cosmetics.

Ella strode to the porthole. "Oh, now ain't that a handsome gent talking to the captain on the dock. Dash shame to be locked in this dreary cabin while he's on board. A woman could run her fingers through those wavy locks."

With her back to the room, Ella didn't see the shocked

look on Mrs. Finnigan's face over the woman's brazen words.

Ella pivoted toward Olivia. "Come see, duckie. This man will put a smile on your face."

Olivia doubted that.

"Come on, now." Ella grabbed Olivia's elbow and tugged her toward the small round window.

The gentleman faced away from them. Olivia's gaze drifted from the top of the man's head of thick dark hair, then down his back to his polished boots. His build, the color of his hair, and his height seemed so much like Anthony's that her stomach gave a little flip.

"Wait until he turns back around." Ella grinned.

Olivia held her breath.

The man turned and glanced at the ship.

Anthony? She must be hallucinating or going mad. It could not be him. Had something happened? Was he here to warn her?

"You look as white as a ghost." Ella's brow creased. "Do you know him?"

Olivia darted to the door.

Mrs. Finnigan gasped. "Where are you going? The captain said we're not supposed to leave the cabin."

Ignoring the woman, Olivia wrenched the door open. As she made her way to the deck, her heart hammered in her chest. Fear and excitement intertwined, leaving her utterly confused. She passed an old gray-haired sailor.

"A woman!" He grumbled and uttered a word she'd heard Atticus say more than once. It definitely didn't sound welcoming. "Off the ship, missy, before we sail!"

Once on deck, several sailors working on the masts peered at her.

One smiled, showing a mouth of black teeth.

Another frowned.

One whistled.

Holding the skirt of her dress up, she ran to the ship's railing.

Anthony glanced up. A smile lit up his face, and all the tension building within her dissipated like morning fog under the full force of a summer sun.

He pushed past the captain and started up the gang-plank.

If her heart beat any faster, she feared she'd collapse. Suddenly feeling unsure, she stood almost frozen.

As if he was unsure as well, his steps slowed. It was as if someone pushed everything around them into a slow, dreamlike state.

Anthony stepped in front of her. "Olivia. My God, I cannot believe I found you. I had almost given up hope."

"Anthony, why are you here?" Her breath caught in her throat as she waited for his answer.

"Because I realized something."

"What?" The single word came out breathless.

"I thought I could let you go, but I was wrong. Good Lord, woman, I love you. I always shall. And if you leave you will take a rather sizable piece of my heart with you, leaving a hollow gap in my chest that I fear I might never recover from."

Anthony's face blurred behind the tears pooling in her eyes.

He cradled her face between his warm palms. "Don't cry, love. Just tell me that you love me as well."

She sniffled. "I do. Desperately."

"Then marry me at St. George's?"

She bit her lower lip. "You want me to marry you?"

"More than anything I have ever wanted."

"Yes, I'll marry you."

She'd barely had time to comprehend what had just transpired when Anthony lowered his mouth to hers and kissed her long and quite thoroughly.

Epilogue

It had become a ritual that one day a week, Anthony and Olivia would go to Gunter's and order ice treats. Over the last year, Olivia had tried every flavor, but strawberry remained her favorite. It had also become a ritual that they follow up with a ride to the British Museum. Occasionally they went in, but on most trips they remained in the carriage and chatted about social events they would be attending or Anthony's flourishing business. Word had gotten around that her husband was a genius when it came to improving the flow of production in a manufacturing environment. New businesses and old businesses all vied for his input. She acted as the business manager and handled the scheduling and accounting.

They had also started a charitable organization for All Saints Orphanage, and a month after their wedding, she and Anthony had traveled to Kent to inform Mrs. Garson and Vicar Finch. At one point during the meeting Anthony had asked to speak to Vicar Finch in private. She wasn't sure what Anthony had said to the clergyman, but when they'd returned the man had looked sallow and ready to cast up his accounts.

Anthony had refused to tell her what had transpired, but she had a feeling it was a threat of some sort. Perhaps informing the clergyman that if he used a birch rod on any of the girls, Anthony would withhold the charitable funds, or perhaps do something even more dire.

"Deep in thought, darling?" Anthony asked from where he sat next to her, having already finished his ice treat.

"Yes, but good thoughts." She slipped the last spoonful of her ice treat into her mouth and released a low moan of pleasure.

As she'd expected, Anthony's gaze grew intense, and as soon as the glasses had been returned to Gunter's, he instructed their coachman to drive by the British Museum, then he tugged the window shades down. Sometimes they didn't talk about social events or business. Sometimes they showed each other with words and actions how much they meant to each other. Usually when in the carriage it was a quick coupling—unlike when they were in the privacy of the home they'd purchased in Belgrave Square. Then it was usually a slow event. She loved him, and she knew without a doubt that Anthony loved her.

"Have I told you how beautiful you are?" he asked, pulling her onto his lap.

She grinned. "Several times today."

"Have I told you how much I love you?"

"I believe this is only the third time today."

He laughed. "I'm slipping."

She cupped his face in her hands and pressed her lips to his. As it always was with them, the noise outside receded as if they were the only two people in the world.

"Anthony." She stroked a finger down his jaw, excited over the news she had to tell him.

"Yes, love."

She watched his face, hoping it would reflect the joy she felt inside her. "I am with child."

His eyes widened, then a broad smile lifted the corners of his lips.

"You are pleased?"

"Very much so. Lately, I have been thinking of children running about our home laughing and giggling. The girls with red hair like yours. Our family, Olivia."

Our family. The thought made her eyes burn. Anthony's face clouded behind the pool of tears that threatened to fall. But they were happy tears. She circled her hands tightly about Anthony's neck and kissed him, and when he kissed her back, she believed she was the luckiest woman in the world.

Acknowledgments

This book wouldn't be possible without the help and support of so many caring and giving individuals. A shout-out to my wonderful editor, Esi Sogah, and the rest of the Kensington team. Thank you to Christina, Dylann, and Diane for beta reading this story when you were dealing with your own deadlines. Thanks to my agent, Jill Marsal. And a special thank-you to readers everywhere who enjoy romance books and support the authors who write them.

Can't get enough of these infamous lords?
Keep reading for a sneak peek of

NEVER MARRY A SCANDALOUS DUKE

The next book from Renee Ann Miller
Coming Soon

London, England

Lady Sara Elsmere released a taut breath and tried not to fidget. Any attempt at blending into the background of the Duke of Dorchester's ballroom was a challenge when wearing a pink gown adorned with enormous silk peony flowers the size of a serving dish.

Father's words replayed in her head. *The gown gives you a youthful glow.*

That statement was utterly absurd. Plain old poppycock.

In truth, the ball gown made her look foolish. Yet, no amount of arguing had changed Father's mind. So, here she was, trying to disappear into the gold-flocked wallpaper and failing miserably.

She desperately wished Father would stop forcing her to attend such gatherings in hopes someone would make her an offer. The gentlemen at these social events had little interest in a twenty-seven-year-old entomologist who collected butterflies and laughed nervously whenever a man asked her to dance.

Sadly, her nervous laugh had started her first season. Excitement had swirled within her in anticipation of dancing. Then Sir Harry had approached, and with each step he'd taken to move closer to her, she'd felt more apprehension. Would she fall? Would she cause him to fall? The thought of making a complete cake of herself became insidious. By the time he'd asked her to dance, she'd begun to laugh. Not a girlish giggle that a man might find cute or endearing, but a high-pitched laugh.

Heads had turned toward her, and the more everyone gawked, the louder her laugh became. At her second ball the same thing had happened when Lord Gilbert asked to partner with her. An utter disaster. Her second ball during that season had been another utter disaster. The same thing had happened when Lord Gilbert asked to partner with her.

Quite understandable that gentlemen at these gatherings avoided her.

Scanning those waltzing, Sara caught sight of her sister being twirled around the dance floor with by some young buck. A bright smile wreathed her sister's face, and her partner had the look of a man who thought everyone envied him.

Sara was sure many did envy the fellow. At just eighteen, Louisa had made her debut in society this year and instantly become the season's incomparable. Every man wished to dance with her, and Sara could not blame them. Her sister was not only beautiful, but she sparkled and thrived under the spotlight.

While Sara collected butterflies, Louisa acted the social butterfly, flittering around with her grace and beauty drawing everyone's regard. How two sisters could be such opposites befuddled Sara's mind. And though at times she experienced a slight spark of envy that Louisa could mingle so easily, she did not truly begrudge her. No, she was happy for her sister. How could she not be when she loved her so dearly?

She searched the crush for her brother. Ned was probably in the cardroom with their host. She didn't particularly care for Ian McAllister, the Duke of Dorchester. He was a scoundrel of the highest order—though the *ton* seemed more than willing to forgive his womanizing, especially when he was serving them an abundance of champagne and French cuisine.

Turning her mind away from the duke, Sara peered at her father, who stood across the ballroom engaged in conversation with another gentleman. Perhaps it was not as much a conversation as it was an argument, for Father's face had turned the same shade of red when she'd balked at wearing the atrocious gown now draped on her person.

Sara nibbled her lower lip and eyed the wide doorway several feet from where she stood. With Father, Ned, and Louisa preoccupied, a better opportunity to slip out of the ballroom might not present itself. She edged toward the opening. She'd heard that the Duke of Dorchester's Richmond estate possessed an exemplary library, and she was on a mission to hide away in it for the remainder of the evening. Surely, afterward, she would garner Father's wrath when they returned home, but she would rather absorb one of his verbal tirades than remain in the ballroom a minute longer.

As fast as she could move, while dragging twenty pounds of silk, tulle, and faux peonies, she slipped through the archway. A sense of elation drifted through her as she made her way down the wide corridor with its red Turkish runner.

A male servant, dressed in a tailored black suit, stepped out of a room and nearly collided with her.

"Forgive me, madam. Are you looking for the retiring room?"

She shifted from one foot to the other, while deciding

how much of the truth to reveal. "Actually, I'm looking for the library."

The man's eyes widened, and he averted his gaze. "Of course, madam, it is the next door to your left."

"Thank you." As Sara moved down the wide corridor, she glanced over her shoulder. There was something unsettling about the way the footman had looked at her—as if she'd startled him—as if she was not what he'd expected.

Well, she had gotten that look enough times in her life. She shoved her thoughts away. Perhaps it was just the guilt of sneaking off that had her overanalyzing the man's expression. Most likely, he thought her brazen for leaving the other guests to indulge in a book.

She opened the door he'd indicated and softly closed it behind her. Gas wall sconces set low illuminated the library, which was one of the largest she'd ever seen, and she'd seen more than her fair share since they were her solace during these gatherings.

The scent of the leather bindings filled her nose as she scanned the soaring mahogany bookcases that lined three of the walls. Each of them had a sliding ladder so the uppermost books could be reached, and in the corner a metal spiraling staircase went to a second-story balcony with even more bookshelves.

Unfettered joy blossomed within her. With such an extensive collection, she felt almost positive she would find something to read that would be more stimulating than the ballroom, possibly even something on entomology.

As she made her way to the bookcases on the right side of the room, she peered up at the ceiling's lovely mural.

Puffy white clouds dotted a blue sky, while winged cherubs, wearing crowns of flowers, fluttered about. The angels held flutes and harps. Such a whimsical scene almost tempted her to lie on her back and stare at it. She tamped down such a foolish inclination and continued toward the bookcases.

So she could read the titles more clearly, Sara removed her spectacles from the pocket sewn into the skirt of her gown. As she scanned the books, she saw titles by George Eliot, Daniel Defoe, and even spotted a book of poetry from Robert Burns. She could not envision the present duke reading the latter. From what she'd heard, he was more likely to engage in reading something more scandalous like *Memoirs of a Woman of Pleasure* than poetry. Surely, the poet's book had been purchased by some dead relation. Sara inwardly scolded herself for such an uncharitable thought, clearly brought about by her dislike of the Duke of Dorchester.

Footsteps sounded in the corridor, along with a man's voice. She spun around to see the door handle being turned.

Had father or her brother tracked her down? She didn't wish to return to the ballroom, not when there were so many books to be explored. Shoving her glasses into her pocket, she made a mad dash for a narrow alcove between two of the bookcases and flattened her body into the space.

The young, widowed Lady Cleary, wearing a bright yellow gown, stepped into the library with the Duke of Dorchester. He closed the door behind him.

Sara swallowed. Why wasn't the odious man with his guests?

That answer came to her as soon as the widow skimmed her palms up the duke's chest and leaned into him.

In response, Dorchester curled his large hand around the back of the woman's neck and brought his mouth down on hers.

Goodness! She should have figured the womanizer would have a liaison in his library. Sara thought of the servant she'd almost bumped into in the corridor and how he'd looked at her. Had he believed she had been heading to the library for an assignation with His Grace? No wonder he had reacted so oddly. She didn't resemble the seductive Lady Cleary, especially in this outlandish gown.

Perhaps, hiding away had not been the most sagacious decision. She opened her mouth to say something, but the sight of Dorchester lowering the shoulder of Lady Cleary's ball gown and kissing the pale skin caused Sara to clamp her mouth tight.

She could close her eyes.

Yes, that would work. She pinched them shut.

Lady Cleary started breathing fast and making mewling sounds. "Mmm. Oh, yes, Dorchester. That feels so . . . Yes, there."

Though Sara fought the urge to open her eyes, curiosity got the better of her and one eyelid slowly lifted.

Dorchester had his thigh between the woman's gowned legs and was rocking into her, while kissing her.

Sara opened her other eye and tilted her head to the side. She wasn't sure why the woman was arching and purring like a cat. What Dorchester was doing to the woman looked rather uncomfortable.

Suddenly the gentleman stilled.

Feeling a shiver of apprehension, Sara clapped a hand over her mouth. Had she made a noise? The possibility caused her heart to pound wildly. So loud, she feared they would hear the erratic *thump, thump, thump* in her chest.

The duke glanced over his shoulder. Though handsome and in possession of striking features, including dark hair, a sensual mouth, and a square jaw, she'd always thought the man possessed an aura of danger. Perhaps it was his piercing blue eyes that looked as if they could scour one's soul to find their weakness.

Trying to make herself invisible to his gaze, she pressed her back more firmly against the wall. One of the blasted round peonies fell off her gown and rolled out of the alcove.

Dorchester's dark blue eyes settled on the faux flower before narrowing in on her like a periscope. He peered at her with the same contemptuous arrogance men at the London Society of Entomologists offered her when she handed in one of her articles for publication.

"Ian, you tease, don't stop. I'm almost there," Lady Cleary snapped, clearly agitated.

He turned back to the woman. "I think it best you return to the ballroom, darling. Something's just come up."

"Yes, I expected that. I can help." Lady Cleary's hands moved to the front of Dorchester's trousers.

He stepped back and out of her reach.

"Ian, what is the matter?"

"I believe I heard a rat."

The widow let out a squeak and inched up the skirt of her gown.

He opened the door. "I think it best you return to the ballroom."

"It's not fair of you to leave me in such a state. Why don't we go into another room," she suggested, sounding hopeful.

"Sorry, darling, I need to deal with this."

"Yourself? Don't you have legions of servants to tend to such a detestable task?"

"I prefer to catch this one myself."

That statement made Sara's heart pound even harder. She normally only laughed when a man asked her to dance, but she tightened the hand over her mouth, suddenly fearful a nervous giggle would commence.

Lady Cleary blinked and appeared ready to question him further, but something in the duke's expression must have halted the action.

The widow's skirts swished as she exited the room.

With a heavy hand, Dorchester closed the door, leaned back against the surface, and folded his arms over his ample chest. "I'm not particularly fond of Peeping Tom who get their jollies from watching others."

Peeping Tom? How ridiculous. She'd not set out to watch his sexual escapade. She'd just stepped into the library to escape the ball.

Her nervousness turned to agitation. She wiped her damp palms on her gown and stepped out from her hiding spot. "It was not my intention to spy on you, and I'm deeply offended that you would even suggest such a thing. Your unfavorable comment leaves me demanding an apology."

Ian drew in a deep breath. The woman obviously belonged in a madhouse if she thought herself due an apology. "You cannot be serious, Miss. . . ."

"Miss Elsmere. Lady Sara Elsmere."

Yes, that was her name. He'd seen her before. The Earl of Hampton's daughter. The one who laughed nervously whenever a man asked her to dance, causing gentlemen to avoid her at these gatherings as if she were a leper.

"I only stepped into the room so I might read."

He cocked a brow at her. "Really?"

"Yes, really. If you think I wanted to watch you. . . ." She waved her hand toward him as she appeared to struggle with what to call what she'd witnessed.

"What did you see?" He stepped toward the middle of the room.

Her already rosy cheeks deepened in color, settling on a shade nearly as pink as her full bow-shaped lips.

"You know," she said.

Yes, he did. He wasn't sure why, but he wanted to hear her try to explain it. He had a feeling she couldn't because she didn't completely understand it, yet the priggish woman was clearly censuring him. He could see it in her judgmental glare. His gaze settled on her sensual mouth, which seemed incongruous with the prim woman. For the briefest of moments, he thought about asking her if she wished to be tutored in what she'd seen.

Ian gave a slight, imperceivable shake of his head to scatter his renegade thoughts. He had no interest in a prim, hoity-toity wallflower who wore her brown hair in a taut bun, while donning a pink frilly garment that hid all her curves and made her look beyond ridiculous.

As if he'd said the comment out loud or she'd gleaned what he'd been thinking, she stuck out her chin. "My father chose this abomination. So don't judge me."

"Aren't you rather old to be having your father dictate your clothing?"

"I am. But if I want his benevolence, I must wear such an atrocity. Now if you will excuse me, it has gotten rather stuffy in here." And with that said, she marched toward the door. Her gaze seemed to settle on the faux peony on the rug. For a minute, Ian thought she intended to retrieve it.

"You may keep the peony, Your Grace. Perhaps your haberdasher could add it to one of your hats, or you could gift it to Lady Cleary for not finishing what you had set out to do."

Ian nearly laughed. It appeared the wallflower was not precisely what he'd thought.

She'd nearly reached the door when a man's panicked voice calling out her name echoed in the hallway. "Sara, where are you? Damnation."

Bloody hell. It wouldn't be wise to be found alone with the woman. Ian moved into the shadows.

Lady Sara opened the door and her brother stepped over the threshold. The man was breathing heavily. His face was ghostly pale.

"Ned, what is the matter?" Lady Sara gripped his sleeve.

Her brother's Adam's apple moved but nothing came out.

"Ned, you're frightening me." She grabbed his shoulders and shook him. "Tell me."

"It is Father. He collapsed."

"Collapsed?" Her voice trembled.

"Yes," her brother replied. "Dr. Trimble said he suffered apoplexy. H-he's dead."

Connect with Us
Visit us online at
KensingtonBooks.com
to read more from your favorite authors, see books
by series, view reading group guides, and more.
Join us on social media
for sneak peeks, chances to win books and prize packs,
and to share your thoughts with other readers.
facebook.com/kensingtonpublishing
twitter.com/kensingtonbooks
Tell us what you think!
To share your thoughts, submit a review,
or sign up for our eNewsletters, please visit:
KensingtonBooks.com/TellUs.